Pan

A Neverland Novel

by Gina L. Maxwell

Here's to loving
our fairytales a
little bit dirtier...

Gina L. ♥
Maxwell

Dear Reader,

While there are no actual magical elements in *Pan*, you'll still need to suspend your disbelief a little more than necessary for a straight contemporary romance. Transforming the original story of *Peter Pan* into a modern-day tale posed its challenges, especially as I wanted to keep some of the more fantastical, iconic moments—like Wendy giving Peter a thimble when he asks her for a kiss—despite setting this in a world where it would be virtually impossible for a twelve-year-old-boy to *not* know what a kiss is.

For me, part of the fun with this story was finding a way to incorporate and modernize those moments, and I sincerely hope you'll appreciate them for what they are and not think too hard about whether everything makes perfect sense. Because although there is no magic in this story, I think you'll find it still lends itself to a healthy dose of whimsy. ;)

If you're having a hard time keeping track of who's who (this is the largest cast I've ever written), there's a Character Glossary in the back of the book, but you might not even need it.

As always, a thousand thanks for giving my book a spot on your shelf and a place in your heart. I hope it stays with you for years to come.

Literary love and kitten kisses,

Gina

For those who still believe in magic, despite living in a contemporary—and often disheartening—world. Never stop believing, never stop reaching for the stars.

CHAPTER ONE

Then…
Age 12
Neverland, North Carolina

W hen someone is lost, it's because there's a place where they normally belong—one where people miss them and never stop looking for them. But me and the other boys have never belonged anywhere but here. No one misses us, and there sure as hell isn't anyone out there looking for us. So I'm not sure why they call us lost.

We know we came from somewhere—we weren't born at the Neverland School for Lost Boys—the only question is where. Not that *I* care to know—if my mother didn't want me bad enough to make sure I stayed with her, why would I? — but the younger boys who wish we had a mother sometimes ask me. I'm old enough to know that storks don't deliver babies to random couples, and even if they did, a stork would never drop an innocent baby—or eleven—into the care of Fred Croc and his wife Delia. But I still don't have the answers they're looking for.

"How long does it take to wash your dirty fuckin' mitts

1

up there?" Croc yells up the stairs. "Get your asses down here pronto!"

The boys and I exchange glances in the rust-framed mirror over the row of sinks in our community bathroom. I hate the fear I can see in their eyes, especially over something as stupid as taking too long to wash their grease-stained hands. Living here is a constant practice in "damned if we do, damned if we don't." We get punished if we take too long to wash up after working our shifts at the body shop, but if we come down for dinner with so much as a smudge, we get punished for that too. If we're lucky, it's being sent to bed without supper. If we're not, we end up with belt marks across our backs.

I wink at them, all younger than me by a couple of years, except for Hook, and speak so that my words don't travel down the stairs. "Dirty work makes dirty hands, am I right, boys?" It's a play on words because not only is our work literally dirty, it's also illegal.

They all snicker and get back to washing and rinsing, the worry erased from their faces for a while longer at least.

Hook rolls his eyes with a shake of his head. "Everything's a joke to you, Pan. When are you gonna grow up? You act like it's normal for kids to be working in a chop shop. This is called a school, but we spend more time busting our asses taking cars apart or putting them back together for a small-time crook than we ever have cracking open our textbooks."

I shrug. "It might not be normal for other kids, but it's *our* normal. There's nothing we can do to change it, so we might as well make the best of things." I wipe my hands on a towel that was dingy white at best last week but is now a shade of soiled gray. Looking over at Hook's overgrown black hair as he bends over the sink that's much too short for him, I add, "Besides, growing up doesn't sound like all that much fun to me. At least here we have food and a place to sleep. Growing up means getting banished from Neverland, and who the hell knows what happens to the kids then."

His ice blue gaze snaps up to glare at me through the mirror. He doesn't like the reminder that we don't know what happened to the older kids who used to live here. Croc tells us that he sends them off to work at a different shop, but he isn't known for his honesty, so we don't really believe him. Hook is two years older than me, and currently, the oldest kid in the house. He'll be the next of us to go.

"Doesn't matter to me," Hook spits out. "I don't care where I go, as long as it's far away from this place."

I study him and try to figure out what his deal is. This certainly isn't paradise, but it's not the worst life I can imagine, either. And, far as I can tell, he has it the best out of all of us. "Says the teacher's pet."

His steely eyes narrow on me. "You got something to say, Pan?"

I square up with him, crossing my arms. "Just that I don't know why you're bitchin' about being here when you're Croc's favorite. I mean, you're the one he's taking under his wing, right? Teaching you how to run the business? That's what you said he's doing when he calls you down at night. Or maybe he's not teaching you anything. Maybe it's something fun like watching TV together, and you're lying because he told you not to tell us what you're really doing."

The other boys mumble their agreements behind me. We don't have a television upstairs. Hell, we don't have anything up here. No books, no toys. Nothing but the beds we sleep on, the dressers that hold what little clothes we have, our imaginations, and each other. Sometimes it's enough for the boys. Other times, it's not.

"You talk too much, Pan."

I smirk. "Yeah, I get that a lot. Doesn't mean what I'm saying isn't true, *James*."

"Call me that again, asswipe," he says huskily, "and see if I don't plant my fist right in your face."

Before I can tell him to go ahead and try, a tiny thing steps in front of me, fists on hips and eyes throwing green fire. "Touch a single blond hair on his head, and I'll tell Croc you were the one who took his pack of cigarettes."

Hook blanches like he's seen a ghost—even I mentally wince at the little sprite's threat—but he recovers quick enough. "What the fuck ever, I'm outta here. Smee, Starkey, let's go."

He doesn't bother to wait before turning on his heel and striding out of the bathroom, but he didn't have to. "Coming, Captain!" they say, and as always, Smee and Starkey follow after Hook like the loyal lapdogs they are, offering apologetic glances at me as they pass.

I give them a small nod. I don't have a problem with either boy. Something about them is drawn to Hook's darker… I don't know what you'd call it. Presence? Attitude? Pissiness? Either way, it's not something I understand, and the rest of the boys don't either. They consider *me* their captain, and rightly so, because I'm the best man for the job. I'm a good and fair leader—all the boys would say so— which is why I don't make them *call* me captain even though I am. Unlike Hook who won't answer to anything else. See? Better.

"Tinker Bell, you shouldn't have done that. You're only nine, and I can take care of myself."

Her usually adorable face screws into an epic scowl. "How about you just say 'thanks, Tink' instead of spouting off dumb facts."

"Thanks, Tink." I ruffle her white-blond hair the way I imagine an older brother might, earning me a grunt of exasperation as she storms out of the room and calls me a *silly ass*, her favorite nickname for me. The tinkling of the bell around her ankle fades as she heads downstairs for dinner, and I turn to the remaining six boys: Tootles, Nibs, Slightly, Curly, and the Twins. "Come on, boys, let's get something to eat."

We shuffle out of the bathroom together, and as we near the top of the stairs, I feel a tug on my shirt. "Peter, are you gonna sneak out again tonight?"

"Tootles, shhh," I whisper, stopping the group. "You want Croc to hear? If he finds out, it's the end of our stories."

Six pairs of eyes widen, and one of the Twins—I don't know which because none of us can tell them apart—says, "But we need to know what happens to Cinderella, Peter!"

They're all whisper-shouting now, some worrying about never knowing if the prince finds Cinderella and the others about what will happen if I'm ever caught sneaking out of the school.

"Lost Boys, listen up." Using their group name does the trick. They all straighten like little soldiers and await my next command. "No more talking. Tonight will be like any other night. Got it?" In not so many words, I reassured them that I plan to sneak out, that I won't get caught, and that I'll bring back another piece of the story they're dying to hear. That we're *all* dying to hear. Even Hook, though he'll never admit it.

The rest of the night is like any other.

We sit at the long wooden table off the kitchen and eat in silence, using our eyes to carry on entire conversations that Croc and Delia never hear. Afterward, we clear our places and head up the stairs, oldest to youngest, except for Tink who has to stay and clean the pots and kettles and whatever mess Delia made when she prepared our barely edible meal.

The loud ticking of Croc's ancient pocket watch echoes up the stairwell. "James," he barks, and we all freeze on the steps.

Hook's entire body tenses in front of me. Man, he really does hate his first name. I wonder if Croc knows that and uses it on purpose. But that doesn't make sense if Hook's his favorite. More likely he doesn't know, and Hook doesn't want to tell him because Croc's temper is known to flare up over the dumbest shit and he's trying to avoid a beating.

Turning around, Hook takes the couple steps down to my level. "You getting the end of the story tonight?"

"Thought you didn't care about the stories."

He looks over and meets my gaze. "I don't."

That's it, that's all he says. He doesn't offer anything else. Just stares at me intently, waiting for my answer.

"Yeah," I say finally. "I am."

Something flashes in his eyes that I can't read. Like a mix of sadness and relief, but neither of those things wash with the boy I know. He's always been a pissy, jealous bastard for as long as I can remember. But since he started hanging out with Croc a couple months ago, he's been an intolerable asshole. He nods once and continues down the stairs as the boys shift to the right to let him pass.

Croc palms the back of Hook's neck when he reaches the bottom. "Come on, boy. I've got lots to teach you tonight." Hook glances over his shoulder at me one last time before they disappear into Croc's office, his expression emotionless like he's made of stone. Something's definitely off with him, but I don't know what.

Slightly pushes past me, followed by the others, jarring me back to the present and my mission at hand: sneaking out undetected. We go through our nighttime routine and get into our beds. Finally, Tink's bell can be heard as Delia leads her up the stairs. While Tink changes in the bathroom, Delia does a bed check, speaking to us as little as possible. We can feel how much she hates us, and we're happy to ignore her just as much as she does. Only Tink has to deal with her much.

As soon as Delia leaves, slamming the door at the top of the stairs behind her, I spring out of bed and do my thing. I jimmy open the window with the loose frame, whisper to the boys that I'll be back soon, and climb up to the flat roof of the building. In minutes, I've made my way over to Barrie Street in the neighboring city of London.

A few weeks ago, I was looking for an adventure when I walked under the balcony of the brick house in the middle of this block and heard a woman talking to her kids. But she wasn't just talking. She'd called it a bedtime story, and it was all about a girl called Snow White and her dwarf friends who all had funny names, just like the Lost Boys. I hid in the bushes and listened to the story floating down to me through the open balcony doors. But she only told them *part* of the story before telling them it was time for bed, and she'd continue the next night. They complained just like I was doing, but inside my head so I didn't get caught, and I knew I'd have to come back to hear more.

I also knew I had to tell the boys what I'd heard. No one had ever told us stories. We'd never heard anything like that before, and just as I'd known they would, they totally loved it. So every night since, I've returned to the same house to get the next part of whatever story she was telling. I'm not sure what I'm going to do when the weather gets cold and the lady stops opening the balcony doors, but I'll worry about that then.

As I approach the house under the cover of night, I hear a different voice. A younger one, soft and sweet sounding. "Nana, the longer you squirm, the longer it's going to take to brush you, you know." Looking up through the rails of the balcony, I see a gigantic dog shifting its weight from side to side and making unhappy grunts. Well that certainly wasn't who I—

Then she rises from behind the shaggy beast, and I forget to breathe. The light pouring out from the room surrounds her like it's protecting her from things that might be hiding in the darkness. I can't see any details of her face, but she's already the prettiest girl I've ever seen.

"Okay, Nana, that's good for now, you big baby. Go on."

The dog performs an oafish hop of gratitude before bounding back into the house. The girl laughs with a shake of her head, then leans on the bannister and gazes up at the stars. She runs a hand down her long braid and lets out a sigh like she's wishing for something. Maybe she wants an adventure, too. I could give her one. I don't know what it would be, but I know that I would search the earth until I found the right one for her.

As for me, I think I just found mine. *She*'ll be my greatest adventure yet.

I want to talk to her, to ask her name, for her to ask mine—

"Wendy, dear, come inside now, please."

"Coming, Mom." And with that, she disappears from sight.

Wendy… My adventure's name is Wendy.

CHAPTER TWO

PETER

Now...

Using the back of my arm to wipe the grease-tinged drops of sweat from my brow, I duck out from under the hood of the Chrysler 300 and turn to grab my— Where the hell is it? Damn it, I hate it when I can't find my shit. I start pulling open every drawer in my tool bench, one after the other. Knowing that what I'm looking for isn't in the bottom drawer full of miscellaneous crap I never need, I squat down and open it to rifle through the contents anyway.

I shove aside a roll of paper towels, a mug of pens, a few dirty rags that I should really take home and wash...and then I freeze. There, in the back corner, is a small black box. The kind that a woman in love would freak out over. Except, if a woman opened this particular box, she'd be sorely disappointed. Any woman except for the one I'd intended to give it to, anyway.

The dust covering it is evidence of how long it's gone untouched—half a dozen years, maybe more—but I know every detail of what's inside without even having to open it.

I pick up the box and swipe my thumb over the top,

displacing the dust as my brain displaces the mental lock on that part of my life. Memories of a distant place and time flood my mind like a dam breaking under the pressure. Cornflower blue eyes, long hair the color of maple syrup, and a musical laugh I'll never forget as long I live.

When I was a boy, I thought she was my forever adventure. But just as they have a beginning, adventures also have an ending, and she had other things to explore. She wanted me to go with her, but even then, I knew there was nothing for me outside of Neverland. So she left, I stayed behind, and I did my best to bury her memory and avoid the ache I feel in my chest every time I think of her.

Fuck. Without opening it, I toss the box back into the drawer and slam it shut. Growling, I turn my agitation to my original problem and call out through the garage. "Which one of you assholes didn't put my 7/16ths wrench back?"

A man with black hair, short on the sides and long enough to curl on top, sticks his head out from the customer service area next to my bay. "Sorry, boss."

I roll my eyes. Even as a grown-ass man, his childhood habit of taking the blame for stuff is ingrained in him as it ever was. "It wasn't you, Carlos. You've been manning the front desk all day."

A boyish smile breaks across his face, popping the dimples in his cheeks that make every female customer swoon. "Oh right. Never mind."

The heavy metal being pumped across the four garage bays from the huge speakers makes it hard for any of the others to hear me, so I make my way down the line.

"Nick, you take my wrench?"

The muscles in his arms bunch, and a sheen of sweat covers his dark brown skin as he drags a wheel from the Jeep on his hydraulic lift and drops it to the ground. "Nah, I've done nothing but new tires and rotations today. People out here acting like it's about to snow in the middle of July or something."

"They can act however they want as long as they're spending money here and not over at Croc's place."

"I hear that," he says, grabbing the wheel to haul it over to the tire changer. "Good luck finding your wrench, man."

I know the next two bays will come up short as well. Thomas is our resident technology geek. Anything that has wires, computer chips, and mother boards, he's our guy. In the shop, that usually means custom sound systems on a fun day or aftermarket alarms or remote starts on a boring one. Either way, I know Thomas won't have my wrench. He has the strictest moral code of anyone I've ever known. He'd never take anything that wasn't his without asking first.

Then there's Silas. He'd never take anything that wasn't his either, but for an entirely different reason. He's an arrogant jackass—and I say that with nothing but love for the guy —who believes he's just a hair better at everything than you are and all his things are of slightly better quality. For lack of a better term, Silas is a one-upper. It usually annoys the shit out of other people, but we accept it as one of the many individual idiosyncrasies that make up our group.

Silas and I are two of the three body work specialists in the shop, but it's rare we get the opportunity to flex our skills. Pulling dents out of doors is child's play when you can take a rusted POS and turn it into an award-winning, custom beauty. But if we don't do the mundane crap that pays the bills, we won't ever have the money to open up the custom rebuild business we've been wanting forever. Something we'll get around to doing someday, but not anytime soon.

"Si," I say with a nod as I pass.

He gives me a chin lift and his signature smirk before going back to sanding the bondo on a Chevy Malibu's quarter panel.

I can hear the arguing before I even get to the next bay,

which is nothing new when it comes to the twins. I find them standing underneath a lifted Toyota, one working on the exhaust and the other replacing brakes, their blond hair sticking up in different directions from running their hands through it as they do when working.

I stop in front of them and cross my arms over my chest, raising an inquisitive brow. "What's the argument today, boys?"

"Hey, Peter," they say in unison.

The one fitting the new exhaust pipe pauses to say, "Numbnuts over there says that a Camaro SS would beat a Mustang GT in a quarter mile."

His brother points a wrench—not my *missing* wrench, I notice—in his direction. "If they're both stock? Absofucking-lutely. Now if you're talking aftermarket mods, that might be a different story."

"What do you think, Peter?" they ask.

The creepy twin thing is something they do often, but I guess when two people are inseparable, it's bound to happen. They do everything together—including women, which is about the only thing they don't argue about. And they can easily turn around a job that has multiple issues in half the time with their tag-team approach, so I've never made them split up. We don't have enough bays for all of us to work separately, anyway. Carlos and Thomas share a bay and switch off with front desk duties since they're the best at customer service.

"Well, in my humble opinion—" There's nothing humble about it because I know everything there is to know about cars. "If you're talking stock and you're driving a Mustang GT, you might get him off the line, but his SS would smoke your ass before you get halfway down the track. So…" I glance at the embroidered name patch on the coveralls of the twin on the left. I wish one of them would dye their hair a different color for chrissake. "*Tobias* is right this time. Sorry, Tyler."

"Aha! Told you, asshole!" Tobias continues to rub his victory in a grumbling Ty's face as I move onto the last bay in our shop.

A pair of shapely legs in jean cutoffs sticks out from underneath the front of a Dodge Challenger, one black combat boot tapping along to the heavy beat of the music.

"Tink, you wouldn't happen to know what happened to my 7/16ths, would you?"

She rolls out from under the car, a huge smile on her face and a familiar wrench in her hand. "You mean *this* 7/16ths?"

I arch a brow down at her. "That'd be the one, yeah."

She raises her free hand up to me, and I help pull her up to her feet. She's wearing a tank top with a chopped-off bottom, leaving her stomach bare except for the grease smudges. I gave up telling her to wear a pair of coveralls years ago. She claims she can't work in restrictive clothing, and honestly, it doesn't hurt business when guys bring their cars in for unnecessary oil changes or diagnostic checks just to get a chance to chat up Tink. It's not like her Daisy Dukes and crop tops are distracting any of us. Tink's always been a non-sexual entity in our group, though we stopped referring to her as one of the boys after she nailed Si in the balls for it when she was twelve.

"Sorry, Peter, I couldn't find mine," she says, looking up at me.

"You need glasses, Tink?"

She furrows her brow under the longer fall of her blond pixie cut. "No, why?"

"Because yours is right there on your workbench."

She follows to where I'm pointing. Her skin flushes as she bites on the inside of her cheek, making the thin gold nose-ring glint in the light. "Well, would you look at that," she says with an embarrassed chuckle. "I swear it wasn't there earlier. But now that I've got you here, Peter, I wanted to ask you—"

"Boss!"

I turn to see Carlos gesturing wildly at me like it's a life or death situation. Shit, I hope the computer isn't on the fritz again. We can't afford to replace it. "Sorry, Tink, hold that thought."

"That's okay, I'll walk and talk," she says, falling into line as I make my way back across the bays, the bell she keeps on a long chain around her neck tinkling with every step. "I was wondering if you wanted to go to the Pitt County car show next weekend and pick out a custom project we could work on together. You know, to sell afterward as another way of bringing in money."

"We don't have the time or space to devote to a project like that right now. We need all our bays operational for the daily stuff that's paying the bills."

"No, I know. But we could make space for it in the pole barn and then after work—"

"Tink, what have I always said about after work?"

She sighs. "When work is done the fun's begun."

"Exactly. We only work as much as we have to, and after that, we work hard at having fun," I say, dropping my wrench off in my bay as we pass. "Which, correct me if I'm wrong, makes me the best boss on the planet."

"You're absolutely the best boss, Peter. You're the best at everything."

I smile down at her. "Won't get an argument from me on that one." We stop in front of Carlos, and I put a reassuring hand on her shoulder. "It's a good idea, Tink, just not for right now. Someday, we'll be able to do stuff like that without pulling overtime hours. Until then, let's keep doing what we're doing."

"*Boss.*"

Carlos is practically bouncing in place as I finally turn my attention to him. "What is it?"

"There's someone who wants to talk to you about a custom rebuild."

I arch a brow in Tink's direction, but she holds her hands up. "Don't look at me. I didn't talk to anyone but you about that."

"Tell him we don't do custom rebuilds right now, but we can refer him to someone who does. Hold on, I think I have a number for J.R. at the Toy Shop in London…" I fish my phone out of the pocket of my coveralls and pull up my contacts.

"It's a *her*, Boss," Carlos corrects. "And trust me, you're gonna want to talk to her."

"Trust me," I say, scrolling through the names in my phone. *Did I save it under the J's or the T's?* "I'm really not."

I hear the door to the waiting area open just as Tink whispers, "Holy shit," making me look up from my phone…and my heart stops.

"Hello, Peter."

A woman with cornflower blue eyes and long hair the color of maple syrup steps into the shop. Her smile is shy, and her small hands twist together in front of her like she's unsure of her welcome. So much time has passed since I've seen her, and yet, she's just as beautiful as that night I saw her standing on her balcony, wearing only a nightgown and rays of moonlight.

"Can you believe it?" Carlos says excitedly. "Wendy's home!"

CHAPTER THREE

WENDY

Then…
Age 12
London, North Carolina

"Night, Wendy," John and Michael call out as they bound into the bathroom that connects our bedrooms.

"Night, boys. Goodnight, Mom."

"Sweet dreams, honey," she says with her usual warm smile as she follows after my younger brothers and closes my door, leaving me alone at last.

Normally, I'm not in such a rush to get through story time—a nightly tradition I enjoy sharing with Mom and the boys, despite growing out of the fairytales a long time ago—but tonight is different. Because tonight I saw a boy hiding in the bushes beneath my balcony. I couldn't see much of him, but I saw his face for a split second before the shadows swallowed him up, and he is most definitely a boy around my age.

The entire time Mom was telling us the end of *Cinderella*, I barely heard a word she said. Not that it mattered, I can recite that fairytale and all the others by heart. But tonight, I had questions running through my mind as I pretended to listen with John and Michael.

Who is he? Why is he down there? Is he still there? Do I know him from school? Has he been there before? On and on, and when I ran out of new questions, I started back at the beginning, practically vibrating with anticipation for the moment I could get the answers.

And that moment is now.

As soon as I hear my mom's footsteps pass my door, followed by the creaks of the old stairs as she rejoins my dad for their night of knitting and crossword puzzles while half-watching *Law & Order*, I throw off my covers and race to the French doors guarding my balcony. Too eager to be slow or quiet about it, I yank them open and rush to the bannister, practically toppling over the edge in the process. Despite my father's rule of never leaning over the railing, that's exactly what I do, squinting my eyes like it'll help me see any movement in the darkness. I look left and right and left again, but there's no one there. My excitement dies. He must have lef—

"What are you looking for?"

Startled at his sudden appearance next to me, I step back and open my mouth for the involuntary scream I can't seem to stop. Thankfully, the boy reacts quickly by covering my mouth with his hand to muffle the sound.

"Shhhh, I'm not going to hurt you," he whispers, slowly removing his hand.

My heart is still racing, and I'm breathing like I just ran a mile. The moonlight bathes him in shades of silver. It's not the best lighting, but I can tell he has light hair, kind eyes, and a half-smile that looks both innocent and mischievous at the same time.

He's a dichotomy—something with seemingly contradictory qualities. I learned that word in school last month, and it became my new favorite. I think a person who is different things at once would be incredibly interesting. Dad just raises an eyebrow at me and says they might seem that way, but it's not really possible. A person is either one thing or another; it's all black and white with my dad, no gray areas allowed.

But the gray areas are where shadows live, and I think the things inside those shadows are likely the most fascinating things of all.

Now that my breathing is steady and the blood is no longer rushing in my ears, I realize that he's studying me, too. His head is cocked to the side, and his eyes are cataloging everything about me, like he'll be tested on it later.

"What's your name?" I finally ask. A small voice inside my head tells me I picked the wrong first question—that there are other things I should be asking of a boy who is somehow and for some reason on my balcony at night—but it's the first question I want an answer to.

"I'm—"

The sound of a door opening and closing below us turns us to stone, and my heartbeat picks right back up where it left off. Why is it so *loud*? The whole neighborhood can probably hear it, for goodness sake. Peeking over the rail, I see my dad taking Nana out. She stops in her tracks and jerks her head up, sniffing at the air. Oh God, if she smells the boy, she'll bark like crazy. Panicking, I grab his hand and pull him into my room, shutting the doors to the balcony as quickly and quietly as I can.

But now I'm paranoid that my mom will come to check on me for some unknown reason, and if I lock my bedroom door, it'll look suspicious. The bathroom! It's the only room I'm allowed—and expected—to lock. Again, I grab the boy's hand and lead him into the large bathroom that connects my brothers' bedroom with mine. After locking both doors, I let out a huge sigh of relief. I'm not worried about John or Michael hearing us; tfhey would sleep through the zombie apocalypse.

"Okay, we should be safe in here."

The boy crosses his arms over his chest and raises his eyebrows. "I could be wrong, but I'm usually not, and I don't think I'm supposed to be in a closed bathroom with a girl."

His statement, while not exactly false, surprises me. It's the way he says it, like he's not exactly sure. "What makes you say that?"

"We're not allowed to be in a closed bathroom with Tinker Bell. We're also supposed to make sure we're not in the middle of changing clothes when she's around. It's why she wears a bell, so we know when she's coming."

I frown. "Is Tinker Bell your cat?"

"What? No, she's not our cat." He laughs loud enough that I have to shush him. Lowering his voice, he says, "Tink is a little girl. The only one, actually. But I told her she's a fairy, so do me a favor and don't tell her any different. It was the only thing I could think of to make her feel better at the time, and after that, it just kind of stuck."

"A fairy? Now I'm super confused. Maybe we should start at the beginning."

"Fine by me, Wendy, but I'd feel better if we weren't in the bathroom."

"How do you know my name?"

"I heard your mom say it. The storyteller *is* your mom, right?"

"Storyteller? Oh, yeah, that's my mom. Um..." I bite my lip and look down at the cool tiles under my feet as I weigh my options.

"You're thinking awfully hard," he says softly. A finger raises my chin before his thumb gently pulls my lip from my teeth, causing my breath to catch. "That looks painful."

"The thinking thing?" I ask absently.

"The lip biting thing," he answers with a crooked grin.

"Oh." In the distance, I hear my parents' voices in the hall outside my room. I hold a finger to my mouth, and we wait in silence, the moment suspended in time, as I wait for the tell-tale sound of their door closing them in for the night. As soon as I hear it, I exhale and motion for him to follow me.

I climb onto my bed, sitting cross-legged, and pat the center for him to join me. Our knees are practically touching as we lean in to speak in hushed tones. "Okay, let's start at the beginning. My name is Wendy Moira Angela Darling. What's yours?"

He sits up a little straighter and says, "Peter Pan."

"Is that it?"

Peter scowls at me. "It's a lot longer of a name than most of the others at the school."

Shoot. I'm so used to everyone having stupidly long names, thanks to an outdated Darling tradition and going to school with a bunch of rich kids, that a normal name sounds almost weird. "I'm sorry, I didn't mean anything by that. Peter Pan is a really nice name. Will you tell me about the others? And about Tinker Bell the fairy?"

His eyes—which I now know are the prettiest shade of crystal blue—light up. "You mean like telling you a story? I've gotten really good at telling stories to the Lost Boys."

"Yes, like a story, but a true one."

Peter shrugs one shoulder. "Okay, but it's not all that interesting. I live at the School for Lost Boys of Neverland. There's ten of us boys plus Tink. She's the only girl."

"Why is a girl living at a school for boys?"

His brows knit together over his straight nose. "I don't know, actually. I never thought to ask. Not that Croc would bother answering, anyway."

"Who's Croc?"

"He and his wife Delia got the school when her aunt and uncle died in a car accident. I don't remember them, but James does, and he says they were really good people. Not like Croc who's a total ass—"

I gasp. "Peter."

"What?"

"Kids aren't supposed to swear."

"They're not?" He pauses to think. "Huh. That's not one of our rules."

"Well, it should be. Or at the very least, you shouldn't swear in the presence of a lady."

"Lady?"

"Yeah, you know, like a girl. Gentlemen—a word for boys with proper manners—don't swear or say bad words in front of a lady."

"That sounds like something a mother would say. Is it?"

"I don't know about *all* mothers, but my mom does. Mostly when my dad gets so worked up about something that he forgets his manners."

"Moms scold fathers and tell bedtime stories to their kids," he says, almost to himself, like he's taking mental notes for a class. "What else do they do?"

He's only given me small bits of information, but I think I'm finally starting to understand Peter's situation. "Don't any of you have moms, Peter?"

"Nope. We have Delia, but she's no mother. She says it all the time, too. So tell me what yours does and then I can tell the boys."

I think for a second about all the things my mom does for me and my brothers. Definitely too many to mention, but I can hit the highlights. "Well, she takes care of us. She makes us meals, does our laundry, helps us with schoolwork, makes us feel better when we're sick or sad, those types of things. And at night, she tells us stories then tucks us into bed with a kiss and—"

"What's a kiss?"

My mouth drops open for a second before I snap it shut. I wait for him to laugh and tell me he's joking, but he's just staring at me, waiting for an answer. How loveless and sheltered would a child's life have to be for him to never have heard the word before? And how on earth do I explain what it is without a demonstration or an example to show him?

I rub my damp palms on my comforter and clear my throat as delicately as possible. "Well, a kiss is," I start slowly as I try to think of what to say, "it's something special you share with someone you care about."

He seems to think about that for a few seconds, then says, "That sounds nice. Can I have one?"

Again, I'm speechless. I've often daydreamed about what my first kiss with a boy would be like, but this is *not* how I imagined it.

"Wendy?" he prods, holding his hand out between us. "Will you give me a kiss?"

Panicking, I open my nightstand drawer, grab the first thing I see and place it in his palm. He looks down at the Monopoly game piece—the stupid *thimble* of all things—then lifts his gaze to mine. My cheeks flush with embarrassment. This has to be the lamest moment of my life. He's going to think I'm *so dumb*. Ohmigod, I want to die.

"Thank you," he says, closing it in his fist. "No one's ever given anything to me before."

Whoa, that's…not what I expected him to say. "Never?"

My heart breaks for him when he shakes his head solemnly. But his mood changes as fast as flipping a switch, and just like that he's excited again. "I should give you a kiss, too."

"Oh, um, I don't think that's—"

He digs something out from his jeans' pocket and holds it up for me to see. "It's called a high crown acorn nut." The mirror finish reflects the lamplight almost hypnotically as he turns it this way and that. Its name makes sense, it really does look like a small metal acorn.

"I got it from a car I took apart today." I'm about to ask what he means about taking a car apart when he continues as though he didn't say anything out of the ordinary. "Usually they're stainless steel or the fancier ones are chrome, but this one is *gold*. I liked that it was different. Special, you know? Like you said, a kiss is something special. So I want you to have it."

I hold out my hand, and when his fingertips graze the center of my palm, it feels like a thousand fairy wings beating in my stomach. "Thank you, Peter. This is very sweet of you."

Peter smiles. "I think I'd like being sweet to you, Wendy. Can I come back tomorrow?"

"Tomorrow?"

He glances at the digital alarm clock on my nightstand. "Yeah, I'd better get back. The boys'll be waiting to hear about the prince finding Cinderella. Guess it was a good thing she lost that shoe, huh?"

I chuckle softly and nod. "Yeah, I guess it was." He gets up and crosses to the balcony doors. "Where's the school?"

Stepping outside, we stand at the bannister as he points off into the distance. "Second star to the right and straight on till morning."

My jaw drops. "It'll take you until morning to get there? It's that far away?"

He laughs. "Nah, I'm just kidding. It's only about a mile or so that way, just past the city limits."

"Oh, that's not bad then."

Despite it sharing a border with London, I've never been to Neverland. I've never even been east of Hampton Street since Dad says it's not safe. The two cities couldn't be more different. London is a large metropolis with a picturesque skyline known for its downtown shopping and 5-star restaurants, all surrounded by a suburban area where people's social calendars are filled year-round with parties, cookouts, and charity events.

We're on the less-affluent east side where middle-class families try to keep up with their upper-class friends on the

23

west. But even London's lower-class is levels above Neverland. I've heard it's a pretty barren place that's more industrial than it is residential. Its only perk is that it's not far from Topsail Beach on the coast, but so are a ton of other towns, so it's not like that's much of a selling point.

"Well, goodnight, Peter Pan."

"Goodnight, Wendy Moira Angela Darling."

One second he's standing next to me, the next he disappears over the edge, and a second after that I hear a *thump* as he drops to the ground. When he steps into the light of the streetlamp, I call out to him in the loudest whisper I dare. "Peter!" He stops and turns to look up at me. "My answer is yes."

"Yes what?"

"Yes, you can come back tomorrow." Suddenly I'm unsure of myself as I realize he didn't ask a second time. Maybe he changed his mind. "If you want, I mean," I tack on quickly.

He grins wide and says something that sounds like, "Definitely my adventure," and then disappears into the night.

CHAPTER FOUR

WENDY

Now...

Peter Pan.

Seeing him again after all these years is positively surreal.

So is sitting in his office of a place he built with the knowledge he gained from his illegal work as a child. Probably not many success stories like that out there, and yet, here he is.

Wearing a grease-streaked wifebeater and a pair of coveralls hanging from his trim waist, he settles his muscular frame —big enough to belong to a heavyweight fighter with extensive tattoos to match—into his worn leather desk chair. He looks so different, nothing like the boy I once knew, and yet...

He looks *everything* like him. Same messy blond hair, same crystalline blue eyes promising adventure, and the smirk that was both innocent and mischievous at the same time. Though, with the way he's looking at me right now, that smirk doesn't seem quite as innocent as it used to. If he keeps that up, he'll burn the clothes right off my body, and this meeting will get decidedly less professional, really quick.

Leaning back in his desk chair with his hands threaded over his flat stomach, Peter studies me like I'm a museum artifact. It takes every ounce of my self-control not to fidget in my seat across from him.

"LB Automotive, huh? That's clever," I say with a nervous smile. "Are all the Lost Boys here?"

"No, Hook has his own crew across town. It's just me, Si, Carlos, Thomas, the twins, and Nick."

"And Tink," I add.

He nods. "And Tink."

"She looked just as happy to see me as she ever did, if that wicked glare was anything to go by."

"You know Tink. She's always had a problem with mothers."

I roll my eyes. "I'm not anyone's mother, Peter. I never was."

"But that's not what we pretended, was it?" He asks the question like it's a demand for admission. For me to admit to the silly scenarios we played out as children. Scenarios that turned more real with every passing year until, eventually, we acted like a true married couple in all the ways that mattered.

Heat swirls in my belly and settles into my cheeks. If I don't change the subject to something more innocuous, he'll be able to read my every thought.

"I'm proud of you, Peter. Despite all the odds stacked against you, you came out on top."

"You doubted I would?"

"Of course not. You know I always believed you could."

A hint of sadness flickers across his face before he sets his jaw, and his walls come down. "Just not if I stayed in Neverland."

The barb stings enough that I wince, but it's okay. I deserve to share the pain.

"Sorry," he says, blowing out a breath and leaning forward to brace his forearms on his desk. "I shouldn't have said that."

"No, it's okay. I never should have asked you to leave. I was being selfish, wanting you to come with me."

"No more selfish than me wanting you to stay." Peter stares into my eyes like he's trying to see our past in their reflection. "But I didn't belong in your world any more than you belonged in mine. You leaving was for the best."

"It didn't break our hearts any less, though," I say softly.

He gives me the signature Peter Pan half-shrug. "Broken things can be fixed; I do it every day. All you need are the right parts, a good set of tools, and the desire to get a little bit dirty and a whole lot sweaty."

The crooked grin and wink he flashes me is *all* mischief, and I hope the flush I'm feeling isn't visible above the scoop neck of my top. But then he chuckles, the sound deep and husky, and I know I have no such luck. "It's good to know some things don't change. Still as proper as ever, I see."

I narrow my eyes at him and lie through my teeth. "I'm not all that proper, Peter."

He arches a dubious brow and leans back again. "No? Then why don't you come over here and show me just how *not* proper you really are, Wendy."

I should've known he'd call my bluff, he always did. Dang it, why do I keep blushing like a schoolgirl with a crush? It's been ten years and half a dozen relationships since I've seen this man. Any butterfly-flapping, skin-tingling, or spark-igniting feelings should be long dead and buried by now

But those half a dozen relationships were never anything to write home about in the bedroom. Not that I would have ever written home about my sex life—oh my God, my parents would have had heart attacks, not to mention, I would've died of embarrassment—and these…these *feelings* that I've always had for Peter, make everything I've ever felt for another man pale in comparison.

"See?" he says, pulling me from my musings. "Wendy Moira Angela Darling, ever a lady. That's okay, Wen. Your properness is one of the things I always liked about you."

I arch a brow. "Then why were you always trying to get me to break the rules?"

Smiling wide, he leans back far enough to pop his feet onto the corner of his desk, lacing his fingers behind his head, which—*Heaven help me*—makes the muscles in his upper arms bulge deliciously. "I'm pretty sure it's Rule #1 in the Bad Boy Handbook: Find a good girl and convince her to break the rules. It might be the *only* rule, actually. And I excelled at it, if I do say so myself. Which of course, I do."

Rolling my eyes, I change the subject before his ego gets too big to fit through his office door. "Well, I'm not here to break any rules now. I'm here to hire you to rebuild a classic car for me."

His eyes narrow slightly, and his feet hit the floor. For several seconds, he just stares at me. "I didn't realize you were here on business."

That pulls me up short and twists the metaphorical knife I've lived with for ten years. The day I left Peter—*chose* to leave Peter—felt like I'd plunged a blade into my chest. I kept telling myself I'd come back, but between college and internships that demanded all my free time, months turned into years, and eventually, I was too scared to come home. I'd convinced myself that maybe Peter had only thought he loved me because he'd never known another girl who wasn't his pseudo-sister. Or maybe he'd moved on and found someone else to share adventures with and dance beneath the stars. It was cowardly, I know, but girl logic doesn't always make the best sense, and my heart had decided not knowing was better than breaking all over again. So I stayed away…until now.

Tilting my head, I ask carefully, "Why did you think I came?"

Something runs through his mind; I can see it just barely there, and then he closes down all over again. Pushing to his feet, he moves to lean on the wall, crossing his arms as he studies me. "I didn't really give it much thought. But business purposes are just as good a reason as any other. Tell me what you need."

Dark clouds hang over us, fat and heavy with all the things we're not saying. But neither of us are ready to incite that storm, so I push it back and focus on my immediate concern. "I'm sure you've heard of the annual Love for Littles event."

"You mean the ritzy party that London's elite uses as an excuse to get dressed up and throw their money around for charity?"

"Yes, I mean the huge fundraiser gala that raises hundreds of thousands of dollars every year for the Children's Hospital of London," I tactfully correct. "This year, the proceeds aren't only going to the hospital but also to a non-profit organization that helps children in foster care, so it needs to be bigger than ever."

"Huh," he says, rubbing his chin. "I'm surprised the hospital board is willing to share, even if it is another good cause for kids."

"Truth be told, they did need a little convincing, but the new social worker at the hospital also runs the Lost Ones of London, so he had some pull."

I make sure to leave out the minor details that L.O.L. is my mother's foundation, which is run by Michael, who also happens to be the hospital's new pediatric social worker. The last thing I want to be accused of is nepotism.

"Okay, so what does this event have to do with you?"

"Right, sorry. The event planner who organized it for

years moved to California to become a wedding planner to the stars or something. It wasn't easy, but," I pause for dramatic effect and for the mental squeal I still do whenever I think about my hard-earned victory, "I won the account."

Peter stares at me expectantly, like he's waiting for the punchline. "For…your financial firm?"

"Oh! I forgot that you— Sorry, no, that's not what I mean. I actually quit being a financial advisor about a year ago and started my own event planning business. See? A proper girl would've stayed in the career she spent years in school and paid a sickening amount of money for, even if it was stressing her out to the point of chronic migraines and severe anxiety."

He frowns, his brows crinkling together. "I don't know, sounds like you made the right choice to me."

Yeah, tell that to my father who's convinced I'm throwing away a solid career in financing to be one step above a children's party clown. Just because I've never done anything larger than birthday parties and baby showers doesn't mean that's all I'm capable of.

Landing this account means the world to me. It's my chance to make a name for myself in this highly competitive industry. My chance to prove that I have what it takes to organize large-scale, big budget events. And maybe more importantly, my chance to show my dad that following my heart— instead of continuing down the path he paved for me—wasn't the biggest mistake of my life.

My mom was more apt to encourage us to chase our dreams, and she was good for countering my dad's extreme practicality. But after she passed three years ago, he's been more rigid than ever with his black-and-white views of the world. Succeeding at something my mom would've encouraged me to do—and something that will help the foundation she started and nurtured after I planted the seed about so many local orphans and foster children needing help—will be my tribute to her memory. For all those reasons, I'm going to make this the best Love for Littles event this city has ever seen.

"So, you're an event planner now. That's great," Peter says. "Let's get to the part where you need me."

I swallow hard. *Why* does he have to say things in a sex-roughened voice? Or what I imagine his adult sex-roughened voice would sound like. This is insane. It's like my brain has situational A.D.D. around him and keeps getting distracted by thoughts of— *Stop it, Wendy!*

In an attempt to walk off my nervous energy and prevent him from seeing all the thoughts running through my wayward mind, I stand and pace the small area in his office as I explain the situation. "The committee wanted a new idea they haven't done before, and I proposed that they do a classic car theme with the highlight of the evening being a customized rebuilt classic car that they could auction off at the end of the night. Lucky for me, they loved the idea, and I got the job. All on my own merit, I might add."

"I'm sure you did. But why come here, to Neverland? Why not go to one of the more prestigious custom design shops in London like the Toy Shop?"

That stops me in my tracks, but I don't turn to face him.

Because I've been waiting for an excuse to come see you... To make sure you don't hate me... To remember the girl who threw caution to the wind and lived for the moment whenever she was with you... To see if there's part of you that still feels for me the way that I feel for you...

I pretend to look out at the shop through the window in front of me, but I'm not focused on anything except his presence behind me. "I'm a firm believer in bringing business to friends whenever I can. I know you're good at what you do, and I think you'd deliver an amazing car." I try one of his half-shrugs on for size and hope it doesn't look as forced as it feels. "Why *not* come to you?"

"Friends, huh?"

Like all those years ago on the first night we met, he's suddenly so close I can feel the warmth from his body. Turning, I come face to chest with him. Normally, I'd look up and meet his gaze, but if I do that, I might melt on the spot. Not that staring at the ribbed cotton stretched over his tattooed pecs is much better. *Come on, Wendy, you can do it. Look up.*

I finally do, and my legs stand firm. Brava to me. "Of course, Peter," I say with a grin and all the nonchalance I can muster. "We've always been friends."

He squints at me, crossing those beefy arms over his chest. I can practically see the smoke coming out of his ears as he thinks everything through. "Okay, fine. I'll do it, but there's some conditions."

"Shoot."

"We'll go shopping for the car together. It just so happens that there's a car show next weekend at the Pitt County Fairgrounds. We'll start our search there. We should be able to find something, but if not, I have some contacts that might be able to help us out."

"Sounds good. I'd like to be a part of that process, anyway. Then I can keep the committee up-to-date on what we bought and what your plans are for it. But is there something we can look at sooner? We only have six weeks before the event, which isn't much time and—"

"Plenty of time," he says, waving a dismissive hand. "Condition two: you help with design choices. Custom accessories, paint job, etcetera. Anything that will be seen by someone, you'll pick it out. Unless you pick the wrong thing, in which case, I'll veto your decision and make the right choice."

Now it's my turn to cross my arms. "Then what's the point of me even choosing?"

"Condition three," he says, steamrolling over my complaint, "since we're *friends* who haven't seen each other in a decade, you need to come to our place tonight for the weekly Friday festivities."

"Our place? Do you all live together?"

"Why wouldn't we? We're family. Families live together."

When he puts it like that, it doesn't sound strange for a group of mid- to late-twenty somethings to be living together like a bunch of frat boys. Wait. "Did you say *weekly* Friday festivities?"

Again, he ignores my question and asks one of his own. "Are you back for good?"

He stares at me intently, and I can feel the weight of my answer on my chest. "No," I say softly. "I'm staying with Michael right now. I'll go home to Charlotte after the job is over."

Peter gives a stiff nod and grabs a business card off his desk. "My cell is on there. Text me the address. I'll pick you up at nine."

I'm a little flustered, what with the deluge of emotions on top of the conditions and plans he's rattled off as though they're foregone conclusions. I'm better when I can plan a presentation and then give that presentation to a quiet audience who later communicates with me via email. So I deserve a bit of a break when all I get out is an *okay* as I stare at the card I'm now holding.

"Wendy," he says, lifting my chin with his finger until I meet his smoldering blue eyes. "I didn't want you to break the rules because of any Bad Boy Handbook."

Using his thumb, he gently pulls my lip from my teeth, stealing my breath with the vivid memory from a lifetime ago that feels like only yesterday. As he holds my gaze, I swear he's not seeing our past anymore. This time, it's as though he's trying to catch even the slightest glimpse of our future, and it makes my wounded heart ache.

"I did it because those times when I watched your face light up from the thrill of doing something you knew you shouldn't, however harmless…those were the moments I lived for. Those were the best adventures I ever had."

Me too, Peter. Me too.

CHAPTER FIVE

WENDY

Then…
Age 12

Peter's been visiting me for about a month, and those precious few hours are the best parts of my week. He can't come every day, though, and it's super hard to get to sleep with my mind racing about why. Though I've learned more about the Lost Boys and where he lives, I think Peter's careful not to give me the more sordid details. It's sweet that he wants to protect me, but it's almost worse leaving it up to my imagination.

Last night he didn't come, and I'm worried he won't show up again. Thanks to my stellar reputation as a good daughter, my parents never check on me after our bedtime routines. If they did, they'd find me not in my bed but sitting on the ground of my balcony with my legs tucked against my chest, searching the shadows and listening in the darkness.

Then I hear it. The soft call of a mourning dove. It's the signal he uses to make sure the coast is clear. If I don't answer back, he knows not to climb up to me. It hasn't happened yet, and I hope it never does. I always want to be here for Peter.

I whistle back, and a moment of rustling ivy leaves later, he's vaulting himself over the bannister. "Hello, Wen," he says with a wide smile.

He's taken to shortening my name on occasion. I almost objected the first time but stopped. Having a nickname that only Peter uses is just another one of our secrets; special things I only have with him. Crossing to me, he offers me his hand, causing my skin to tingle where our palms touch.

"Hello, Peter."

"And how are you this fine evening, m'lady?"

Sometimes he likes to pretend we're grown-ups and tries to speak proper like the fairytale characters I tell him about. It's fun to act like we're in our very own fairytale and can do whatever we want. I giggle and let him pull me to my feet. "I'm well, thank you, kind sir. And how are—" I gasp when he turns his face toward the light spilling out from my bedroom. "Peter, what happened?"

His eye is black and blue with a nasty cut that looks like its struggling to stay closed over the curve of his cheekbone.

"It's nothin', don't worry about me. I'm fine, I promise."

I capture my lip between my teeth and try not to fuss over him. "Is that why you didn't come last night?"

He nods. "Wouldn't stop bleeding and I didn't want to upset you. Maybe I should've waited until it was healed. But I missed you, Wen."

Gah! Sometimes the things this boy says makes my knees shaky. "Come on, get inside. I have stuff that can help that angry gash."

"Wendy, I'm a man," he grumbles on his way into my room. "I don't need to be tended to like some kid."

I've heard mom mention my father's "fragile male ego" when he thinks he's being babied. The irony is that he complains about it even as he gives her puppy dog eyes and waits for her to bring him soup and a cool cloth for his fore-head when he's sick. This must be how Mom feels.

I roll my eyes behind his back and order him to sit on my bed before getting the supplies I need from my bathroom. Arranging myself next to him, I use the warm washcloth to clean the dried blood from the cut, then gently hold it there to soften the skin with the heat.

"I'm going to apply this butterfly bandage. I don't think you need stitches, but it's going to take a long time to heal if the skin can't stay together."

He holds still and barely winces when I push the edges closer and secure the adhesive strip. "I'll have to take it off in the morning or Croc will be suspicious."

"Oh, right. Well, even having this on for eight hours or so should help."

"What's that?" he asks, watching me open a small jar.

"It's a salve my mom uses for John's bruises. He's in Tae Kwon Do, and sometimes, the sparring gets a little out of control." As I smooth the ointment over the discolored skin, a smile spreads across his face, and I can *feel* him staring at me. Now his cheeks aren't the only ones with color. "What?" I ask self-consciously.

"You'd make a great mom, Wendy."

"Oh, thank you. I mean, I hope to be, someday. I'd like lots of kids."

Suddenly, he sits up straighter, and I can practically see the lightbulb floating over his innocently mischievous head. "Holy shh—" My left eyebrow arches at him like I've seen my mother do more times than I can count, and to my surprise, it works. "—oot," he finishes. "I have an idea. You can be a mom to the Lost Boys."

My mouth gapes open. "You want me to be a mom to you and the Lost Boys?"

"No, not me, I don't want a mother. I'll be the dad. Dads are the leaders of their families, after all, and that's what I am

—their leader. Except for Smee and Starkey, but whenever Hook's not around, they follow me, too."

"Peter, you're not making any sense," I say. "How can I possibly be a mother to the Lost Boys?"

"You can come with me sometimes at night. I'll sneak you in, then you can tell us—I mean, them—bedtime stories, and tuck them in just like a mom does."

"Are you crazy? You want me to sneak out of my bedroom in the middle of the night? What if I get caught? What if my mom checks on me, or Croc catches me at the school?"

"No, yes, you won't, she won't, he won't," he says, counting the super-fast answers on his fingers.

I'm speechless, utterly speechless. Wait, no I'm not. "You *are* crazy, Peter. Do you realize that I've never broken a rule in my life? Never! And something tells me there's a certain amount of finesse needed for breaking rules without getting caught, and as a strict rule follower, I *don't have that*."

"But I do." He pulls his shoulders back, stretching his T-shirt across his chest. *Why am I noticing that?* "I break rules all the time, and I never get caught." Gingerly touching the bandage on his cheekbone, he frowns. "Well, almost never."

Instinctively, I reach up and lightly trace the outer edge of his bruise. His hand encircles my wrist, and we both freeze. Those fairy wings are back in my belly, and I forget to breathe as a crooked grin spreads across his face. I stare into his blue eyes sparkling in the lamplight, promising unexpected adventures and stories untold.

I think about the other boys and Tinker Bell at the school, without anyone to care for them or look after them. Not properly like children should be. Would it be so horrible if I took a small risk to offer them some much needed nurturing? My parents have always raised me and my brothers to help those less fortunate than us, so they would probably even approve. You know, if it wasn't for the whole "sneaking out of my room at night to go with a strange boy I barely know, to go to a city I'm not allowed, to sneak into a place run by a couple who takes pleasure in abusing children" thing. But besides all that…

"Okay," I whisper.

Hope and excitement flash in his eyes. "Okay?"

"Yeah, okay." Taking a deep breath, I utter the words that will begin our story. "I'll go with you to Neverland, Peter Pan."

CHAPTER SIX

WENDY

Now...

Peter picks me up right on time in a dark green muscle car. He holds the door open for me, and I settle onto the pristine tan leather. "What kind of car is this?"

He props his arm along the top of the door and leans in, pride beaming on his face. "She's a 1970 Hemi 'Cuda, one of only 666 made. She's a rare beauty with a ton of horsepower. Just like her owner," he adds with a saucy wink before closing me in.

I barely contain my nervous giggle as he walks around to slide behind the wheel. I feel awkward and excited—just like in the early days of our relationship—so my plan is to make idle conversation as a distraction. Though, whether I'm trying to distract *him* from noticing or myself, I have no idea. "Did you restore it yourself?"

"From the wheels up." He turns the key, and the engine roars to life like an angry beast on the hunt. A couple of hard revs actually rocks the car in place.

"Whoa," I say, quickly fastening my seatbelt. I brace my

hands on the dash as he pulls away from the curb in a way that would flunk a driving student. "So, what—"

"Why did you quit being a financial advisor to be an event planner?"

The suddenness with which he interrupts my inane chatter breaks my train of thought, and I have to take a moment to switch tracks. "I told you, it was stressful. I don't work well under pressure."

Taking his eyes off the road for longer than I'd like, he pins me with a knowing look. "You forget that I know you, Wen. And I know that's a bunch of sh—crap."

I bite the inside of my cheek to keep from laughing. I'm still not one to cuss, but I've grown out of being scandalized whenever I hear others doing it. I haven't seen him in ten years, but I highly doubt Peter Pan, ruffian mechanic and leader of the Lost Boys, doesn't swear like a sailor on a daily basis. So the fact that he caught himself to avoid offending me is melting my insides and making me feel things I'm not ready to feel for him again. Not yet.

"I don't know what you're talking about," I say primly, "and I'd appreciate it if you'd pay attention to the road instead of me."

"Fine, I'll let it go for now." Though he turns his attention back to the stretch of highway ahead, somehow, I become even more aware of his presence, like the space between us is shrinking with every passing second. "But for the record, whether or not I'm looking at you, I'm always paying attention to you, Wendy." His voice is low and rough. "It's impossible not to."

Oh God. How could I have forgotten about the things he used to say to me? The things that reach deep inside and touch my soul, my heart. Peter was always so guileless. It was one of my favorite qualities about him. It's like he had an inability to lie to you.

Although, being one hundred percent honest *all* the time

had its downsides too. Don't ask him if he thinks you look fat in those pants because he might just tell you "yep" and then not understand why you storm off in a huff or burst into tears.

But by that same token, when he expressed how he felt about me, I knew it to be the absolute truth. He wasn't telling me things I wanted to hear. There was no fear of being manipulated for ulterior motives like other girls worried about with their boyfriends. Peter simply told you what he thought, what he felt. All the time, every time.

So now I have to wonder, is he still like that? Or has he learned that a little deception can go a long way in getting what you want from a girl? What are his intentions with these conditions of us spending so much time together? He could still be hurt about how things ended between us. Maybe he wants revenge, to make me feel things and then break it off in some kind of twisted history-repeating-itself game.

I don't want to believe he would do anything like that. But the truth is I have no idea. And it's that uncertainty holding me back, reminding me I can't just return to Neverland after a whole decade and pick up where Peter and I left off, like nothing ever happened. No matter how much I might want to.

We drive the rest of the way in silence. I wish I could say I paid attention to how we got to the large three-story home in the middle of nowhere, but I was too consumed by my own thoughts. But as he pulls off the road onto a dirt driveway, it's impossible *not* to notice.

Dozens of cars are lined up in several rows off to the side like a fairgrounds parking lot. People are everywhere—in the front, on the wide wrap-around porch, and spilling from the back onto the sides of the house—carrying Solo cups or bottled beer, laughing and dancing and even wrestling.

"Welcome to the Lost Boys' Lair."

"*This* is what you meant by Friday festivities?"

"This is it. One big party."

I try to take everything in as he walks around to open my door, and I climb out of the car. "You do this *every* week?"

"Why not? You have a better idea on how to spend a Friday night?"

Grabbing my hand, he leads me up the porch steps through a screen door that squeaks as it slams shut behind us. It's not packed enough to be sardine status, but it's not exactly empty, either. "Do you know all these people?"

Peter looks around like he's never considered it before. A few seconds and a half-shrug later, he says, "Most of them. Probably. Maybe."

"All of Neverland must be here," I say as a couple of girls wearing very little clothing brush by me.

With a smug grin, he answers, "Likely. Come on, the real fun is out back."

Peter leads me through the main floor that's set up like the ultimate man cave. The front room is a gamer's paradise with a gigantic TV—seriously, those Call of Duty guys are *life-size*—surround sound, and special chairs that vibrate every time the player's character gets hit. Spectators are cheering and booing like it's a modern-day gladiator arena and not a farmhouse living room.

The next area may have been a dining room at one time but is now set up with a full bar, complete with stools, a ton of alcohol, and a swarthy bartender pouring drinks into red plastic cups while flirting shamelessly with the steady stream of women. Peter nudges me closer and catches Carlos' gaze.

"Hey there, Boss." He hands Peter a glass stein of beer, then flashes his dimples in my direction. "Glad you could make it, Wendy. Beer?"

"I don't suppose you have Stella back there, do you?"

Thick, black brows furrow together. "Who?"

"Never mind, I'll just have a bottle of whatever's easiest." His smile returns as he grabs me a Bud Light and twists the top off for me. "Perfect, thank you."

Peter takes a long pull of his beer then salutes Carlos with his glass. "Thanks, man, see you later."

"Good luck in the games."

"Games?" I ask.

"Don't need luck when you're the best," Peter answers with a smirk and starts to tug me away.

"Chief's here tonight."

That stops Peter in his tracks, but his amusement only grows. "Really?" Carlos nods. "Good. Winning's more fun against an equal."

I don't have time to ask for clarification as he leads me through the kitchen and out another screen door. Music blares through a set of speakers taller than me, and somehow, I can still hear the din of the crowd. The property is large enough that I can't see where it ends, and there are people *everywhere*.

A large bonfire seems to be the main focal point with a crowd of at least fifty people around it. Beyond that, tiki torches are lit in smaller groupings around what appear to be… "Huh. Games."

"Cool, right?" he says, looking out like a king surveying his land. "We have a few pits for horseshoes over there and three sets of cornhole over there. But the *real* fun is way in the back."

I follow his line of sight to where a dozen or so people are standing. My jaw drops. "Are those…? Are they throwing…?"

"Tomahawks, hatchets, axes. Whatever you want to call them, the answer is yes. Come on, I'll show you."

I'm too stunned to fear for my safety as we approach an area with axes flying at huge wooden targets. I'm also so engrossed in the actual axe-throwing that I don't notice who's doing the throwing until I hear my name in stereo.

"Wendy!"

I turn my head to see two large men bearing down on me

with arms outspread. I barely have time to brace myself before I'm the filling of a very tight twin sandwich. Despite feeling like my ribs might puncture my lungs if the boys get any more enthusiastic, I find myself laughing.

"Back off before you break her." Peter yanks them off by their shirts, but it doesn't dim their smiles a bit.

"Tobias, Tyler. My God, I can hardly believe it. You're so…so…"

"Huge?"

"Sexy?"

"Huge and sexy?" they finish together.

I laugh at how they're still speaking in unison like they share a brain. "I was going to say handsome. Is that acceptable?"

"No," Peter growls at the same time as the twins shout, "Hell yeah," and it makes me laugh all over again. No sooner do they start bickering about which of them I missed more when I hear another blast from the past.

"I'd recognize that laugh anywhere. Hiya, Wendy."

Before I even lay eyes on him, the cocksure tone that says he knows just a little bit more than everyone else gives him away. I smile and answer in kind. "Hiya, Silas." He's exactly how I would've imagined him to be. There's no dichotomy when it comes to Silas; what you see is what you get—arrogance with the extreme good looks to back it up. Model-gorgeous with sharp features, a full mouth, and a head of shoulder-length hair that makes you think a woman's hands were plowing through it moments ago. "It's been a long time. How are you?"

Grinning wide, he winks and says, "Better than any of these dipshits." Peter's hand strikes like a snake, smacking Silas in the back of the head. *Whack.* "Ow, man!"

"Watch your language."

"Seriously?" he says, rubbing the back of his head.

"Peter, he's a grown man now, not a ten-year-old boy."

45

"I don't care," he says, daring Silas to say otherwise with a narrowed glare. "They didn't swear in front of you before; they don't need to do it now. A little manners won't kill 'em. Now apologize to the lady."

"Sorry, Wendy," Silas grumbles, appearing properly dejected. Even though Silas always acted like he was better than everyone else, he still always deferred to Peter's leadership, and that obviously hasn't changed. Not with any of them, it seems.

"No apology is necessary," I say pointedly at Peter before smiling back at Silas, "but it's appreciated all the same. Are the others around?"

"They're never far." Turning around to where people are still throwing axes, he calls out, "Lost Boys, look who I found!"

There's a pause in the flying axes before I'm surrounded by faces that are familiar yet so different. My heart fills near to bursting as Nick and Thomas hug me like I'm their long-lost sister—or like once upon a time I pretended to be the mother figure they so needed at their tender ages.

From the corner of my eye, I see an axe go flying, end over end. until the blade is embedded dead center of the bullseye. Peter laughs as he walks over to grasp the forearm of the giant who'd thrown it. I didn't realize my mouth was hanging open until Nick closes it for me.

He's the definition of "mountain man" personified. Long, wavy brown hair is pulled back in a man-bun tied with a leather thong, his chiseled face is sporting a groomed beard that still somehow looks wild, and tribal tattoos mark his tan skin (I know this because *sweet baby Jesus* the man is only wearing a pair of worn jeans).

Also, because he's literally the size of a mountain. At least six-foot-five and whatever someone weighs when he's that tall and has only two-percent body fat.

"Chief, been a long time," Peter says. "What brings you to Neverland?"

The mountain smiles and walks down to wrest his axe from the large wooden target. "Figured it was time to check on my sister, make sure she's not getting herself into any trouble."

Speaking into his ear so as to not draw attention to myself, I ask Thomas who the man is and what he's a chief of. Thomas leans down and says, "Remember Tiger Lily?" I nod. "That's her half-brother, Gray Wolf."

"He's chief of the Piccaninny tribe?"

"No, that's just it," Thomas says. "He's *not* the chief. He would've been, but his mom had an affair with an outsider, so he's never been fully accepted by the tribe."

"Then chief is an ironic nickname? Isn't that insulting?"

"Look at the guy. If he was insulted, no one would dare use it. I think Gray was the one who actually started it as a joke. He's pretty easy-going. Until he's not."

I see what Thomas means. The mountain man seems rather jovial, drinking beer and flipping his axe around by the handle as he talks. But I can also sense something else. Like that gray wolf he's named after is lying in wait, ready to attack the moment something goes sideways.

Peter grabs an axe from a large chunk of wood—the handle is painted black and the metal head a dark green, like his car, with a gold "P" on each side—and turns back to Chief. "The only one of us who sees your sister on the regular is Tink," Peter says. "She's always on the track, doesn't even take time out for Friday festivities anymore."

Chief grunts thoughtfully and runs a hand over his beard. "Guess I'll have to crash her pad if I want to see her, then. In the meantime, who wants to see me crush Pan in a battle of the axes?"

Beers are raised with cheers, and people choosing sides and placing bets. There's so much commotion, I don't even realize Chief has come up next to me until he speaks. "And who might *you* be, little one?"

"Oh, I'm—"

"Into blondes, actually," Peter interrupts with a wink in my direction, and *why am I blushing?* "Yeah, sorry there, Chief, but you're just not Wendy's type. Better luck next time."

"Wendy. As in *the* Wendy?" At Peter's nod, Chief smiles wide. "I've heard the stories of your adventures together. Every time this guy gets drunk, he doesn't shut up about—"

"Blah blah blah, are we throwing axes or gossiping over tea?"

Chief laughs as he walks over to get into position. "Let's go, Pan. To the winner goes the spoils."

"You're on." Peter flips his axe in the air and catches it smoothly, joining his opponent.

"Wait," I say to Thomas in a mild panic. "Am I the spoils?"

"No, of course not. Peter would never do that." I breathe a sigh of relief until I notice the frown marring his face. "At least I don't think he would."

"Thomas!"

"Come on, we'll be able to see better over here."

My concern is apparently my own as we move off to the side, so we can see all the action. I'm about to press for a better confirmation that I'm not about to be a trophy when Peter reaches back with one hand and drags his T-shirt off in one smooth motion. Every thought in my head evaporates, and my mouth dries up like the Sahara as I watch his muscles ripple, making the ink in his skin come alive.

"You look like you could use another beer." Silas appears next to me and exchanges my empty bottle for a fresh one. I hadn't even realized I'd drank it all.

"Thanks," I croak, then clear my throat and try again. "Thanks, Si."

"No problem." His lips are quirked to the side, but thankfully, he keeps whatever his thoughts are to himself, sparing me any further embarrassment about my reaction to a half-naked Peter.

I quickly learn that the men are playing the best two out of three games. Nick explains the points system, so I can follow along with everyone else, and then I lose myself in the excitement. There's something extremely primal about watching a couple of tall, muscular men drinking beer and throwing hatchets, the sheen of sweat making their suntanned skin glow in the firelight. Every time Peter strikes a bullseye, the crowd cheers, and he crows arrogantly with his fists raised.

I find myself laughing and cheering along with everyone else, and it's such a relief to not be stressing out about work or responsibilities. This is one of the things I miss about being around Peter. When I was with him, I lived in the moment. All the constant pressures and anxiety about my grades and my future, they melted away whenever he was near. It's impossible not to enjoy life with Peter Pan. He makes even the simplest pleasures an epic adventure, and it's been a long time since I've had one of those.

With a win each, it comes down to this final game. Chief is done, having thrown five times already. They were all bullseyes except for one. If Peter scores three or less on this last throw, he'll lose. A four will tie them up. But a bullseye wins him the whole thing.

The contest has grown in popularity, with almost everyone on the property now crowded around these two men and their targets. Tink sauntered up a while ago, but she didn't join me and the rest of the Lost Boys, choosing to stand on the other side with Chief's cheering section—though I noticed she's not actually rooting for the big man. As Peter pauses to drink his beer, I see another familiar face.

"Hook," I whisper. Wearing black from head to toe, a

scruffy dark beard, and a somber expression with cutting eyes that challenge the world, he looks like the president of a motorcycle club.

Silas looks over and confirms with a nod. "Yep, that's him all right. Captain Happy Pants and his Crew of Crazies."

I study the group of men with him but only recognize Smee, with his reddish-brown buzzcut and Starkey, with his unique shock of white hair and dark eyebrows. The rest look like they could all be featured on *America's Most Wanted,* so I'm not about to go and make my introductions.

"Shut up, Si," Thomas says, crossing his arms and glaring at the man who's like an older brother to him. "Back up off 'em already. The Pirates have never done anything to us."

My heart melts as I look up at Thomas' scowl. My sweet, little Thomas. He might not be little anymore—in fact, he's downright huge like the rest of them—but it's nice to know behind the manly-tough exterior is still the tender boy I once knew. Whatever girl snags his attention will no doubt be treated like the center of his universe.

Silas claps a hand on his friend's shoulder. "Sorry, T, I was just joking around. You want me to grab you another beer?"

"Nah, I'm good. Besides, you'll miss finding out who wins Wendy."

I gasp. They laugh. I'd completely forgotten all about that stupid comment. Now I have a hoard of frantic butterflies in my belly as I watch Peter get into position. Not that I plan on letting myself be pimped out for any reason, much less a stupid competition, but still.

"Don't you dare miss that bullseye, Pan!"

The words are out of my mouth before I can hold them back—apparently all it takes is a couple of beers to loosen my tongue—and it causes him to stop and arch a brow in my direction. "Do you really have so little faith in me, Wen?"

I score my bottom lip with my teeth. "No."

"You hesitated."

"No, I didn't."

Peter points his axe in my direction. "Yes, you did. I think it's time to up the stakes. Hook!"

"Fuck off, Pan," he drolls.

I'm not sure why Hook is even in the crowd. He's the picture of I-don't-give-a-crap, his expression positively blasé. Walking back to him, Peter grins. "Come on, man, give me your bandana. Promise it'll be worth it." A spark of interest flashes in Hook's glacial blue eyes before he unties the black cloth around his wrist and hands it over.

"Uh oh," I say, "I don't like where this is going." But apparently, I'm the only one because as Peter blindfolds himself, the crowd cheers him on.

"Chief, set me up in front of the target, brother."

"Oh, this is too much," Chief laughs, positioning Peter. "You're as good as mine now, little one."

Peter doesn't bother to respond but the deep breath he draws in, like maybe he's not as sure of himself as he wants everyone to think, isn't very reassuring. "Count me down."

Chief leads the crowd with his fingers. "Three! Two!"

"Oh my God, I can't look." Clapping a hand over my eyes, I blind myself as much as the man holding the axe and hold my breath…

"One!"

CHAPTER SEVEN

PETER

I swing my arm forward, release my grip, and let my axe fly.

In the half-second it takes to arc through the air, I can feel the buzz of excitement from the crowd vibrating in my blood, the warm summer breeze cooling the sweat on my skin. But most of all, I can feel Wendy's presence. She makes everything around me brighter, more intense. I didn't realize how muted my world was without her until she walked back into my life. And I'm going to do everything in my power to keep her from leaving a second time.

Starting now.

I hear the *thwack* as the blade sinks into the wood. Before I can even yank Hook's bandana off, the deafening cheers tell me I've won. Sure enough, my axe is dead-fucking-center of the bullseye. Stretching my arms out to the sides, I crow at the moon then turn, just in time, to see Wendy Darling leaping at me. I catch her in mid-air and swing her around before setting her back on her feet.

"Peter, that was amazing!" Her smile is easy, and her blue eyes bright. Uptight Wendy has left the building, at last. And it only took a couple of beers and a fake contest to do it. "I can't believe you actually did it!"

Capturing her chin with my hand, I arch a stern brow at her. "I know. That's a problem we'll have to fix."

"What is?"

"You believing in me." I give her a teasing wink just to see that pretty blush color her cheeks, but I'm not exactly joking. I *do* want her to believe in me. I want her to believe in *us*.

I release her to give her a second to let that sink in while I accept the congratulations and adoration due for an amazing win over an axe-throwing champion like Chief. Eventually, the crowd settles down and disperses to their previous entertainment, and my opponent makes his way over. He's amused as hell as we clasp each other's forearm in our usual way.

"That was ballsy, my friend. Damn fine win."

My smile somehow gets bigger. "Yeah, I know. I'm sure you'll get me next time. You hangin' around?"

"No," he says, turning serious. "Think I'll go find my sister."

Something doesn't sit right with me about him wanting to check on Tiger Lily. The princess of the Piccaninny tribe is the most independent, self-reliant woman I've ever met, and she's never once needed her older brother's help. He never even got to intimidate her dates. With her ball-crusher rep, she does fine all on her own.

"What's going on?" I ask. "Anything I can do to help?"

"Nothing right now. Just some things I've heard that I want to talk to her about."

I nod. "Keep me in the loop. You know the Lost Boys think of both of you as extended family. We're here for you, whatever and whenever."

"Appreciate that, brother." We clap each other on the shoulders then break apart. "Now go enjoy your prize. You earned it with that fucking stunt, man."

"Yes, I did. Later, Chief," I say, taking Wendy's hand and leading her toward the house.

"Why didn't you cuff *him* for cursing around me?"

I look back at her over my shoulder and the wry twist of her smile makes me chuckle. "Even *I'm* not dumb enough to lay hands on Gray Wolf, sweetheart." I nod hello at Tink and Nick sitting on the back porch as we jog up the steps. "Besides," I say as I hold the screen door open for her, "it's not like I plan on cuffing everyone who swears in front of you. Just the Boys because they know better and still need to show you respect."

She rolls her big, gorgeous eyes as she passes me. "Like the respect you showed me when you made me the trophy of a contest? What if you'd *lost*?"

"I wasn't serious about making you the prize, woman. Chief knew that."

"You're lucky because I *would* have been serious. Seriously *pissed*."

Stopping us at the bottom of the staircase off the kitchen, I press my forehead to hers. "I rarely lose, Wen, but I never lose when it matters. And you will *always* matter."

She does that lip-biting thing that drives me crazy, spurring me on to my original goal, pulling her up the two flights of stairs that will take us to the third story of the house.

"Where are we going?"

"My room."

She's flushed and a bit winded when we reach the top, but I want to make her hot and breathless for entirely different reasons. I don't bother turning the light on—she'll want to explore and take everything in, and there's nothing she needs to be looking at right now except me or the back of her lids when I finally kiss her.

And I *am* going to kiss her.

I shut and lock the door before positioning her against it.

Bracing one of my hands high above her head, I settle my other one on her hip and lean in close enough that we share the same breath.

"Tell me why you quit your career to start party planning."

"This again?"

I say nothing and wait her out.

"Why do you want to know so badly?"

"Because from the time you were young, you had plans on following in your father's footsteps and helping people secure their futures—your words, not mine. It's why you left to go to that fancy college." *It's why you left me.* "So, what changed?"

The only light in the room is from the half-moon outside, but it's enough to see her pale eyes searching mine as she thinks about her answer. Or rather, which answer she's going to give me—the truth, or another lie.

Finally, she says, "I missed the magic."

"What magic is that, Wen?"

"The kind you brought into my life." I hold my breath as she raises one hand and lightly strokes my jawline with her fingertips. "I needed a way to find it again. To find that spark of wonder in the world."

I do my best to swallow past the brick in my throat and rasp out, "And you found it with party planning?" I don't mean for it to come through, but the doubt is clear in my tone.

She drops her hand and exhales a quick laugh. "I know it sounds weird, and with some jobs not as much, but other-wise…yeah, I have."

"How? Tell me how."

I have so much time to make up for. Ten years is a long time to not see the girl you fell in love with once upon a time. In that decade apart, she matured mentally and physically, experienced things that shaped her and changed her.

And it all happened without me.

But now she's back, and I'm hungry. Hungry to know her, to know who she is and who she still aspires to be. Hungry for her attention, her touch.

Her body.

Her heart.

I might not have her forever, but for however long I *do* have her, I will feast on everything she is, and everything she offers.

"I have a better idea. Why don't I *show* you?"

"Okay, how are you going to show me the magic of party planning?"

"I'm doing an event a week from Sunday. You could come with me."

"I'd like that a lot. Is it one of those black-tie things? I can check my closet, but I'm pretty sure the last time I wore something fancy was…well, never."

She laughs softly, like she doesn't want to disturb our shadows embracing on the floor. "No, it's nothing like that. You'll fit right in just coming as yourself, Peter Pan."

"Great. Now that that's settled…" I close what little distance is left between us. Bringing my hand up from her hip, I free her bottom lip like I did hundreds of times in another life. "You've always been so hard on this poor lip of yours," I whisper, soothing it with the pad of my thumb.

Her breathing is shallow, and her gaze drops to my mouth, right where I want it. Dipping my head, I hover just out of reach, teasing my lips over hers, until her eyes flutter shut, and I know she wants this just as much as I do.

"I've been dying to do this from the moment you stepped into my shop."

Then I claim her lips like I once claimed her heart—fully, almost desperately. Even growing up as I did, I'd never *needed* anyone. Not until Wendy. Not until I asked her for a kiss, and she gave me a thimble. From that moment on, I needed her like I needed air.

Wendy mewls in the back of her throat and opens to me, inviting me in with a tentative swipe of her tongue, and I take it. Anchoring one hand in the mass of waves and wrapping my other arm around her back, I lift her off the ground as I plunge inside the wet heat of her mouth with a growl. She wraps her legs around my waist, notching her sex over my throbbing cock that's trying to punch a hole through my jeans, dragging a tortured groan from my chest.

I need to feel her beneath me, for her to feel my weight pressing her into the mattress and remember that she belongs to me as I much as I've always belonged to her. Crossing to my bed, I lay her down and cover her with my body, settling my hips into the heaven between her legs.

Fucking Christ, no woman has ever fit so perfectly with me, and I rock my pelvis against her as though driving my point home, even though she has no clue what I'm thinking. It doesn't matter, though, because she gets the message, arching up and throwing her head back with a keening moan. I see my opening and go for her neck, licking, sucking, nipping every square inch as I grind my hips in small, agonizingly glorious circles.

Her nails score the bare skin on my shoulders. "*Ohmigod, yes.*"

My heart would beat right out of my chest if it weren't for her breasts pressing against me and holding it in. But there's too much material between us, and the soft cotton of her shirt is suddenly scratchy and offensive. It has to go.

Grabbing the bottom of her shirt, I pull it up and stop before I even get to see what color bra she's wearing. "What," I say, "is *that*?"

I can't tear my eyes away from the sexy-as-hell jeweled star nestled inside her navel, but I can hear the blush in her voice. "To everyone else it's just a belly button piercing. But for me, it's a memory of how to find you."

Second star to the right and straight on till morning.

God, I was such an idiot kid back then, it's a wonder I was ever able to convince her to come with me. I was so young and ignorant about the world—being almost completely cut off from society will do that to you. Being around her made me nervous and sometimes self-conscious. Though I did my best to hide it, it caused me to say some pretty nonsensical things. Thankfully, she always seemed to like what I said, even if it *was* kind of dumb.

But I'm not that boy anymore, not where it counts. And I'm going to reward her for finding me again, even if it takes all night.

I fuse our mouths together again, our tongues tangling and bodies pressing in all the right places, when I hear three sharp knocks on my door.

"Go away!"

"Peter, you need to come outside, *now.*"

Through labored breaths, Wendy asks, "Is that Tink?"

I nod. "Get someone else to handle it, Tink. I'm a little busy right now."

She snorts so loud I can hear it through the door. "Yeah, I just bet you are. But the cops are here arresting Starkey, and *Hook is going apeshit.* You're the only one he'll listen to, Peter."

I grit my teeth. "Fuuuu—*ugh.*"

Wendy giggles. "Just *say it.*"

Scowling at her, I say, "Don't tempt me, woman. I have to go down there, but you can stay up here if you want." I reluctantly push myself up from the bed and pull on a T-shirt.

"No, I'll go with you." My cock screams at the unfairness as I watch her get up and set herself to rights again. Smoothing her hair back into place, she says, "I think maybe this is a good thing. We probably shouldn't jump into…um, whatever…right away. You know?"

I do know, but I don't agree. I think we should absolutely jump into anything and everything. But telling her that isn't going to do much but scare her away, and the only place I want Wendy Darling is here.

"Yeah, you're probably right," I choke out with a smile, then open my bedroom door to a seething sprite on the other side.

Wendy offers a warm smile. "Hi Tin—"

"Took you long enough, jackass," she tosses out at me before spinning on her heel and jogging down the steps.

"Tink, watch your lang—"

"Bite me, Pan!"

I scowl, not liking how rude Tink's being to Wendy, but then again, I suppose that's nothing new. Wendy, however, is laughing behind her hand, her blues eyes twinkling with amusement. "You've been upgraded from 'silly' to 'jack', I see."

"Still an ass, though," I say wryly. "Come on, let's go wrangle some Pirates."

"Sounds like an adventure."

It does sound like one, but when we make it out of the house, reality isn't quite as charming. Three squad cars are parked, their cherries spinning and lighting up the whole front half of the property. My room faces the back of the house, or I would've seen them as soon as they pulled up. The rest of the scene is one big shit show.

Two cops are holding Starkey down on the front of a cruiser as he struggles in his cuffs. Silas and Nick are doing their best to hold back Hook, who's shouting obscenities at the cops, barricading him from getting to his friend and threatening to throw cuffs on him too.

"Stay on the porch," I tell Wendy, not wanting her to get in harm's way.

I give her a quick kiss and head down the steps. Before I even reach him, Hook wrests himself from the boys' grip. With a beastly growl, he lunges forward and cold-cocks one of the officers right in the face, blowing his nose wide open.

The cop doubles over, screaming in pain as blood gushes through his fingers.

I wrap my arms around Hook's upper body and drag him to the bottom of the porch where I can pin him against the wooden railing. "Are you fucking insane? You want them to haul your ass away for assaulting a LEO?"

"Yeah, I *do*. They're arresting him on bullshit charges. If they're taking people in for no goddamn reason, they might as well take me, too, but they *won't*."

Hook's eyes are wild as he pushes against the forearm I have across his chest. If his face is any indication, someone had already gotten a couple of hits in before the boys tried to restrain him. Looking over my shoulder, I notice one of the other cops favoring his right hand with swollen knuckles like he'd just used someone's face as a punching bag.

And what Hook said doesn't make sense, now that I think about it. Why *isn't* he getting arrested? I just watched him assault a police officer to the point he'll probably have to have his nose reset, and none of them are making a move to cuff his ass. It doesn't make sense.

I look back at Hook, and suddenly I can see what others probably can't. James is worried. Like, really fucking worried. For Starkey? But why? I'm pretty sure every other guy on Hook's crew has done time, including Hook, and he's never acted like this.

"What's really going on here, man?" There's a war going on behind those arctic blue eyes as he debates how much to tell me, or whether to tell me anything at all. And just when I think he might actually reach out for once in his miserable life, I see the iron gates slam shut.

"Starkey's never been on the inside before."

"Why so interested in Starkey's well-being? I mean, other than the fact that he's been one of your loyal lapdogs from the time we were kids. Smee did time. I don't remember you getting all bent out of shape then."

"Starkey's too damn soft," he says gruffly. "He'll get eaten alive unless I'm there to protect him."

"What're they charging him with?"

"I don't know, because they won't *tell me!*" Hook's voice goes from normal to shouting so loud the veins in his neck pop out, and he's pushing on me to get free again.

One of the cops behind me calls out, "We told the kid and that's all that matters."

"Bullshit! Only thing you told me was my rights."

Chancing a look over my shoulder, I see the two officers on Starkey yank him up from the hood and drag him to the back door.

"Captain!" he screams. "I didn't do nothin', I swear. I kept my nose clean like you said. You gotta believe me. *I didn't do nothin'!*"

"I know. I'm gonna get you outta there. Keep your head down and don't ask for trouble, you hear me?"

There's a helplessness in Hook's eyes and a sliver of fear shaking his voice that he's trying desperately to mask with his signature gruffness. But I see his truth, and I'm more than shocked. I'm *floored*.

He claims Starkey has no more of a place in his life than any other member of his crew.

But he's fucking lying.

He cares about that kid. He might even love him, in his own way. And that tells me everything I need to know about this situation. For now, anyway. Hook might not want to admit it, but on some level, buried way deep down, he's my friend. He's a Lost Boy. Family.

So I'm going to do everything I can to help him. Even if all it means is helping him cope with Starkey doing time until he gets out. Because let's face it, it's not like I have any connections with the law, so there's probably not a whole helluva lot I *can* do.

Hook's shoulders sag with defeat as the cops drive off

with their alleged criminal, and I can finally release my hold on him. "I'm sorry, Hook, but you getting arrested with him wouldn't have helped him any."

Already his eye is starting to swell and the dried blood trailing from his lip into his beard cracks with his humorless laugh. "You're so fucking naive, Pan. It's a good thing you never left Neverland. The real world would swallow you up and spit you back out."

I have no idea what he means by that, but he doesn't give me a chance to think about it before he stalks off toward his motorcycle, the rest of his crew falling into line behind him.

"You're welcome, by the way!"

His only response is flipping me off, which I've come to think of as Hook's version of a high-five, so I return the lewd gesture, even if he doesn't see it.

"Are you okay?" Wendy comes up beside me and rests a hand on my arm. "That was really intense. I can't believe they didn't arrest him for assault."

"Yeah," I say, the gears in my brain turning as I slip an arm around her waist. "Neither can I."

CHAPTER EIGHT

PETER

Then…
Age 13

Wendy's an angel, I swear. She's made it to see the boys once a week for the last several months. We don't sneak her out more than that because we don't want to push her luck, but I still go to her as much as I can. We don't do anything all that exciting. Mostly talk about our days, listen to another part of a story to bring back to the boys, and she's also been showing me how to use a computer and this thing called Google that'll tell you anything you want to know.

Sometimes, we just lay down side by side on her balcony and stare up at the stars. When she starts to get sleepy, I make her get up and go to bed. I wish I was bigger. Then I could wait until she falls asleep and carry her in. I hope I won't always be the same size as her. It'll make it harder to protect her when I need to.

Anyways, tonight isn't a great night. It's the first time Wendy's visited when we've been punished for some imaginary thing Croc claims we did. I don't think any of us really listen to the reasons anymore. Telling him we didn't do whatever it is only makes him angrier, so we just keep our mouths shut and take whatever punishment we've got coming.

I'm glad tonight it was just being sent to bed with no supper. I know she's real good at fixing us up, but I hate that she ever has to see that stuff. It's the uglier side of our reality, and I can make myself forget it just as quick as it happened, but I don't think Wendy can. It's in her eyes when she looks at the boys sometimes, and I don't want her remembering those things. I want her to think of only happy thoughts, all the time.

"Tootles," Wendy says in her best motherly voice, "could you please pass the mashed potatoes?"

I smile as I watch Tootles pretend to pass a heavy bowl to Nibs, who passes it to one twin, who passes it to the other, who gives it to Slightly, then Curly, and finally to Wendy.

"Thank you, boys. Tinker Bell," she tries again, "are you sure you don't want to have dinner with us?"

"You mean *pretend* to have a *fake* dinner with *fake* parents?" Tink shoots back from where she's pouting on her bed. "Thanks, but no thanks."

"Tinker Bell," I say in my best fatherly voice, "that's no way to talk to your mother."

"She's *not* my mother. I don't have a mother. None of us do, and you shouldn't want one, either. They're horrible witches."

Wendy frowns. "That's not true at all. My mom is great."

"Congratulations, you have the one nice mom on the planet."

Tink's attitude is always super pissy when Wendy shows up. I think she likes being the only girl. Maybe she feels like Wendy is taking her spot in the group, but that would never happen. Besides, I like Wendy in a totally different way than I like Tink, so that means Wendy isn't replacing her. I should explain that to her, and then maybe she'll like Wendy.

"Tink—"

"Shut up, you silly ass, I don't want to hear it."

The boys gasp at her foul mouth around Wendy. They know better than to use swear words in front of her, but Tink doesn't play by the rules. I figure the problem with Tinker Bell is she's so small that she can only be all good or all bad, but not both at the same time. When Wendy's not around she's great to everyone. But when Wendy visits, she's horrible to everyone, even me.

"All right, boys, back to your dinner."

Everyone except Hook, who's hanging out with Croc— something that's been happening more and more lately— pretends to dig into the food in front of them. We're all sitting in a circle on the floor, eating an imaginary buffet of our favorites. Wendy goes around the table and asks everyone about his favorite thing about today, and each of us makes up something outrageously fantastic.

"Boys," Wendy says when we all pretend to be stuffed so much we can't eat another bite. "Why do you all have such strange names? Those can't be your real ones, are they?"

"Peter's and Hook's are real," Curly says with excitement, like he's happy at least a couple of us know our names.

Wendy looks to me, and I tell her as much as I know. "Hook and I are the only ones who can remember being called by our names before Croc and Delia took over the school. But we don't know the other ones, and they never cared what the other boys' names were, so they gave the kids nicknames they could remember."

I go on, nodding at each of them as I talk. "Curly is obvious with his hair. Nibs is short for Nibbles because he chewed on everything when he was little. I'm not sure about Tootles and the twins don't even have nicknames because no one can tell them apart. Slightly is because he thinks he's slightly better than everyone else. Tinker Bell because she likes to mess around with cars and she wears that bell. I don't know about Smee either. But Starkey is because of his stark white hair."

"Or," the kid says, "maybe it's 'cause of a star that has a key."

"Or maybe that," I say doubtfully. "But probably the other thing."

The sound of someone coming up the stairs makes us freeze, but I give the all-clear signal. I can tell the difference between Croc or Delia's steps and Hook's. We hear him punch in the code to get into the room. It's a system Croc put in to keep us prisoner at night—once you're on this side, you're locked in until he lets you out in the morning. But even if you did make it out of the room, there's an alarm system on every exit and window on the main floor. It's why I never get caught going out the second story window.

Hook walks in and doesn't even look at us, just walks like a zombie into the bathroom for his nightly shower. As soon as the door closes behind him, Wendy is back to our conversation.

"Okay, so I have an idea, but you can tell me if you think it's stupid." The boys are excited and beg her to tell them. Wendy always has the best ideas, so I'm just as curious. "What if I gave you all names?"

I'm not sure what they'll think of that—seems to be a mix of confusion and blind enthusiasm coming from the younger kids.

"I'll try to come up with some that sound similar to what you're called now. That should make it easier to get used to them. But then you'd have real names instead of pretend-sounding ones."

All the boys light up at the thought of Wendy giving them special names, and I have to hand it to her, she's come up with another great idea to give them a bright spot in their lives.

"It's settled, then," she says with a big smile. "I'll have names for all of you the next time I visit."

"Leave me out of it," Tink says. "I like my name just fine."

I sigh. Such a grumbly little fairy. But Wendy doesn't let it affect her.

"I think you're absolutely right, Tinker Bell. Your name is really pretty and unique. Way better than my boring name."

I lean in, so I can whisper in her ear. "I like your name, Wen."

She blushes and ducks her head, hiding behind the waterfall of caramel colored hair. "Thank you, Peter. I like your name, too."

"Is it time for a bedtime story yet, Mother Wendy?"

That makes her smile. "Yes, my sweet Tootles, it's time for a bedtime story. Everyone in bed, and father and I will come around to tuck you in."

For the next half hour, we go through our weekly routine of tucking the boys into bed—except for Tink, she doesn't want to play, and not Hook, he's too old to play—and telling them a story. Then I sneak her out of the school, across the city lines, and back onto her balcony where our night began.

Usually we hug and say goodnight, and there's all this weird energy between us, like there's something missing. I started holding her hand sometimes, and it's nice, but I want more. I just never knew what that more was. Until tonight.

"Well, goodnight, Peter," she says, pulling out of our hug.

I don't know how to start this except… "I snuck onto Croc's computer in his office for a bit today."

She gasps. "Are you crazy? What if you'd been caught? I told you to use mine—"

"I looked up what a kiss is, Wen."

Her eyes widen, and her mouth drops open like it always does when she's shocked. And now I have all sorts of ideas on what I want to do with those lips. *Thank you, Google.*

67

"I…um…"

I take a step closer. "It's okay, I get it. I didn't know it then, but I put you on the spot and you…" I chuckle, unable to help myself. "Well, you improvised with something that is *not* in fact a kiss. What is this, anyway?"

I hold up the small silver piece she gave me that first night. Her face is covered by shadows, but I know my Wendy, and I know she's most definitely blushing right now.

"It's a thimble," she says, embarrassment clear in her tone. "And not even a real one. It's a Monopoly game piece."

At that, I raise my eyebrows. I think we played that before. "Like the iron and the dog? That game?"

"That's the one. Oh God, you must think I'm so stupid."

She covers her face with her hands, but I pull them away. "Not stupid, Wen. Creative. You're always so creative, even when you panic."

Laughing softly, she says, "Thank you."

"You're welcome." I use my fingers to tuck her hair behind her ear, then trail them lightly across her jaw. "Can I give you a kiss now, Wendy? A real one, I mean."

For several seconds, she doesn't say anything, and I think I've screwed up. But then she nods her head and her eyes fall to my mouth. My knees almost buckle from relief.

Slowly, I lean in, inch by inch, second by second, until my lips touch hers. They're soft and warm, and I want to live here like this forever. Her hands come up to fist in my T-shirt and mine land on her hips. I don't want this to ever end, but she has to go inside and get some sleep, or she'll be tired at school tomorrow.

Forcing myself to pull away, I try to steady my breathing with no real luck.

"Wow," she whispers, her eyes still closed, and suddenly, I feel ten feet tall.

I take a deep breath, ready to let out the excitement before

I explode, when her hand claps over my mouth. "No, Peter," she whisper-scolds. "No crowing or you'll get us in trouble."

"Oh, right, sorry. Habit," I whisper back. She rolls her eyes then shoos me away, telling me it's time to go, so I do. But before I hop over her balcony railing, I need to say one more thing.

"Hey, Wen?" She stops at the doors, gripping the handles as she looks over. "For the record, that really is called an acorn nut."

I watch her muffle a giggle right before I drop to the ground with the biggest smile on my face. I think I'm going to like kissing Wendy Darling more in the future.

CHAPTER NINE

PETER

Now...

C hugging the last bottle of water from the bucket of melted ice, I realize I underestimated the amount of work it would be to clean out the pole barn. I bought this property seven years ago, and this outbuilding has served as basically a catch-all for our shit. Anything the boys have tinkered with over the years—a golf cart, one of Lily's old stock cars, and a rusted out 1953 Indian Chief motorcycle to name a few. Plus, a couple of suped-up riding lawn mowers, and more tires of various sizes than we'll ever know what to do with.

The sun has started its descent, which means it's at the perfect angle to shine its fiery rays of hell on me as I'm working, making this that much more unbearable. I'm glad Wendy's not here right now because I'm soaked through my wifebeater and stink worse than the junk I'm cleaning out. Wiping an arm across my forehead, I grab a truck tire in each hand and carry them over to the stacks I've started in the back. I let them drop to the ground, and my effort is rewarded with a plume of dirt rising up to swallow me like a mini sandstorm before re-settling over the cement floor. Maybe I should do some sweeping.

"Why don't you close the bay door to keep the sun out?"

Turning to search for a push broom, I see Tink perched on the section of counter I'd cleared off earlier. She's in an orange baby tee with a "TLP" logo on it and a pair of black Dickies with combat boots, which means she's on her way to the track to work with Lily—or as the public knows her, T.L. Picc, the girl climbing the ranks of the amateur race circuit and fast on her way to becoming the first female driver in the American Stock Car Racing Association.

"Two reasons, sprite," I answer as I spot the broom that might be dirtier than the floor. "I wouldn't be able to see since the electrical is totally fucked. I think field mice chewed through the wires, which means I need to get an electrician out here because my name's not Zeus so I don't mess with contained lightning."

She laughs, and it makes me smile. It's good to hear. Tink's been in a bitchy mood since Wendy showed up two days ago. It's always bothered me that she seems to hate Wendy so much. No matter how many times I tried to explain when we were kids that Wendy wasn't going to take her place in the group, it never made a difference. Tink would cross her arms, purse her lips, and insist she had her reasons.

Eventually I gave up trying to convince her otherwise, but I did demand that she stop being nasty to Wendy. Tink had reluctantly agreed to respect my order as her captain. And if you didn't count the occasional comment muttered under her breath, she'd done as I'd asked. If I can't get her to like Wendy now that we're adults, I hope she'll still keep her promise from when we were kids.

"The second reason is that if I closed this place up right now, I'd cook like a Thanksgiving turkey."

Tink scrunched up her nose at that. "Good point."

"Heading to the track?"

"Yeah, Lil wants to work on her times. Wanna come?"

"Normally I would, but I have to get this place in order."

"Why, are you nesting or something?" She covers her mouth on a dramatic gasp. "Peter, are you pregnant?"

Peeling off my sweat-soaked shirt, I hold my arms out. "Does this look like I'm pregnant to you?"

She offers an apologetic wince and says, "I don't know, you might be retaining water right in this area."

She points in the direction of my washboard abs—yeah, washboard, because that's what I work my ass off for in our home gym—so I retaliate by throwing my balled-up shirt at her. Instead of Tink squealing in disgust and trying to dodge the gross sweat bomb, she catches it with one hand and arches a single *is that all you got* eyebrow at me. I should've known better. Tink is anything but a typical woman. Kind of hard to be when you're raised as the only girl of eleven kids.

"Seriously, though," she says. "Why are you doing this?"

"I need to clear a space to rebuild an old car, just like you said."

Launching herself off the counter, Tink tosses my shirt behind her and comes up to me with excitement lighting her green eyes. "Holy shit, Peter, that's awesome! I have so many ideas on customization and how we can supe up the engine so that it'll beat even Lil's car."

"Sorry, sprite, but we can't do any of that fancy stuff with this one." Her face falls, and it kinda kills me to know this is about to get worse.

"Why not?"

"Because this car is going to a charity auction with a bunch of old, rich dudes. So no upgrades, no suped-up engines, no fancy paint jobs. Not this time. But we can still rebuild it together, you and me."

I can see her putting the pieces together, bit by bit, as storm clouds fill her eyes. "This has something to do with Wendy, doesn't it?"

Blowing out a breath in resignation, I try to put a Band-Aid over Tink's metaphorical old wound. "She's organizing the Love for Littles this year. It was her idea to make it a classic car theme and bring us the business. Pretty cool, huh?"

"I can't believe this," she hisses. "She's doing it *again*. Ten whole years go by, and it took all of two minutes for her to butt her nose into our life and take over."

"Damn it, Tink, she's not taking over." Needing to move through my frustration, I walk over to the bucket of melted ice. I lean over and dump it on my head, hoping that cooling my body will help cool my rising temper, then I shake the excess from my hair. "She's commissioning us for a job. One that will pay us enough money, or at the very least give us local recognition in the quality rebuilds arena, that we can secure more of the kind of work *you* want us to be able to do."

She crosses her arms in a violent huff and shoots fire from her eyes. "That's not the point, Peter."

Planting my feet, I return her glare. I'm hot, hungry, in desperate need of a shower, and grouchy from not being able to see Wendy since I dropped her off Friday night. Not to mention the shit that went down with those cops and Hook has been needling me all weekend. I'm in no fucking mood to deal with Tink's childish issues.

"It *is* the point. You wanted to work on a car with me, and now we have the opportunity to do that. It doesn't matter how. And just because we can't go all out with this one, doesn't mean we won't get to do cooler stuff in the future. So you can either get over your shit about Wendy and do this with me, or stay pissed about irrelevant details, and I'll get Si to help. Choice is yours."

She punches her fists down at her sides, although I'm pretty sure she'd have rather aimed them at my face. "You're such a jackass sometimes, Pan."

As she storms off, I sigh and mutter, "So you've mentioned. Several *hundred* times."

I'm hoping she calms down at the track and reconsiders doing the job with me. She's got a week before I'll have a car in here, so she has until then.

CHAPTER TEN

WENDY

"Wow, I can't believe how *big* it is." I look over at Peter and the amused smirk on his face gives away his train of thought. Smacking his arm, I clarify. "I was talking about the car show, Pan."

"I know." He turns his head and that adorably cocky smirk my way. "For now."

I can't help it, I laugh harder than I probably should. He's too much, and yet, I still can't get enough of him. From the first night he appeared on my balcony, Peter was a dancing flame, drawing me in and providing the warmth and light I was missing in my rather dull life.

I knew it was risky to love a boy so different from me—one who was being neglected, treated like free labor, and physically abused. But somehow it never seemed to affect Peter. His childlike spirit, boyish charm, and love for adventure were never tainted by the shadows surrounding him.

Unlike poor Hook. Even when we were kids, I knew things were somehow different for him. Peter and I were sixteen when Hook was forced to move out of the school. It was odd not to see him in his bed, broody and pretending not to care about the rest of us. I always hoped that wherever he was, he'd found happiness and someone who loved him despite himself.

Considering what I saw last week, I'm guessing things aren't all that different, which makes me sad for him. I also feel bad for poor Starkey. I wonder if John might be able to help.

"The show is divided into three main sections—parts and services, rebuilt and shiny, and what we want, which is old and rusted-out. We'll head over there and go through every aisle until we find what we're looking for," Peter says, drawing me back to the present.

"Sounds good," I say with a smile.

As he leads me down the rows of cars that have seen better days, he stops occasionally to ask questions and talk specs with the owners, and I find myself embarrassingly aware of how attractive this adult version of Peter is. Not that I didn't notice the second I laid eyes on him, but there's no harm in taking a second—or fiftieth—look. He's always been a perfect ten in my book, and that definitely hasn't changed with how well he fills out those worn jeans and stretches the gray cotton of his LB Automotive T-shirt to capacity. But getting to know him again, like *this*, is gaining him points that shoot him way above a ten.

Owns his own business: +1 point

Employs and still lives with all the Lost Boys and Tink: +2

Throws hatchets shirtless in a manly display of rippling muscles and tattoos: +1000

Yes, I know, it's crass and beneath my upbringing as a lady, but I don't care. That did it for me. A *lot*. Which, combined with the beer, is what I'm blaming my poor decisions on last Friday when I practically jumped Peter's bones in his room. Between the memories of him axe throwing and him grinding his *other* weapon between my legs that night,

I've had plenty of fodder for my frequent "de-stressing" sessions over the past seven days.

"Everything okay?" he asks, studying me.

"I'm fine, why?"

"You look a little flushed."

"Oh?" I automatically press my hands to my cheeks, like I'm checking their temperature. "No, I don't think so. I mean, maybe. It *is* kind of hot in here, don't you think?"

"Wen, they're pumping the AC so hard in here, I'm surprised there's not frost on the windshields."

"Really? Huh. Hey, how about that one?" I point to the next car and walk over to it.

He joins me and arches a brow at my lame distraction, but he doesn't call me on it, so maybe he just thinks I'm weird and not lusting after him in public. I'll take that. Let's hope it's that.

Finally, Peter looks at the car and shakes his head. "It's not that a 1950 Oldsmobile 98 is a bad choice, but I think we should look for a convertible. Better for enjoying a drive along the coast."

"I like that idea. Okay, then, moving on."

I get bold enough to place my hand in his and thread our fingers together as we start walking. He gives my hand a light squeeze that I feel around my battered heart like a soothing balm. But when he places a warm kiss just below my knuckles, everything inside of me sparks to life. If I don't get my mind on something else, there will be no end to the flushing I do.

"Tell me what happened after I left. How did you get LB Automotive started?" When he doesn't answer right away, I glance up. His lips are in a tight line and tension brackets his eyes. "Peter? You told me you had a job lined up that offered living quarters and everything. Is that not what you did?"

"Nah," he says, his face relaxing with the reappearance of his half-grin. "I wasn't ready to jump into a steady job right away. I wanted the freedom to come and go as I please and work if I wanted and play when I wanted. You know me, Wen, I'm more interested in adventure than adulting."

I arch a dubious eyebrow. "Well, you must've adulted at some point, or you wouldn't be where you're at today."

He shrugs. "Yeah, I did okay. I lived pretty simply, so I was able to save almost every dollar I made working odd jobs for cash. In three years, I was able to buy the house, which was in foreclosure. When the boys and Tink came of age, they moved in with me, and we all worked on repairing it and making it what it is today."

"I love that you're all still together. When did you open the shop?"

"Five years ago. Bought it for cash from an old guy looking forward to retirement on the outer banks," he says, stopping briefly to check something in the interior of a convertible. "A Bel Air would be great, but this is a '55 4-speed, and not everyone can drive stick. Let's keep looking."

"Okay. So what happened to the school after all the boys were gone?"

Peter grunts. "Rumor has it that Croc intended on breaking his promise to Delia about not getting any more kids —he ran out of free workers when they all followed me—but before that could happen, the place went up in flames."

"Oh wow. I'm not surprised, though. With the way the lights flickered all the time, it was probably their faulty wiring. Thank God it happened after everyone was gone."

"Yeah, except it wasn't the faulty wiring that turned it into a steaming pile of ashes," he says, his tone flat. "It was Hook."

I drag in a sharp breath and stop in my tracks. "Did he get caught?"

"Never even tried getting away. They found him standing there with empty gasoline cans at his feet, watching it burn. Did two years of a five-year sentence."

"Poor James." Over my initial shock, I start to walk again. "He's always seemed to take life so much harder than the rest of you."

"He's also the toughest of all of us. Don't worry about him, he's fine."

Peter probably knows better than I would, seeing as I'm only just returning and haven't seen him in twelve years to know any different. But I'd always thought Hook harbored a sort of perpetual sadness like some people do. They have different ways of hiding it, like with laughter they don't really feel. But his mask of choice was anger, and I believe he felt every bit of it. Though sometimes his mask would slip, and I'd catch a fleeting glimpse of his inner sad little boy, and it would break my heart.

Peter whistles like a construction worker appreciating an attractive woman as she passes. Luckily, he's not whistling at another woman but at an old sports car of some sort.

"Man, what I wouldn't do to fix this girl up."

I stop in front of it, but he continues on down the side, caressing the body like it *is* another woman. "Should I be jealous?" I tease.

He glances up from where he's leaning over the taillight and studying the sleek lines of the car from back to front. "Possibly," he says, rejoining me. "This is a 1969 Ford Mustang Boss 429 Fastback. They made less than nine hundred of these in '69, so she's pretty rare, just like my 'Cuda."

Looking at the faded black paint and patches of rust, I add, "she's also in pretty bad shape."

"Yeah, she is. I could bring her back to her former glory, though."

"So then why don't you? If you enjoy rebuilding cars, why aren't you buying junkers like this and selling them for profit once they're fixed?"

With one last longing glance, Peter steers me back down the aisle for our original mission.

"I don't have the extra money up front for projects like that. You might get a car for only a couple grand and think it mostly needs just cosmetic stuff. But then once you take it apart, all these other problems come out of the woodwork and you need to sink in more money than you thought, which is eating into your profits. Plus, there's no guarantee you can sell it once it *is* fixed and then you're really screwed.

"It'd be fun, sure—Tink's actually been wanting to do it for a while now—but building up enough capital to do something like that would mean longer hours at the shop, so we could take on more work to save up. And I don't want us spending all our time busting our butts with no down time. We work to live, not the other way around."

I understand that concept—after all, I left my career because of that very reason—but it doesn't have to be a permanent thing. If he makes a business plan and—

"Your turn," he says, interrupting my thoughts. "What was your life like after you left?"

"Dull and boring, mostly. I wasn't a partier in college or anything like that. I spent my time studying and getting good grades. I got my bachelor's in financial planning, interned for three years, then got my CFP Cert before finally landing a spot at a big firm in Charlotte that catered to very wealthy people with very large portfolios."

We turn a corner and head back down the next aisle with Peter surveying the cars as he listens. "And what was *the* moment?"

I frown. "Which moment?"

He turns his head to look at me. "The moment you realized you couldn't do it anymore."

"Oh, that. I think I knew it a long time before I actually did anything about it. But the defining 'straw that broke the camel's back' was when a client chose to miss his daughter's dance recital in order to discuss his stocks. He took her Face-Time call during the meeting. She was backstage, about to go on as the lead, and I saw the look on her face when he told her very matter-of-factly that he had a meeting he couldn't get out of.

"The man had all this money, tons of assets and properties, and talking about it with me—something that could have been handled over an email—was more important to him than his own child.

"I just couldn't do it anymore. I couldn't spend my life catering to the filthy rich whose families came second to their bank accounts. I couldn't continue to surround myself with people who stopped believing in magic."

Peter stops me in the middle of the aisle and turns me to face him. He steps in so close I have to tilt my head back to meet his gaze, but I'd bend over backward to see those electric blue eyes if I had to. The world around us evaporates as he frames my face in his roughened hands and brushes his thumbs over my cheeks.

"I'm glad you never stopped believing, Wen. When you left—" He pauses, swallows, and sets his jaw like he's determined to get this out. "When you left it was the thing I was scared of most. That you'd stop believing and forget all about me."

Reaching up, I hold onto his wrists and make him a promise. "Never."

That single word seems to ease his tension as a lopsided grin cracks his stoic expression. Just when I think he's about to kiss me, something catches his eye behind me.

"I think we found our winner." He rushes me over to a huge convertible that was probably a cherry red back in its heyday but looks closer to pink now. "Damage from the sun and salt, but nothing too bad. The richies at your event would love this once she's fixed up."

"What is it?"

"A '57 Chevy Bel Air. It's an automatic, fuel-injected, and has some other perks like power steering and a power top. I think it's perfect."

I wish I could see what Peter sees because I can't share his enthusiasm. It's missing the side mirrors. Actually, that's not entirely true. One of them is dangling from its cord over the door. The windshield has a huge crack going through it, and the leather seats look like Michael from the *Halloween* movies went to town on them. And that's just what I can tell as a car-ignorant person.

"I don't know, Peter, maybe we should look for some- thing a bit less…needy."

"This is the last row of junkers. If we don't get something here, I'll have to start scouring the classifieds and who knows how long it'll be before I find something."

"And you're sure you can get it done in time? The event is in five weeks. If I show up without a car to auction off, I'm beyond screwed."

I'd have to return to Charlotte with my tail tucked between my legs and a tarnished reputation. Word travels fast in this industry, and there's no way I'll get hired for anything other than birthday parties if I fail. Not to mention the well- meaning "I told you so" lecture I'd get from my father as well as feeling like I let my mom down. I absolutely *cannot* mess this up.

"I'm sure," he says. "Remember how I said we needed to fix that problem of you not believing in me? Let's start right now, with this. I won't let you down, Wendy."

He has a point. I came to him for this because I believed he could do it. There were other, totally unrelated reasons, too. But the pertinent one at the moment is his ability to come through for me on this.

Smiling, I say, "Okay. Let's buy ourselves a car."

Peter grabs my face and kisses me soundly, leaving me reeling while he negotiates price and delivery with the seller.

As he haggles over the price, I get an alert on my phone about tomorrow's event, and all my current excitement goes right out the window.

"Crap, now what am I going to do?"

"What's wrong?"

Looking up from the email I just got, I sigh. "The event I'm bringing you to tomorrow is at the Children's Hospital. I'm throwing a Disney themed party, and the model I hired to play Cinderella just canceled on me. So now I have a princess party with no princess."

Peter plants his feet, crosses one arm over his chest, and rubs his chin with his other hand. "A princess, huh? Would it matter if this Cinderella has some tattoos and a pixie cut?"

"Well, I have a wig so—" I stop, realizing what he's saying. "No way can you get her to do it. Not in a million, trillion years."

"Now what did I just say about you believing in me?"

His signature cocky smirk plays across his face, and I can only laugh in response. This is either going to be absolutely amazing, or Peter's going to need an ice pack for a very sensitive area of his body.

CHAPTER ELEVEN

PETER

"You've gotta be kidding me."

Dragging a hand over my mouth to wipe the smile off my face, I clear my throat and try to keep the humor out of my voice. "Maybe take out the piercings."

There's a second where I can see her contemplating a dozen ways to tell me off, but she thinks better of it and relents. Taking out the thin rings in her nose and left eyebrow, then the numerous ones decorating her earlobes and cartilage, she drops them all in a paper cup.

Instead of her usual bold makeup style, she did a great job emulating the picture we printed off as a reference. It's been years since I've seen her so fresh-faced and innocent. With the wig, accessories, and the pale blue ballgown, it's really quite the transformation.

"I still look ridiculous."

"No, you don't, Tink." Moving in behind her, I place my hands on her shoulders and give them a reassuring squeeze through the puffy sleeves. "You look like Cinderella."

She gives me a disgusted glare in the full-length mirror. "Really? Because I don't remember any mention of Prince Charming being attracted to Cinderella's punk edge."

"Then you're Tinkerella. The white glove covers up most of your ink and who cares about what's showing. You're like a coloring book. I bet the kids will get a kick out of it."

She sighs and tugs the gloves up as high as they'll go. "I can't believe I let you talk me into this."

"Correction, sprite." I turn her to face me and point an accusing finger back at her. "You agreed to repay the favor you owed Wendy."

"From when we were kids." Crossing her arms, she sits in a huff on the hospital bed, a sea of blue poofy stuff practically swallowing her whole.

"You didn't put an expiration date on it."

"So she sent you to collect, couldn't even do it herself."

"Wrong. It was my idea to talk to you, not hers. She's not the type to ask for help, especially from a girl who's anything but friendly toward her. You still could've said no."

"I never welch on a debt, and I don't like them hanging over my head, either." Tink fidgets with the black velvet choker around her neck. "Plus, I couldn't stand the thought of a bunch of sick kids being disappointed."

"That's my point, sprite. You can act like a badass fairy all you want, but underneath all that armor, you've got a soft heart." She drops her eyes to her gloved hands in her lap, but I lift her chin. "It's okay, you know. To care about people outside our family."

"Our family is all we have, Peter. It's always been us against the world."

"That's true," I say with a nod. "But it doesn't have to be that way forever. I know it's scary to let outsiders in. But if we don't give them a chance, we'll only ever have each other."

"What's so bad about that?"

"Nothing's *bad* about it, Tink. Having each other is a great thing—it's been *every*thing—but what if we could make it even better?" I lower myself into the visitor's chair by the door and think about the images of a future I've imagined in my quietest moments. "Picture our family as it is now, but only bigger, with more people who love us and we love back. And who knows, maybe eventually, we'll have a bunch of Lost rugrats running around the farm."

"*What?*"

The look of sheer horror on her face is enough to make me burst out laughing, which is when our hostess for the afternoon bustles into the room like her dress is on fire. Speaking of her dress: short-sleeved and white, it fits her up top, flares at her waist, and ends above her knees. She looks like the angel she is to me, and all I want to do is wrap my hand in her long braid, pull her close, and show her how to sin. *Not the time or the place, asshole.*

"Okay, everyone is ready in the activity room so it's time — Oh, Tink," Wendy says with a soft inhale. "You look absolutely perfect. Seriously, thank you so much for doing this."

Tink gets to her feet and smooths the huge skirt into place. "Yeah, well, these kids have enough problems. A flaky princess shouldn't be one of them."

"I couldn't agree more," Wendy says with a small smile, hugging her clipboard to her chest.

"Plus," Tink adds, "this makes us square."

Wendy shakes her head. "I don't understand."

"A long time ago I told you I owed you a favor." Wendy's eyes widen as she remembers how our night of playing Ghost in the Graveyard ended. Tink doesn't give her time to rehash any specifics. "Since I don't usually spend my time walking around as a Disney character, this is me doing you that favor. That makes us square. Got it?"

Wendy nods. "Absolutely. Totally square."

Getting to my feet, I rub my hands together and grin. "Let's get this party started, ladies. Remember, Tink, you're a sugary-sweet princess now, not a foul-mouthed mechanic."

She gives me a sarcastically sweet smile and flips me off

as she passes. I laugh and take Wendy's hand to follow her down the hall.

"Peter," she says softly. "She'll be okay, right? With the kids, I mean?"

"Trust me, Wen. It's going to be fine." I cross the fingers of my free hand just in case.

Tink stops in front of the doors to the room to wait for her cue while Wendy and I go on ahead. I wasn't sure what to expect, but I never would've imagined what I see as the doors swing closed behind us.

Chandeliers made from white Christmas lights and gold tinsel hang from the ceiling, along with blue balloons dipped in gold glitter and yards of blue netting billowing out from the center to the walls and down to the floor.

A gold-painted cardboard grandfather clock reads a couple minutes to twelve and a huge cutout of a pumpkin carriage is set up in the corner with two Merry-Go-Round horses.

A couple dozen kids are talking animatedly with each other and the nurses. Some are wearing only tiaras or top hats with their pajamas while others are in full princess or prince costumes, but all of them are practically vibrating with excitement.

And my girl is no different, the way she's beaming with pride. "Welcome to the ball, Peter."

"Wen, this is… This is really amazing what you did."

One little girl notices us standing by the doors and squeals. "Miss Darling, is she here? Did you bring her?"

The kids turn into a bunch of chatterboxes, all talking over each other, but Wendy regains their attention with a single question. "Who's ready to meet Cinderella?"

Their answering shouts are loud enough to be heard in Australia, so thankfully, Wendy doesn't make them wait any longer. She pulls the door open and in sweeps Tink. Actually, it's less of a sweep than a few hesitant steps inside the room.

The tiny humans who aren't tethered by IV bags or other equipment rush up to her like teens backstage at a boy band concert. Her eyes open wide, and she pulls her hands up by her shoulders as they swarm around her, making her look even more like a demure princess.

From the corner of my eye, I notice Wendy draw in a deep breath and hold it. I give her hand a squeeze and hope my instincts were right about this, about Tink. It only takes her a few seconds to regroup, then little by little, she relaxes and starts interacting with the kids. And it's only a minute later that Tink lights up with the biggest smile and starts hugging the little princes and princesses before making her way around the room to the ones who can't come to her.

Tink gives every child individual attention—commenting on how wonderful they look, asking their names, and sometimes dancing with them to the soft classical music coming from a hidden speaker.

"She's amazing, Peter. The kids are completely infatuated with her."

I wrap an arm around her shoulders. "I never had any doubt."

Looking up at me, she raises her eyebrows. "None?"

I grin and hold my thumb and forefinger about an inch apart. "Almost none."

She chuckles and leans into my half-embrace before leaving me to go wrangle the kids for pictures with the princess in front of her carriage. Everything was going great until one of the little girls lifted up Tink's dress and gasped.

"Where are your glass slippers?"

The entire room stops what they're doing to stare at her black boots that were hiding under all that poof. Well, shit. I guess you can take the Tink out of the mechanic shop, but… Covering my mouth to muffle my laughter, I wait and see how she's going to get herself out of this one.

"Well, um… My glass slippers are…uh…"

"Extremely uncomfortable, so I told her to wear whatever she wants."

A little girl wearing a yellow dress squeals and points to the man who just arrived wearing a princely white and red uniform trimmed in gold. "Prince Charming is heeeeeeere!"

The buzz of excitement over a new character come to life is contagious, spreading from one kid to the next. All the nurses giggle and whisper to each other, their eyes tracking his every move as he crosses the room. Even Tink—the least girlish-acting girl in this place, despite her current attire—is blushing like crazy. But I've never seen Tink swoon over anyone before, so that could be the embarrassment over her boots.

The prince speaks quietly to Wendy who's smiling from ear to ear. Then he touches her arm, and I'm on the move. Before I get to them, he joins Tink in front of her cardboard carriage, bowing low to her and kissing her gloved hand as she does her best to curtsy.

"What was all that about?" I ask Wendy, failing at sounding casual.

"What do you mean?" She doesn't even look at me. Apparently, Prince Charming is hard for a girl to tear her eyes from.

Screw casual. I cross my arms, hoping it makes me look less like I'm pouting and more like a tough guy protecting his territory. "The flirty stuff between you and that prince guy."

That's when her head snaps up, and she locks eyes with me. "Flirty stuff? With *Michael*?"

"Michael?" I study him again and try to picture a little kid with sandy blond hair and chubby cheeks, but I don't see it. What I remember of Wendy's baby brother is hard to reconcile against this tall, dark-haired man with chiseled features. "*That*," I say, nodding toward the man talking to the children with Tinker Bell's hand tucked into his arm, "is your brother?"

"In the flesh. He had something come up earlier and wasn't sure if he'd make it, so I didn't want to mention it to the kids. Michael is the new social worker of the pediatric department, and he's also the director of Lost Ones of London."

"Isn't he a little young for all of that?"

She nods. "Only twenty-three, but my baby brother is a bit of a genius. He graduated high school a year early then went to college and finished his master's in social work at twenty-one."

"Wait." I try to remember something she said on that first day… "*Michael* is the guy who convinced the board to combine the charities for the event?"

"Yes, and he's the one who told me about the event coordinator opening. But he didn't have any say in that. I got the job on my own merit, in case you were wondering."

"Come on, Wen, I would never think that. You're not the type to ride anyone's coattails."

"Thank you for that," she says. "Not everyone thinks that way, though. That's why it's so important to me that I nail this event."

"You will, don't worry." I take another look at the man who was the youngest of our group, even if he was only an honorary Lost Boy we saw on occasion. "So that's Michael. I'm still not seeing it."

"You'd probably recognize John a bit easier, but Michael was only thirteen when I left home," she says. "Plus, he used temporary hair dye for his part today. I told him he didn't have to go that far, but he insisted that the kids get an accurate Prince Charming."

"Doesn't seem like he has any issues with his less-than-accurate Cinderella."

Wendy follows my gaze and grins. "I wonder if he knows it's her. Michael had a huge crush on Tink when they were kids, but she's only ever had eyes for you."

"What? No, she hasn't."

Turning, she looks at me incredulously. "Peter, you're kidding, right? It's obvious she has feelings for you. Why do you think she hates me so much?"

I arch one of my eyebrows. "Because she doesn't like mother figures, and she liked being the only girl in our group. She's got a good heart, but she has a serious aversion to outsiders."

"Uh huh," she says with more sarcasm than I like. "And she *still* hates me because…"

I cross my arms, a pillar of strength and rightness. "Because of that last thing."

"About outsiders."

"Yes," I reiterate. "Outsiders."

"Okay, we'll go with that, then."

Finally she relents, but the fact that she's biting on her lip to keep from smiling is a dead giveaway that she doesn't actually believe me. Am I wrong? Tink's never said anything that would make me think she has feelings for me.

Michael's leading Tink in a dance around the middle of the pretend ballroom. I can't hear what he's saying to her, but she's staring up at him, smiling and even laughing. *That* is what a girl looks like when she's into someone.

Most of the time Tink is sassing me, rolling her eyes, or calling me an ass. All things a pseudo younger sister would do. Which means I'm right and Wendy is wrong. Thank hell.

"Lady Darling," I say, bowing and taking her hand. "Will you do me the honor of dancing with me?"

"You know how to waltz?"

Straightening to my full height, I curl my lip. "Hell no. But I do happen to remember how to sway back and forth, high-school-slow-dance-style."

Laughing, she sets her clipboard down and wraps her arms around my neck. "In that case, Lord Pan, I'd love to high-school-slow-dance with you."

I pull her close until our bodies are flush. I love how she still fits against me, even though I'm much bigger than I was ten years ago, and she's filled out in all the right places. It's like no matter how we change over time, our edges are fluid, always melding together perfectly.

"I get it now," I say, looking around the room—the attention to small details that make huge impacts, the happiness radiating from the children, the smiles on the nurses' faces. "I get why you became an event planner."

A soft grin turns up the corners of her mouth and lights up her eyes. "You do?"

I nod. "I see the magic here, in what you do. You've created a world for these kids where their illnesses can't touch them, at least for a little while. On the surface, it might look like simple cardboard cutouts, balloons, and enough glitter to cover all of Neverland…" Wendy chuckles and traps her lower lip between her teeth. "But underneath that is the magic of freedom. Freedom from whatever problems they might have in the real world. And that's a career worth having."

She turns her head and takes in the scene she created. "Children inherently hold their own magic on the inside—it's in their hearts, their imaginations, and the way they so easily suspend their disbelief." Shrugging, she looks up at me again. "I just helped them see it on the outside, too."

"Don't make it sound like a small thing, Wen. It's amazing what you did."

Color seeps into her cheeks, and she lowers her gaze to my chest. "Well, not every job is as amazing as this one." She scrunches up her nose. "It's harder to make old, stodgy rich folk see the magic outside of their wallets."

"I have no doubt you'll make their stuffy event magical—I mean, the theme is classic cars, so I'm not sure it gets any better than that. But if they don't see it, that's *their* problem."

"It's also a little *my* problem since it's my company name

on the line, and this is the kind of job that can make or break me."

"Like I said before, don't worry about that. I'm going to build you a boss Bel Air that's going to rake in tons of dough, and Wendy Darling is going to be the charity event queen in all of North Carolina."

She chuckles, saying she hopes that's the case, but I have complete faith in her. Wendy can do anything she sets her mind to. Slipping my arms around her waist, I lean my forehead against hers as we continue to sway together.

"You know," I say, turning on the Pan charm with a mischievous grin, "I can bring a whole different kind of magic into your...life."

Wendy rolls her lips in as her blue eyes dance with amusement. She does a quick check to make sure there's no one in our immediate vicinity, then whisper-laughs, "Did you just refer to your penis as being *magical*?"

I waggle my eyebrows at her ridiculously. "Hasn't it always been?"

"Oh, for sure."

"That sounds too sarcastic for my taste."

"Wellllllll..."

"Well *what*?"

"Hate to break it to you, big guy," she begins with a slight wince, "but while it was magical in many ways, I never got to the big finale, if you know what I mean."

I stop swaying, my joke no longer funny. "Are you—" Before I say anything more, I need to get away from the mixed company. Grabbing her hand, I lead her out of the room and into the empty hall. Caging her in with my hands braced against the wall, I start again. "Are you saying that you never came?"

"Peter, it's extremely common—"

"Not with me, it's not," I growl.

"I mean for *that age*. We were young and inexperienced."

She smiles and raises her hands to my face. "No one starts out as Casanova."

All I get out is a grunt. Even with being inexperienced, making love to Wendy had still been the most amazing experience of my young life. Then again, considering she was my first, and I *did* reach the big finale every time, I doubt it could have been anything less than mind blowing.

I grin as I realize I have the chance to redeem myself. "You know what this means, right?"

"Hmm?"

"You need to give me a chance to make it up to you."

"I do, huh? Just like that? Whatever happened to getting dinner first?"

"Oh, we'll do dinner first," I say leaning in, "then I'm gonna give you enough magic to make you fly."

Her gaze settles onto my lips, and her voice is breathy as she fists the sides of my shirt. "I like the sound of that."

"You'll like the feel of it even better." With that, I claim her lips like I intend to claim her body. And her orgasms.

"Jesus, you gotta be kidding me."

We startle apart to find a pissed off Tinkerella standing there. Wendy's immediately worried. "Tink, is everything okay with the kids?"

"They're fine. Michael's entertaining them while you two play tonsil hockey in the hall." I arch a brow of warning at her, and she backs down. "Anyway, I gotta change and head to the track. I'll leave everything in the room."

Tink stalks down the hall and disappears into the hospital room. I'd be pissed about the cockblock, but we wouldn't have been able to do more than that kiss anyway.

"I should get back in there. A lot of them get tired quickly, and we still have to play games."

"Yeah, I need to take her back, anyway. About that date, how's tomorrow night sound?"

"A Monday night date? Peter, I have a ton of work to do

this week, and *you* need to get started on that Bel Air, or I'll be screwed, and not in the magical way."

I laugh. "We can't have that happen again. I suppose the boys can have festivities without me this week. Friday?"

"Friday works."

"Great," I say and kiss her before walking backward to the room. "Be ready at seven, Wen. Dinner first, then I'm giving you flying lessons."

CHAPTER TWELVE

WENDY

Then…
Age 17

I should be studying for my economics final, but instead, I'm getting ready to meet Peter. Then again, it's not like any of my classmates are studying right now either. It's a Saturday night, and most of them are dancing the night away at our Junior Prom. I could've gone, too—I was asked by three different boys in my class—but I can't go with Peter, so I never even considered it.

Running a brush through my long hair, I check my appearance one last time. He told me to wear something nice tonight, but not too nice. When I asked him what that meant, he furrowed his brow and twisted his lips as he thought about it, then finally answered, "A dress. No, a skirt and casual top. But something you won't mind if it gets dirty. Not that it'll get dirty, dirty. Just maybe messy. But not—"

I'd laughed and held up my hands in surrender. "Never mind, I'll come up with something."

In trying to decode that less-than-specific explanation, I settled on a flouncy, pale pink netted skirt that hits at mid-thigh with my favorite Paramore white baby-tee with the band's name splashed across the front in hot pink. Dressy-casual, achieved.

Glancing at the clock, I realize I'm going to be late if I don't leave right now. I pick up the small, gold acorn nut that sits in a special dish on my vanity. It's my ritual to give the "kiss" a kiss every time I sneak out to see my secret boyfriend. And like Pavlov's dogs, that simple, silly ritual elicits a visceral reaction in my body. The butterflies take flight in my belly, and I get all tingly from head to toes, knowing I'm about to be in Peter's arms.

It sucks being seventeen and not getting to talk about my boyfriend like other girls do, but I can't take the chance of anyone piecing together who I'm seeing and it getting back to my parents. I'd come home from school to find my balcony sealed off with freshly painted drywall.

But it only feels like I'm missing out on the typical girl-friend stuff when I'm not with him. As soon as I see him, hear him, touch him, the rest of the world fades away, and nothing else matters. So, I do my best to hold on to those memories between our visits, and when I really miss him—which is often—it helps to hold his "kiss" and feel its metal begin to warm against my palm.

"Do you really think kissing that thing brings you good luck?"

I put it away and cross my room as I address my brother who's leaning against the frame of our shared bathroom. "It's been five years, John, and I haven't gotten caught yet. Neither have you, for that matter, so you're welcome."

A couple of years ago, John caught me climbing back onto my balcony after one of my nights with the Lost Boys. Once I explained who I was meeting and why, he decided the price of his silence was tagging along for the occasional adventure. He'd been thirteen, which was right around when I started sneaking out on my own, so I couldn't exactly argue that he was too young. Michael, on the other hand, was only ten at the time. We only took him with us every once in a great while, and we never stayed out long.

"I'm not one for superstitions," John says. "I like cold, hard facts. If there's any luck involved it's that we're lucky to have very trusting, possibly even oblivious, parents who never check on us after we come upstairs."

"I don't care, as long as it stays that way." Sitting on my bed, I start to pull on my low-top, white Chucks.

"Heard any news about Hook?"

I stop tying my shoe to look up at him. He's studying the calluses on one of his palms like they're the most fascinating things he's ever seen. Like he doesn't care about what my answer is, when I know he does. Much like Starkey and Smee, John had been drawn to Hook since the first time he saw him. Not that James paid much attention to the star-struck thirteen-year-old boy hanging off every word he said, but John never seemed to notice.

"No, no one has," I say, shaking my head. "It's been a year, John. He's always been a loner. I'm sure he found a nice place to settle down and make a good life for himself."

He shrugs noncommittally. "Yeah, okay, just wondering. Tell Peter I said 'hey'."

"I will." I finish tying my shoes and head out.

My conversation with John set me behind schedule, so as soon as my Chucks touch the ground, I take off. On nights we spend outside of the school, we have a meeting spot at the city limits. It's a good thing we've been running the mile in gym all semester, or I'd be doubled over, gasping for air before I even made it a few blocks.

Finally, I see him. My knight in shining armor atop his trusty steed. Or, more accurately, my boy in a white T-shirt atop his mildly rusty motorcycle. Instantly, I feel lighter, the stresses of every day teenage life melting away more and more the closer I get.

"I was beginning to worry you couldn't come," he says.

"Wouldn't miss this for the world," I say with a huge smile, even though I don't know exactly what *this* is. The details don't matter, as long as we're together.

He turns his body enough to pull me in for a searing hello kiss, one arm wrapping around my waist and his other hand sinking into the hair at my nape. I love the way he kisses me. A kiss from Peter—a real one, not an acorn nut or pretend thimble—is no mere thing. He doesn't kiss me with only his mouth but his whole body. His arms hold, hands clench, chest presses, and legs interlock. It's not a kiss, it's a claiming, as though proving to the world, or maybe just himself, that I am truly and happily *his*.

He kissed me for the first time when we were thirteen, and about a year after that, our kisses morphed into those of the French variety. Over the last three years, we've transitioned to really hot make-out sessions, heavy petting, and some intense dry humping on the rare occasion we're alone for long enough to get that intense.

Lately, though, it feels like we're teetering on the line of the next important step. I'm talking *the* step. We've been together for five years already, and I know we'll be together for at least fifty-five more. I'm excited to share something so special with him and also crazy nervous for about one million valid reasons. But even with all that, it also feels like the time is right. As long as he makes the first move, because I'm too chicken.

Reluctantly, we pull apart, and he starts the motorcycle's engine. "Ready for our prom date?"

A big smile splits my face. "Is that what this is, Peter? An evening at the prom?"

"It will be if you ever climb onto the back of my bike."

Laughing with giddy excitement for whatever he has planned, I hop onto the seat, tuck my skirt under my legs to hold it down, and band my arms around his waist as we take off. The May night is still warm on my skin, even with the wind rushing around us and tunneling through my hair. I love being on the back of Peter's bike with him. It's euphoric. Like we're flying among the stars, up where the realities of our world can't touch us, and we can be anything we want. We're free.

Ten minutes later, I can smell the ocean and taste the salt in the air, and a few minutes after that, we're pulling onto the sands of an abandoned beach. Or maybe not so abandoned.

"Peter, go further down, so we don't interrupt them," I say as we approach what looks to be a midnight picnic for someone.

"We can hardly interrupt ourselves, Wen."

He stops the bike next to the blanket and helps me off as I look at the simple spread. A box of doughnuts, a six-pack of Coke, and my old boombox are set up in one corner next to the old backpack I gave him to use for when he's on his bike. But there are two things he definitely didn't bring in the backpack.

"Tiki torches? Where on earth did you find those?"

He rubs a hand at the base of his neck and gives me a sheepish smile. The kind he gives me when he knows he's about to be in trouble. "I got 'em from a house down the beach a ways."

"You *stole* them?"

"No! I *borrowed* them. They don't even know they're gone, and I'll put them back as soon as we leave, I promise. I didn't have any candles, so that was the best I could come up with."

And now my heart is a melted puddle of *awwwwww*. Seriously, this boy says the sweetest stuff to me without even trying. "Thank you, Peter, this is the most thoughtful thing anyone has ever done for me. I absolutely love it."

He grins and puffs out his chest a bit. "Of course you do. Now, take off your shoes and socks," he says, leaning down to turn on the easy listening radio station, "and show me how we dance at prom."

I giggle as we race to unearth our feet and drop everything on the blanket. He leads me to where our bare toes can sink into the sand, then turns and awaits my instruction. Smiling, I place his hands on my waist and wrap my arms around his neck. "Now we just sway back and forth, like this."

"That's it?"

"Mm-hmm. There are lots of ways to dance fancy, but this is what we call high-school-slow-dancing."

"I can definitely handle this," he says, as he slips his arms all the way around me, pulling me in close.

Sighing with contentment, I catalog every detail of this moment. The soft music mingling with the sounds of water lapping at the shore, the moonlight bathing us on one side with the firelight on the other, and the ocean breeze swirling around us like protective magic, keeping the rest of the world at bay.

Peter's taller than me now, and although his frame is still small, he's all toned muscles. A few years ago, he and Hook decided that all the boys and even Tink needed to start working out when they could. They didn't have traditional equipment, but they used their own body weight for resistance or grabbed whatever they found to use as weights. The kids are still small, but they're stronger than they were, and more importantly, Peter says it's instilling that habit in them so that even after he's gone, they'll continue to work at getting stronger.

I didn't understand why they were so adamant about it until the night Nick told me the story of how Peter and Hook stood in front of the boys when Croc intended on belting them for some minor infraction. Then it all made sense. In their world, strength equals safety. Things haven't been perfect—Croc still manages to get in some "discipline" when Peter's not around to stop him—but the situation has improved now that they're getting better at defending themselves.

"What are you learning with Ms. Mills right now?" I ask playing with the ends of his shaggy hair.

Ms. Mills is a teacher who Croc had to hire a couple years ago to get the kids up to state education requirements for their ages. If they didn't bring her on, the state would've shut down the school and put all the kids into regular foster care homes. I'd like to say that Croc and Delia complied out of a desire to keep the children together and because they loved them. But the reality was that they didn't want to lose their monthly checks from the state or their free labor at the shop. Regardless of the reasons, it resulted in the Lost Boys all staying together while finally getting an education, which is great.

"She's teaching me about *Romeo and Juliet*. You ever hear that story?"

I doubt there's a high school kid on the planet who hasn't studied Shakespeare's most popular story, but I don't say that. Instead, I smile up at him and nod. "We read it last year in Drama Lit."

He nods, too, a serious look on his face. "I hated the end. Two people who love each other that much should end up happy together forever. Like in all the stories you told us as kids."

"Those were fairytales, Peter. The whole point of those is to have a happily-ever-after at the end because ultimately, they're all love stories. But *Romeo and Juliet* isn't a love story, it's a beautiful tragedy with a powerful message."

"You sound like Ms. Mills," he grumbles. "I think that Shakespeare guy should've let her wake up before he drank the dumb poison. Or the grown-ups should've just let them be together from the beginning."

Chuckling, I say, "then it wouldn't be much of a story worth telling."

"Yeah, I guess so. I still say all stories need a happy ending, though. Like ours."

I stare up at him, searching his face for signs of his two default settings, humor or arrogance. But all I see are sincerity and assurance. "How do you know our story will end happily?"

"Because we love each other." No hesitation, not even a flicker of doubt.

Sometimes I forget how naive Peter is about life, how cut off he and the others are from the rest of the world. Pop culture references escape them completely, and all they know of the adult world is what they see working at the shop. I've never even brought up my plans for college to Peter because I don't want to ruin our present by talking about the future. Eventually I'll have to, but not yet.

For now, living in the bubble we've created for ourselves is all I want. But it's hard not to worry about possible scenarios where we end up as a metaphorical version of Romeo and Juliet's tragedy.

"But what if…" I pause, unsure if I should say it. "What if, in the end, our love isn't enough?"

He lifts a hand to caress my cheek with his fingertips and tuck some errant strands of hair behind my ear. I can see the flames from the torches dancing in the reflection of his eyes, and I imagine that it's his fire burning for me that's shining through.

"It will be," he says with steel in his tone. "I know it the same way I know the stars are shining above us. Our happy ending is written in those stars, Wendy Darling. No matter what happens to us here on earth, that will never change."

I might not have his unshakable faith that everything will work out, but I have enough hope to match it. Maybe with enough of both, two kids who never should have met, much less fallen in love, will get their happily ever after, after all.

"I love you so much, Peter."

"Love you more, Wen."

He dips his head and seals our confessions with a sweet kiss. But like an ember falling onto dry tinder, what started as a spark turns into a raging inferno. Peter lifts me up without ever breaking our kiss, and my legs wrap naturally around his hips like they've done it a thousand times.

In a few quick strides, we're back at the blanket, and he lowers me slowly until I'm lying down with nothing but the boy I love and the moon above me. And as I stare up into those beautiful eyes I know so well, I see the first hint of uncertainty I've ever seen on Peter Pan. Holding himself up with one arm, he cups my face with a trembling hand.

"Wendy…"

My whispered name on his lips is a plea and a question all in one. With a soft smile, I reach up and smooth the crease in his brow. Then I meet his gaze and pray he can now see the fire inside of me that burns for only him, shining through my eyes as I answer.

"Yes, Peter," I say, pulling him down until he finally settles his weight over me, pressing me and the blanket into the sand. "Please. I don't want to wait any more."

It's true what they say. Prom night *is* magical. Peter proved that with his thoughtfulness and love. Then he proved it with his body and soul, and we were children no more.

CHAPTER THIRTEEN

WENDY

Now…

"Time for dessert," Peter says suggestively, raking his gaze over my white top and pale-yellow capris like he can see right through them.

I lock up from nerves as possible scenarios of how this starts and where it happens run in my mind. Peter didn't want us to "have to deal with people" on our date, so I talked Michael into staying over at John's tonight, and Peter brought over take-out from a nice Italian place. We decided on a more casual set-up on the living room floor with everything spread out on the coffee table. For my part, I'd lit some candles and put on the easy listening station, bringing back memories of one of the best nights of my life.

Grabbing my wine glass, I take a big sip to take the edge off. "Okay, but we should go into my room because I don't want to…for lack of a better word, *taint* any of Michael's furniture."

The biggest smile breaks across his face as he reaches into the paper bag next to him and pulls out a clear container with a huge piece of tiramisu. "I think as long as we're careful putting it in our mouths, we should be fine eating it right here."

"Oh my God. I— You know what? Never mind. I'm just going to stop talking now."

His deep chuckle at my expense shouldn't endear him to me even more, but it seems there's little Peter Pan can do that doesn't cause my heart to sink deeper into emotional quicksand. Fighting it only makes it worse, so I might as well embrace it.

For the next month, anyway. Then I'll go back to Charlotte, where I've made a home and started to build a name for myself, and my life will return to normal. *Normal.* Suddenly that word feels like a synonym for boring, complacent, and ordinary. None of which can be used to describe life with Peter. Again, I'm reminded of how much fun we had together, how freeing it was just being around him. Things I'm rediscovering every time I've been with him in the past three weeks.

"I think Donatello's has the best tiramisu in the area, but you tell me what you think."

He holds the fork out to me, and I accept the bite. No sooner does it hit my tongue than I'm moaning my appreciation. Creamy decadence melts in my mouth. The bitterness of the cocoa powder and espresso-soaked ladyfingers melts together with the sweet custard and mascarpone into one perfect creation.

"Told you," he says, taking a bite. I grab my own fork to scoop up a healthy chunk, and as soon as my mouth is full, he says something that almost makes me choke. "Tell me about your love life."

I hedge with an attempt at distraction before I realize my mistake. "Tell me about *yours*." What am I saying? The last thing I want to hear about are his myriad of conquests in the bedroom. Oh, shoot. Maybe that's not even the case. Maybe he fell in love with a girl, and they were serious, but something happened that prevented them from being together, and he's never gotten over her. That scenario would be way worse.

"Nothing to tell."

I've never been so happy to see his nonchalant shrug. I quietly exhale the breath I've been holding as the knot in my belly begins to loosen.

"I mean," he continues, "I've had my share of fun over the years—more than some guys and less than others—but I've never wanted any kind of relationship."

"Why not?"

"Did that once," he says, holding my gaze. "Didn't work out."

I swallow hard, unsure of what to say. That "way worse" scenario *is* what happened, except I was the girl. *Am* the girl. And that makes me feel strangely giddy and sad all at the same time.

"Your turn. I figured you would've been married with half a dozen kids by now."

It wasn't for lack of trying. After I graduated college, I tried finding someone to share my life with. It was the next box to check off in my multi-step plan—date exclusively for two years, get engaged for one, stay newlyweds for another year, then start our family and live happily ever after.

But it never worked out that way. The men I dated were nice—they cared about me, had great jobs, came from good homes, and kept diverse financial portfolios. They were also predictable, creatures of habit and structure, and staunch rule-followers. All traits that I shared, which made us perfectly compatible in almost every way.

Which is why I inevitably broke it off every time.

"I never found what I was looking for."

"Which was what?"

Peter abandons his fork in favor of turning toward me, so I do the same. We're only inches apart; yet, it might as well be a mile. We've been building up to this moment since last weekend, since I stepped into his office three weeks ago— maybe even since the first night we met—and every second I'm not in his arms is torture. I know he feels the same way, I can see it in his eyes. But he wants his answer, and he won't budge until he gets it.

"Passion," I say. "Spontaneity, maybe some rule-bending. I wanted that sense of magnetism, of being helplessly drawn to someone. To know that no matter how far apart life pulled us, we would always come crashing back together. I wanted adventure and magic and…" I take a deep breath and finally admit what I've known for years. "You, Peter. I wanted *you*."

Reaching up, he cups the sides of my face, his fingers slipping into my hair as his blue eyes stare into mine. "I'm yours, Wen. Always have been. Take what you want, and I swear, I'll give you all that I am."

My heart squeezes as I realize what he needs. The first night we made love, he'd held back because he wanted to make sure I was ready to take that final step with him. He'd known it wasn't a question of what I wanted, merely when I wanted it. But after everything we've been through—the hard choices, the heartache, the time apart—he needs me to *choose* him.

So I do.

Fisting my hands in his shirt, I pull him to me and make my choice clear with a searing kiss to end any doubt. His lips are warm and firm, and every time we kiss feels like coming home in a way I wasn't prepared for. Ten years is a long time, and who we were then is a far cry from who we are now, and yet, our teenage selves are still here, reconnecting beneath the adults discovering each other for the first time.

Satisfied that I made the first move, Peter takes control. He parts my lips with his and thrusts his tongue inside, demanding I give back all that I take. A whimper escapes my throat as I climb into his lap, needing to be closer, to finally eradicate the space that's separated us for far too long. Straddling him, I settle onto his hard cock, straining against its denim prison, eliciting a painful sounding groan from his chest.

"I'm sorry, did I hurt you? I'm a little rusty—"

"The only way you'll hurt me is if I can't ravage your sweet body like I've been craving for the last three weeks."

Oh…well then. "As long as it happens in my room, feel free to ravage me as much as you like."

Setting his jaw, he gets to his feet with ease, despite me clinging to him like a stripper on her pole, then strides across the apartment. In seconds, he's found my guest room and laid me on the queen size bed.

I'm about to complain about him not joining me, but the words die on my lips when he strips off his shirt, exposing all those cut muscles and bad-boy tattoos—separate pieces of art that form one cohesive masterpiece, stretching from his pecs, over his shoulders, and down his arms. I want to take my time, to study each one and ask about their meanings, the reasons he chose to permanently etch them into his skin.

But not now.

Now I have other things I want to focus on, namely the massive one contained by the fly of his jeans. Lifting up on my elbows, my hungry eyes dip down to where my thoughts have strayed and watch as his erection flexes against the denim.

He unbuttons and opens the zipper with slow, deliberate movements. When he palms himself through his underwear, I have to fist my hands, so I'm not tempted to sit up and yank everything down to finally bare him to my hot gaze.

"Keep looking at my cock like that, Wen, and all my plans for taking things slow will go right out the fucking window."

The heat of his threat feels more like a promise I hope he'll keep. It melts over my spine and pools warmth into my empty, aching sex. Trying to hide my intense visceral reaction, I quip, "My, what language, Mr. Pan. And here I thought you were a gentleman."

His feral grin proves that any attempt at teasing him was lost with the breathless way I uttered the words. Operation Aloof is a fail, and I can't even muster up enough self-respect to care that he knows how far gone I am.

Leaving his jeans hanging open—dang it, why aren't those off yet? —he lowers himself to the bed and half lays over me, enough to assert his dominance without obscuring his view of my body.

"You and I both know that's just another thing we pretend. I might be respectful of you as a lady, but there's not a damn thing gentlemanly about me, especially not when it comes to getting you under me. So you're gonna have to give me a pass on the foul language in times like this."

The thought of Peter—*this* version of Peter, with his muscles and tattoos and all-around hugeness—being unrestrained in the bedroom sends shivers of desire through me. I want that. I want *him*. So, so badly.

"Good," I tell him, skimming my nails over his scalp as I push my hands through his hair. "Because in times like this, the last thing I want you to be, is a gentleman."

"Same goes for you, Wen. When we're together, I don't want the reserved and proper lady. I want your raw, uncensored emotions. Nothing exists outside you, me, and the stars you fly with when I make you come. Deal?"

"Deal," I answer without hesitation.

Satisfied, Peter divests me of my top and pants, leaving me in my white lace bra and panty set. Suddenly, I feel way too exposed and self-conscious. I've never put much effort into working out, and my curves are soft as opposed to the toned physique of girls like Tinker Bell. Remembering how much emphasis Peter always put on being strong, I'm worried he'll find me lacking. I try crossing my arms over my belly, but he shackles my wrists above my head in one hand and shakes his head disapprovingly.

"I can see the thoughts in your eyes, and I want them gone. Not just now, but forever. You're perfect, Wen, and you always will be."

I arch an eyebrow. "Even if I gain a bunch of weight?"

The muscle in his jaw tics, and his eyes narrow at me. "I don't like you challenging my opinion of you, Wendy Darling. I will *always* find you beautiful." His free hand covers my stomach, his fingertips toying with the waist of my panties. "Not because of how you look, but because of how you look when I do things like this."

In one fluid motion, his fingers slip beneath the silk and pass over my mound to part my slick lips and tease my swollen clit.

"Ohhhh," I moan, my eyes closing as my pelvis lifts, chasing his touch.

"That's it, baby," he coos to me, nuzzling into my neck and nibbling my ear. "Just like that."

His fingers continue their magic, circling around my bundle of nerves, then grazing across the top and causing my hips to jerk from the jolt of pleasure that shoots through me. His mouth finds my breasts, licking and sucking on my nipples through the silk of my bra. Big wet spots make the thin material see-through, and the friction of it rasping against my sensitive flesh creates a live wire of electricity straight to my sex.

The tension in my belly builds and builds, but every time I'm balanced on the edge of climax, he backs off, only to start all over and drag me back to the precipice. When I think it can't get any worse, he slips two fingers into my soaked channel and begins to work them in and out of my body like he's playing an instrument that exists for him alone.

I gasp and whimper, mewl and moan. My body is no longer under my control. It writhes under him, alternately begging for more of his torture and trying to escape it. I passed *flushed* forever ago, and now I'm catching fire, burning for him without any hope of dousing the flames.

"Christ, you're so fucking beautiful like this. Tell me it's all for me, Wen. That no one else makes you feel this way."

"No one," I groan. "Only you, Peter. Only...*you ohmigod.*"

He changes his movements inside me, curling his fingers forward to hit my G-spot—something that none of my other lovers ever cared to find. He finally releases my hands to leverage himself up on one arm, and I take advantage of the sudden freedom to grip his shoulders, using him to anchor myself to this world, this moment. I feel caught in this place of uncertainty, unable to stay where I am but afraid of where I might end up if I move on.

Peter kisses the breath out of me then presses our foreheads together as he stares deeply into my eyes. "Let go, Wen," he rasps. "Fly for me, angel. Fly high."

He presses his thumb to my clit as he adds a third finger, thrusting deep and giving me wings. I scream his name as my first orgasm detonates, ripping through me with a vibrating force that bows my back and blurs the world around me. My limbs quiver with aftershocks as I soar among the stars for an eternity contained in the span of seconds. In the distance, I can hear gruff words of praise as I float back to earth, guiding me back to where I'm lying on my side, gathered against Peter's firm chest with his hand stroking my hair.

"There she is," he says with a rare soft smile that makes my heart as weak as my legs right now. "Welcome back."

"Peter, that was...I..." Have no words, apparently. Thankfully, he isn't expecting any.

"Shhhh, you don't need to say anything. All I want you to do is feel, remember?"

I nod as he pulls my top leg onto his hip, which is when my head clears enough to realize that while I'd been blissed out from orgasm, he'd shucked the rest of our clothes and sheathed himself in a condom. I'm briefly disappointed that I missed that show until the head of his cock notches at my opening, and I no longer care about anything other than him finally filling me to capacity.

"Yes," I mewl. "Please, Peter, I want you."

"I'm yours, Wen," he rasps against my neck. "Take me. Take all of me."

Pushing his hips forward, he uses his body to invade mine, driving all the way to the hilt with one steady thrust then holding still, letting me adjust around him. Both of us are breathing heavy, not from exertion, but with anticipation.

We can pretend that we're merely two people rekindling an old flame for the sake of mutual fun, but we know it's more than that. This moment *means something*. It holds weight. Like the magnets inside our chests are turning toward each other, and if we go through with this, that undeniable pull will fuse us together even stronger than before.

If I was thinking clearly, I'd realize that it's not the best idea to start something that can't be anything other than a soul-deep connection when I have no plans on staying. Or *had* no plans on staying. The way I feel right now makes me think uprooting my entire life and essentially rebooting my company in a new location isn't that big of a deal. Because as Peter finally begins to move, I'm overwhelmed with the emotions and physical sensations battling for dominance, and all I want is to stay like this with him forever.

We find our rhythm, the one written only for us, as we hold each other's gaze. Sweat slicks our heated skin and dampens the hair on our faces. He's warrior-beautiful, his chiseled jaw set, cheeks ruddy, and eyes bright with lust.

Over and over, he fills me, stretches me, pushing me higher and higher. And every time I'm sure that I can't take any more, that the next time he plunges inside will be the one to drag me over the edge, he pushes me higher still.

"Fuck, you're so goddamn tight. Hot. Perfect," he grinds out between clenched teeth. "Only you, Wen. Only you."

He hooks my leg over the crook of his arm, opening me wider for his punishing thrusts, hitting me deeper than I ever thought possible.

"Oh my God," I gasp.

"Come with me, baby. Come right fucking now."

He changes the angle of his hips and alters my universe as I know it. My breath catches in my chest as the orgasm rolls through me like pulsing waves, pushing a tingling warmth into my extremities as I ride the swells. My sex clenches around his cock, again and again, demanding his release, and with an animalistic roar, he gives it to me, emptying himself in powerful streams that I can feel even through the latex.

As I struggle to come back to myself, I'm vaguely aware of Peter disposing of the condom in the small waste basket by the bed, then freeing the covers to pull them around us. Too weak to move, I let him roll me onto my other side and press my back against his chest. He tucks one arm under my head and snakes the other up the center between my breasts to splay his hand possessively over my heart.

"And so, my adventure returns," he says gruffly in my ear. "You know what this means, Wen?"

"What, Peter?" I whisper through my climax-induced haze.

"You left me once. That was your chance to be free of me. This time, I'm not letting you go. Not without a fight."

I close my eyes to stem the tears as the last of my walls crumble to the ground, leaving my heart vulnerable and his for the taking. Again. Seconds later, his breaths are deep and even, as though stating his intentions for me worked like a mental Ambien.

Placing my hand over his, I release the breath I'd been holding since his declaration, and I vow to stop fighting fate. There's no use. Peter and I were destined for each other from the time we were twelve. Maybe we were meant to take separate paths for a time, to grow as individuals, before coming together as a couple, and now that we've done that, we don't have to be apart anymore.

With a smile on my face, I follow Peter into oblivion and dream of our happily ever after. It's perfect and amazing, and everything I ever hoped for...except for that tinkling bell that won't stop echoing in the distance.

CHAPTER FOURTEEN

PETER

My fingers twitch at my side as I prowl like an agitated lion out in front of Mermaid Lagoon, the pool hall we frequent after the races. The rest of the gang, with the exception of Tink and Lily who went home to shower first, is already inside, ordering pitchers of beer and claiming our favorite spot in the back next to a couple of electronic dart boards.

We're at week four of Wendy returning to Neverland, and I can count on two hands how many times we've seen each other. The last time was earlier this week when she carved out an hour to choose all the accessories and finishing details for the Bel Air, as per my condition #2. At the time I made it, I'd wanted the additional excuse for her to spend time with me, which turned out to be unnecessary. She's more than happy to oblige me in that respect. The issue is our schedules.

The closer we get to the big fundraiser, the busier she gets, and so do I, since I'm having to haul ass on that Bel Air, but it doesn't mean I don't hate the distance any less. With this commission job Wendy tossed my way, I'm getting a small taste of what it would be like if we took on more custom projects outside of our normal LB jobs, and I don't mind saying it kind of sucks.

I'm used to an even amount of work and play—I treat it as a rule, actually—but the past few weeks, I've been working nights after my days, and the only fun I have to look forward to are Friday festivities. I hadn't been to a race since Wendy's been back, but when she insisted she couldn't come out last night, *I* insisted she come out with us tonight.

Tink and I put in a few hours with the Bel Air this morning before heading out to Neverland Speedway with the boys to hang out and support Tiger Lily. I'd wanted Wendy to see Lily race, but her day went longer than planned, so she's meeting me here instead. Except, she's ten minutes late now, and I'm on the verge of hopping in the Cuda to—

"Peter!"

I stop mid-stride and look over to see Wendy raising her hand as she makes her way through the parking lot. Even from here, I can see her bright smile, and it threatens to fucking cut my legs out from under me. I don't know how I earned the love of an angel like her, and I don't care. I'm not dumb enough to question the universe and risk it making things right. My plans are simple: treasure the hell out of her and never let her go.

Making love to her last Friday had been an earth-shattering revelation. It was like returning to the one place I belonged in this world and discovering a new one all at once. I used to be a Lost Boy, but the night I met Wendy, I became *found*. I belong with her, *to* her, and there isn't an adventure big enough to pull me away.

When she's only a few feet away, I rush up and wrap my arms under her ass to lift her with a possessive growl. She squeals and puts my shoulders in a death grip. As if I'd ever fucking drop her.

"Bout time you got here, woman. What took you so long?"

Smiling down at me through the curtain of soft, caramel-colored waves, she says, "It's something you do as a responsible adult, called work. Have you heard of it?"

I grunt. "Yeah. Not a huge fan, though. Now *you*, on the other hand, I'm a huge fan of."

Thanking whatever gods influenced her to wear a shirt that bares her stomach, I kiss the satiny flesh mere inches from my face. I intend to stop there, but temptation gets the best of me, and my tongue slips past the dangling star into her navel. I can *feel* her gasp at the intimate invasion. Glancing up, I know by the way her pupils expand and her lips part, that just like me, she's imagining a much harder part of my anatomy pushing into a much wetter part of hers.

Threading her fingers through my hair, she pulls my face away from her stomach and glances at the big picture window behind me. "Put me down, you big brute, before we cause a scene."

I reluctantly loosen my grip as I turn, letting her slide down my body, so she feels the steel rod I'm now sporting behind my zipper, then ease her onto her feet. Though we haven't seen each other in days, we've talked on the phone and texted plenty. And my sweet, proper lady has divulged some very improper desires that I haven't been able to stop thinking about for five goddamn days.

"That wasn't even close to causing a scene, Wen." Crowding her against the window, I lean in and graze my lips along the shell of her ear. "A scene would be pushing you onto your knees in front of all those people, so you could show them how much you want to worship my cock. They'd watch as you rub your face over it through my jeans like a kitten with catnip, begging me for it while your pussy makes a damp spot in those cute little shorts of yours for everyone to see. *That* would be a scene."

I punctuate the fantasy with a sharp nip on her earlobe, eliciting a satisfying whimper. I sense someone stand next to us and pull back to see who's stupid enough to interrupt us. *Fucking Chief.* He's leaning casually on the building with his arms crossed and a shit-eating grin on his face, as per usual.

He left his long hair down around his shoulders and rolled the sleeves up on his T-shirt, prominently displaying his heritage tattoos—Samoan on one arm and Piccaninny on the other—as a firm middle finger to any tribe members who might be around. Considering the Piccaninnies owned Mermaid Lagoon, chances are high. I hope I don't have to get into a bar brawl tonight. An injury will put a serious damper on my plans for Wendy later.

Not that Chief looks like he gives a fuck about my plans. With his perpetual smile and mischievous nature, you'd never guess at the kind of pain the giant keeps hidden. His sister and I are the only ones he's ever let in enough to know the real Gray Wolf. To the rest of the world, he's a carefree nomad, the life of every party, and an international ladies' man to rival James Bond.

"Can I help you?" I ask dryly. Wendy turns her face into my chest and laughs, but I'm not nearly as amused at the interruption. Then again, the Lagoon isn't the place to get all keyed up over the myriad of filthy things I want to do to Wendy Darling, so it's probably for the best.

Chief moves his hands up and down, gesturing to his gigantic frame. "Do I look like I need help with *anything*? Wendy, what do you think?"

When she unburies her face, he waggles his eyebrows at her, making her laugh all over again. "No, Chief, you look very…"

"Watch it," I grumble.

"Capable." She turns that gorgeous smile up at me. "Is that acceptable?"

"I was hoping for idiotic, but I suppose that works, too." I plant a long kiss on her lips then face a chuckling Gray. "Girls on their way?"

"Be here in five. Come on, I want to buy the lady a beer."

I grab hold of Wendy's hand and lead her inside where everybody's already got games going and a few pitchers empty. The boys all shower Wendy with hugs and cheek-kisses, just like always. As I look on, something kicks against my breastbone, hard.

This is perfect. This is what I want. This is what I've always wanted.

When we were kids, we had plenty of adventures together—some with Tink and the Lost Boys and others by ourselves. In reality, they were simple games like playing make-believe or Ghost in the Graveyard, but to us, they were much more than that. They were our way of escaping our prison.

Our adventures today aren't all that grand, either. Just a group of friends who like having fun and letting loose, whether it's a party at the house, a night at the races, or hanging at the Lagoon; we always have a damn good time building on the memories we made the week before, and the week before that. Now that Wendy's back, I want her to be a part of that again.

Don't get attached. She's not back for good, she said so herself.

I mentally snarl at my brain trying to piss on my parade. She'd said that before. As in, before I willingly sacrificed my battered heart at the altar of her body and told her in no uncertain terms that I wasn't letting her get away from me a second time. She never argued with me, so that has to mean something. At least I don't think she did. I blacked out right after and slept the dreamless sleep of a dead man—a damn satiated one at that.

"You love her," Gray says next to me as we watch the twins play Wendy and Thomas in a game of pool. When she misses the cue ball entirely, Silas laughs so hard beer comes out his nose, which makes Wendy double over with laughter.

Without taking my eyes off her, I smile and answer him honestly. "Always have."

"What are you gonna do when she leaves?"

My face falls. "Who said she's leaving?"

"A little fairy told me she's going back to Charlotte in a couple weeks after the fundraiser is over."

Tinker Bell. What Wendy said to me that day in the hospital about Tink being in love with me has been weighing on my mind. She doesn't act any differently toward me than she always has, and she sure as hell doesn't act like other women when they want my attention: no coy glances or giggling at everything I say or "accidentally" brushing up against me.

But I can't come up with a more logical reason for her to despise Wendy, and I hate that I can't reconcile the two points for an easy answer. I'll have to talk to her about it eventually, but not until after the fundraiser. We've been having a great time rebuilding the Bel Air together, and I don't want to ruin that with a difficult discussion that could just as easily happen when she doesn't have the opportunity to yank the jack and crush me under a ton of steel.

"That was her original plan," I say, "but I'm working on changing it."

"And if she won't?"

I chug the rest of my drink, trying to drown the possibility of being faced with the same choice I had ten years ago. The beer suddenly tastes sour, but I manage to force it down. "Then I put Si in charge of the shop and follow her."

In my periphery, I see Chief whip his head over to stare at me. "You'd leave the Lost Boys?"

Last time, I couldn't. They were still under Croc's care, and I didn't know how he'd treat them if I wasn't around, so I had to stay. I'd told Wendy I had a job lined up that offered room and board, but I didn't take it because it was at Croc's other shop—the place where Hook had gone after he left the school—and they made the illegal shit we did as kids look like, well, child's play. I knew if I went there, the boys and Tink would follow me, and we'd never be free.

So I lived on the streets during the summer and homeless shelters when it was colder, worked odd jobs for cash, saved my money, and kept tabs on the kids until they got out.

I'd needed to stay back then, just as Wendy had needed to go. But now…?

"No matter where I go, the boys and I will always be family." Tearing my eyes away from her, I meet his steady gaze. "But she's the air I breathe. I can't live without her, Gray, not again. If she goes, I go."

"Damn, brother, I never thought I'd see the day," he says, his grin returning as he slaps me on the back. "Peter Pan, all grown up."

I chuckle—and wince from the Grizzly-sized hand print probably imprinted on my shoulder blade—and pour myself another beer. "Let's not get carried away."

"What are we laughing about, boys?" Wendy asks as she steals my beer and takes a long drink.

"You, trying to play pool," I say, reclaiming my beer. "It's not a javelin you need to throw across the bar, Wen. It takes more finesse than that."

"Feel free to show me how it's done, Pan." Again, she relieves me of my glass, but this time, she holds it away as her gaze drops to my ass for a hot second. "Then I'll enjoy the show of your tight backside every time you bend over the table."

My mouth hangs open as Chief roars with laughter. "Carlos," I bark. "How much has she had to drink in the ten minutes since we've been here?"

"Only one, boss!"

Wendy giggles and snakes an arm around my waist. "I'm not drunk, Peter, I'm just having fun with you."

I pull her in close and smirk. "You want fun, woman? Let's get out of here, and I'll show you all kinds of fun."

"You can't leave yet," a voice says from behind me, "we just got here."

"There she is," Chief announces loudly, enveloping his little sister in a bear hug, complete with sound effects, before releasing her. "You almost gave me a heart attack when you went into that wall tonight. You owe me like six beers."

"Not the first time I crashed, won't be the last, big brother."

It may not have been the first time she's crashed, but it's the first time I've seen her lose a wheel. As Lily was taking turn three in the twenty-fifth lap, her driver's side front wheel flew off out of nowhere. She escaped injury by keeping a clear head and managing to slow the car down to about twenty before hitting the wall, but it fucked her car up enough to take her out of the race.

"It's my fault," Tink says next to Lily, her features stormy and her blond hair sticking up like she's been pulling on it.

Tink and Tiger Lily have been best friends since the night we rescued Lil when we were kids. The two are similar in temperament but couldn't look more opposite. Tink loves her heavy eye makeup, but Lily hardly uses any. One is pale and petite with a platinum pixie cut and the other is tan and tall with black hair down to her ass.

Chief resembles his Samoan father, but Lily is a younger version of their mother, regal as a runway model with sharp brown eyes that can slice you to ribbons. She does her best to balance her duties as the chieftain's daughter while still pursuing her racing career, both of which require her to be professional and a bit of a hardass. But around us, she's fun as hell and just another one of the boys as far as we're concerned.

Except for maybe the twins. I have a feeling those two have plans for the Piccaninny Princess, and they're just biding their time before acting on them. If they like their balls where they are, they'll wait until her brother moves on. Then again, Lily's just as liable to take a tomahawk to their dicks as Gray is, so either way, it'll be entertaining to watch.

"What do you mean?" I ask Tink.

"I was the last person to tighten the wheels before she hit the track."

Lily put her hand on her friend's shoulder. "Hey, enough already. I know you did everything right. It was just a bad lug nut, it's no one's fault, okay?"

Wendy chimes in with, "I agree, Tink. I don't know anything about cars, but I know you'd never risk one of your friends' safety. It must have been a fluke."

Our feisty fairy rolls her eyes and mutters that she needs a drink as she heads over to where Si is already holding out a beer for her. I give Wendy's waist a quick squeeze, letting her know I appreciate the attempt and not to worry about the brush-off.

"So, the rumors are true," Lily says, drawing attention to the fact that this is her first-time seeing Wendy since her return.

I can feel Wendy's ribs expand against my side and then hold like she's bracing herself for another less than warm welcome. Tiger Lily lifts her chin slightly and studies Wendy, as though deciding the fate of a traitor who abandoned her tribe. I'm not worried, though. Wendy earned Lily's respect long ago, and that's not easy to break.

Finally, Lily's sharp brown eyes soften over her warm smile. "Wendy, it's really good to see you. Welcome back to Neverland."

Wendy sags with relief and returns the smile. "Thank you, it's great to be home for a bit. I wish everyone was as glad to see me," she says with a glance in Tink's direction.

Lily waives her hand in the air. "Ah, she'll get over it.

Come on, I need a beer and a partner for pool. You can catch me up on all the exciting things you've been up to."

"Okay, but you might want to rethink me being your partner. I kind of suck at pool," she says with a chuckle.

"That's okay because I'm awesome at it." Lily loops her arm through Wendy's and leads her back to the group, shouting at the twins. "Hey, knuckleheads, rack 'em up, so I can kick your asses."

Tobias and Ty exchange a heated glance as Lily sashays past them. Chief must've caught it, too, because his eyes narrow and his shoulders tense. Running interference for my boys, I step in front of the mountain and ask him what's been on my mind since Tink mentioned it.

"You think someone's messing with Lil's ride, don't you? It's why you came."

His steady gaze swings to me, and he lowers his voice. "I'd heard some things and wanted to check on her myself. She's getting noticed, and if her rankings stay the way they are, she could move up to the big leagues in another year or even sooner. But not everyone is happy about the idea of a woman, and a Native one at that, playing with the white boys in the professional circuit."

Fire sparks in my veins at the thought of anyone coming after Lily. She might be privileged in her world, but she's considered trash by a lot of people in ours, and she's had to claw, scratch, and fight to get where she is today. I'll be damned if we're going to let any small-minded assholes get in her way now.

"Any idea who those someones might be?"

He shakes his head. "Not yet. But I'm not leaving until I know it's handled."

"Agreed. I'll talk to Hook, see if any of his contacts know anything."

Chief scoffs. "He barely tolerates you. What makes you think he'll help?"

It's true. "Captain" James Hook and I have never been your typical friends, but I at least have his respect, and more than that, we have a shared past. Though, our experiences at the school were vastly different. James had it way worse than any of us. For years I'd been oblivious to the hell he was going through, until I walked into the storeroom of the shop at the wrong time. I didn't even fully understand what was happening before I was on Croc and knocking him unconscious with the fire extinguisher I'd been putting away.

As soon as he'd collapsed in a heap on the floor, I realized what I'd interrupted, and so many things finally made sense. I'd wanted to puke on the spot, but Hook had jacked me against the wall and threatened my life if I so much as got heartburn over it or thought of spilling my guts about what I'd seen. I swore not to do either.

That instance didn't earn me any favor with Hook—at least none he'd ever shown—but it tied us to each other in a way no one else will ever understand. So, are we friends? Probably not. But like I said before, we're still family. He would no sooner let someone mess with one of us than we would with him. It's just how it is. It's orphan law.

"Don't worry about it, I'll talk to Hook. I need to check on the situation with Starkey, anyway. And we'll both keep an eye on Lily. I'll tell the twins they're joining her pit crew to see if they find anything suspicious behind the scenes."

Growling, Chief says, "Not them. They're like dogs panting after a bitch in heat with her. They'll be too distracted."

"Yes, they are, and no, they won't," I argue. "Their interest will only make them more vigilant. Trust me, if you want her protected, they're the ones you want doing it."

"Fine, but if they touch her, I'll cut their balls off and feed them to Tasi."

I snort. "I don't think your wolf will get the chance before your sister turns them into her version of fuzzy dice for her mirror."

A proud grin splits his face. "True. Let's go, I'll beat you in a game of darts."

Laughing, I follow after him to where the others are milling around. "You don't stand a chance against me, big man." Stopping behind Wendy, I lean in and speak in her ear. "And later tonight, neither will you."

Her lips curve coyly as she stares up at me through thick lashes. "Sounds like my kind of adventure."

Damn straight it will be, I'll make sure of it. Tonight, and every night.

CHAPTER FIFTEEN

Then…
Age 15

"All right, is everybody clear on the rules?" Peter asks, and we nod our heads.

This is the first night all of us, including my brothers, have ventured out of the school together. Peter had the idea of playing Ghost in the Graveyard at the several acres of field Croc uses to store all of the junked and parted out cars. We chose tonight because it's a full moon with a clear sky, so we can easily see where we're going while still using the shadows of night to our hiding advantage. The place is almost eerie with the hundreds of old or broken cars sitting in silence as far as the eyes can see. Some of them are by themselves while others are in clusters or even piled five or more high against the bluff that borders one of the sides.

I was worried this might not be safe, but Peter said as long as we stick with the younger kids, we'll know what we can and can't hide in. For my part, I'm going to stick with the cars on the ground.

"Then it's time to pick partners. The older kids are me,

Wendy, Hook, Silas, and John. I'm assuming Smee and Starkey will be with Hook, which means Carlos, Tink, Nick, the twins, Michael, and Thomas all need to partner up with the rest of us."

"How come John and Wendy get to be big kids?" Michael pouts.

John ruffles our baby brother's hair. "Because Wendy's fifteen and I'm thirteen, that's why. You need a -teen in your age to be a big kid, and 'ten' doesn't have it. Be thankful you're here at all. Am I right, Captain?"

Hook lights his cigarette and cocks a brow at my brother like he's questioning why John dares to speak to him. I don't know why he even came out with us because all he does is say how lame we are. But sometimes I think that's just an act and he secretly likes being with us. I'm not sure he's all that happy about John trying to be his best buddy, but as long as he's not mean to my brother, I won't say anything.

Michael rolls his eyes on a sigh. "Fiiiiiiine."

"I'm with Peter."

I'm surprised it took Tinker Bell so long to stake her claim. Peter doesn't see it, but that little girl is infatuated with him. I think it's cute, actually. He's protective of her, so it's natural she'd have a crush on him. I don't mind. Her life isn't easy, and I'm glad she has someone like Peter to look out for her.

"Okay Tink, you're with me," Peter says. "Anyone else?"

"Me!"

Again, no surprise there. Michael has serious hero worship when it comes to Peter, and he's been sweet on Tink since I brought him to the school for the first time two months ago. But I'll feel safer if he's with me. Peter and Tinker Bell are liable to hide in one of those gigantic car towers, and Michael doesn't have that kind of scrappy agility. Not caring that it makes me the bad guy, I tell Michael he has to be with me. Thomas joins us, the twins go with John, and Nick and Carlos pair up with Si.

We play over and over, each team taking turns being the Ghost and hiding until someone announces they found them, sending everyone sprinting back to the safety of home base as they try and tag someone to be the next Ghost. After about an hour, it's finally Peter and Tink's turn.

"All right," I say to the group, "everyone face the truck and count, so they can go hide."

As we all turn toward the rusted-out Chevy pickup we're using as base, I can hear Peter and Tink scurry away. I count, and the little kids dance with anticipation of the moment they get to take off into the "graveyard."

Suddenly, Hook grabs my wrist to get my attention and shushes the boys to be quiet and not move. At first, I don't understand why, and then I hear it. Men's voices off in the distance. I look back, but Peter's nowhere to be found. Knowing him, he's at the farthest and most remote hiding spot in the entire place. I can't let the boys be caught, but it might not be necessary to move them if the men don't plan on coming in much more.

"Let's go see what they're here for," I whisper to Hook.

He seems surprised by my suggestion but nods. We motion for the boys to stay put with John and Si in charge of the younger ones, then we make our move, sticking to the shadows as much as possible and ducking behind vehicles. Soon, we find three men about fifty feet away, walking in our direction.

"Such a nice night for a stroll, don't you think? Let's go, sweetheart."

One of the men yanks on something…and that's when I realize the third person isn't a man at all. It's a girl about my age, maybe a little younger, with rope bound around her wrists and used like a dog leash to pull her along.

I clap a hand over my mouth to muffle my sharp inhale,

even though it'd be impossible for them to hear me from this distance. Next to me, Hook tenses as his hands curl into fists against the car we're hiding behind.

"That's Davey and Tito, two of Croc's crew," Hook whispers. "And that girl is Tiger Lily of the Piccaninny tribe. Croc uses her as a driver for his car boosting business."

My head whips to the side to stare at him. "He *steals cars*?"

"Jesus Christ, Darling. You didn't actually think the work we do at his shop is legit, did you?"

"I know it's illegal to make children work, but I didn't know that *what you do* is illegal, too," I whisper back angrily.

Hook shakes his head and mutters, "You and Pan fucking deserve each other."

Ignoring that snide remark, I argue, "She doesn't even look old enough to drive."

"She's not, legally. But kids on the res start driving at a much younger age because there's no rules about it there, and she's *good*. Like, wheel-man for a bank heist good."

I don't even know what to say to that. Girls at my school were worried about snagging the latest fashions at the London mall and gaining the attention of boys they liked. I can't imagine any of them, myself included, driving a car at breakneck speeds, much less for illegal purposes.

"So you all know her?"

"No, Croc deals with her separately. I've seen her a couple of times when she drops off cars at night, though."

"For fuck sake, how much farther, Davey?" The complaint from the one not holding the rope swings my attention back to them.

"Another hundred yards at least," Davey says. "You want people to hear the bitch scream?"

Tito glances over his shoulder at her and shrugs. "I don't know, she ain't fought us yet. Maybe she's not gonna."

"That's because she hasn't had my cock in her yet. She'll

scream plenty then." Davey laughs like he can't wait to hear her torture spill from her lips, like it would be the stuff his dreams are made of.

My blood turns to ice in my veins, and my stomach rolls. They plan on raping that poor girl. And they plan on doing it right around where the boys are waiting for us. Hook must have realized the same thing because he jerks his head for me to follow him, and I do, darting over the same path we took a few minutes ago.

But before we reach the base, I pull Hook up short. "I need you to get my brothers home safely and the Lost Boys back to school."

"What are you talking about? We're all fucking leaving."

I swallow and shake my head. "No, I can't. I have to do something to help her."

"Like what?" he asks angrily through clenched teeth.

"I don't know, I'll think of something."

"You realize what'll happen if you get caught?"

"Yes," I say, glancing back to make sure they haven't gotten this far yet. "But I also know what happens to her if I leave."

"Wendy," he says tightly like he's never used my name before, and I think it might actually be the first time. "The boys and me, Croc will—"

I put a hand on his arm. "I know. That's why you have to get them back, in case these guys run to their boss. They can't see you out here. Find Peter and Tink on your way out and then get my brothers home. *Please*." When he balks at the plan, I add, "I'll be fine, I promise."

He curses a blue streak. "You'd better be or Pan will castrate me in my sleep. Don't do anything stupid. Just make them think the place is haunted or something."

"Yeah okay, now *go*."

I hold my breath as I watch him take off running to where my brothers and the Lost Boys are waiting. When I can't see him anymore, I search the area and try to think of a plan. Thirty seconds later, I have one. I'm not confident it's great, but I'm out of time when the men come into view.

Davey pushes Tiger Lily back onto the hood of a car, tying the end of the rope to the steering wheel through the missing windshield so that her arms are stretched high above her head. My heart is beating so loud I'm afraid it'll lead those barbarians right to me, but then at least they wouldn't be focused on their plans for her.

The sound of a belt buckle loosening as Davey stands in front of a stoic and shockingly calm Tiger Lily spurs me into action. Grabbing the trailer hitch I found on the ground nearby, I throw it as hard as I can in the direction of the shop. My prayers are answered when it crashes into something metal, making a huge *bang* that startles the men.

"What the fuck was that?" Tito asks.

"How the hell should I know? Go check it out."

Tito unsheathes a large knife from his side and stalks off, mumbling under his breath about the unfairness of being the new guy.

Crap! I suppose it was too much to ask for them *both* to go check it out. I like Plan B a whole lot less, but I guess that's pretty typical; otherwise, they'd actually be Plan As. Since I'm not particularly crafty when it comes to devising ways to take down a man twice my size, I'm taking a play out of Peter's book. Last month, he told me about how he took out Croc with a fire extinguisher—not that he told me why. For my sake, I hope he wasn't exaggerating what a blow to the head can do. I want him unconscious, so I can untie Tiger Lily, and we can make our escape before Tito returns.

Taking a deep breath to steady my nerves as much as possible, I pick up my makeshift weapon—a broken piece of wood about the size of a baseball bat—and grip it in both hands as I sneak out from my hiding spot. God, the moon's soft glow might as well be a spotlight for how exposed I feel right now. Luckily, Davey's too busy listing off all the disgusting things he wants to do to hear me creeping up behind him.

Just as he starts to lower his pants, I raise the wood over my head. I quickly calculate my height versus his and make a snap decision to even the playing field with something I've seen John do in his martial arts classes. Using my foot, I kick the back of Davey's knee, causing it to buckle.

"What the—"

Before he can finish his sentence, I swing as hard as I can. The reverberation from the impact shoots through my hands and up my arms, making me drop the wood like it stung me. Davey groans and slumps to the ground.

"Oh my God, it worked," I say, slack-jawed. Then I gasp when the man braces his hands on the ground and shakes his head like he'd just gotten a little dizzy.

"No, it didn't," Tiger Lily says. Fear freezes me in place, but the girl lifts her legs into a back somersault on the hood of the car until she's kneeling upright at the top. Reaching through the open windshield she starts working on the knot with her bound wrists just as Davey gets his feet under him. "Run!"

"I can't," I whisper. What made me think I could do this, that I could save her? I'm not as brave as Peter or as strong as Hook; I don't even know how to defend myself like John. I'm just a girl who couldn't stand the thought of another girl being violated, and now I've made matters worse.

Davey turns to see who assaulted him and a sickly grin slides onto his face. "Two for the price of one. Must be my lucky day."

"Not tonight, asshole."

From the corner of my eye, I can see Tiger Lily free the knot. She slides down the hood then plants her feet at the edge and launches into the air at her would-be attacker. Her flight happens in slow motion with the pale moonlight glinting off her long, raven-black hair as she lets out a war-cry worthy of a banshee. She collides with him, and they both go down. I retrieve my piece of wood, thinking maybe I can get in another hit. Surely, he can't withstand *two* cracks to the skull, right?

But things go from bad to worse as Tito runs back over, gigantic knife in hand, ready to save his partner in crime.

"Davey, what the fuck is— Hey, who are you?"

Oh no, oh no, oh no…

"She's *mine*."

My heart soars to see Peter sprint into the small clearing, heading straight for Tito. Who has a knife.

"Peter, *no!*"

But he never even slows down. The look on his face is one I've never seen. If I hadn't known him before this moment, I'd be scared of him. It promises pain and wrath, and his silver-glinting eyes are as bloodthirsty as his opponent's knife. Just before Peter gets to Tito, he drops between the man's legs like he's sliding across home plate, then pops to his feet on the other side and uses the same kick method I did.

A tiny yell with the jingling of a bell distracts me, and I turn just in time to see Tink fly into the fray, jumping onto Davey's back. Like a hissing kitten, she spits and claws and scratches her much bigger predator, distracting him enough that Tiger Lily gets in a crotch shot. Davey growls as he cups the injured area with one hand and throws Tink off with the other.

"Knock it off, you nasty pig!" Adrenaline floods my veins as I run over with the wood held high and shouting my own battle cry fueled by hate and disgust. With every ounce of strength I didn't know I possessed, I bring the weapon down with both hands like Thor with his mighty hammer. The wood breaks in two, and this time, when Davey collapses to the ground, he doesn't make a sound or the slightest twitch.

The girls and I stare at him as we try to catch our breaths. Tink walks over and kicks him in the ribs. I arch a brow at her.

"What? Just making sure he's not awake is all," she says, crossing her arms.

"Thank you," Tiger Lily says to us, wresting the knife from Davey's belt.

"You're welcome," I say as I watch her place it between her feet. "I don't know how you managed to stay so calm like that. You must be really brave."

She makes quick work of sawing through the rest of her bindings, then stands. Definitely a little younger than me, but she's taller and graceful like a dancer. "It's got nothing to do with bravery. They wanted me to scream and cry and beg them for mercy, but I knew they were going to rape me no matter what, so I kept my mouth shut. They were already getting what they wanted, I didn't have to make it fun for them, too." Tiger Lily flips the knife in her hand, end over end, like she's been playing with sharp objects since birth. Smiling wickedly, she says, "But I would've gotten my revenge eventually when I hunted them down, sliced off their balls with their own knives, and fed them to my dogs."

"Oh, okay then," I say, swallowing hard. *That got dark real—* "Oh no, *Peter.*"

Spinning on my heel, I run over to where Tito is on the ground, unmoving but still breathing, with the girls right behind me. Peter is sitting against the side of a car, breathing hard and holding his side. He's covered in sweat and dirt, and pain brackets his eyes.

"You're hurt." Concern swamps me, but my words come out like an accusation, as if I told him not to do that.

"Nah, I'm fine."

Tink crouches down and flicks Tito in the face before smiling over at her hero. "You got him good, Peter."

"Sure did, sprite," he says tightly.

Off in the distance, we can hear dogs barking and a man shouting commands at them to search.

Tiger Lily frowns. "Croc is coming. We need to go."

I reach down to help Peter get to his feet, but he groans and sits back again with a pained grunt. He takes his hand away from his side, and that's when I see it. Blood. So much blood.

"Oh my God, Peter," I cry as I fall to my knees at his side and try to examine his wound. But every time my hands get near him, he brushes them away. "Peter, stop, let me see."

"It looks worse than it is, Wen, I swear. He got me on the side is all. But you guys have to get out of here. I'll stay." Tink and I immediately protest. "Hey, listen to me. If I'm the only one here, I can tell Croc that I was out screwing around when these guys found me and tried to bring me in. They're not gonna say otherwise because if Croc knows they tried messing with his prize driver, there'll be hell to pay. With my story, it makes them the heroes and the victims, so they'll keep their mouths shut, and he won't know the other kids are sneaking out or anything about you, Wendy. That's the way it has to be."

"He's right," Tiger Lily says. "It's everyone's best option. I know a back way out of here. We can take that to where I have a car stashed. I'll make sure they both get home, I swear on my honor."

"Thanks. Wendy, gimme a second with Tink, would ya?"

I rise and take a few steps off to the side, my stomach flipping so much I feel sick. Tink leans in so Peter can whisper something to her. A few seconds later, she backs away, and I drop to his side. The barking is getting louder, and the last thing I want to do is leave him here. Getting caught by Croc with what happened to his men could mean punishments like Peter's never had before, and he's had some bad ones.

Tears stream down my face as I try begging him one last time. "Peter, please come with us. We can help you."

"Shhh, you know this is the only way to spare the others. I need you to get out of here, Wen. If Croc ever finds out about you, I'd—"

He takes a steadying breath as though he needed to cut himself off before he said something I wouldn't want to hear. Peter's always protecting me, even from himself, even now. I might be young, and I might be naive, but if there's anything in this world stronger than the love I feel for Peter Pan in this moment, I don't want to know what it is. Because this is everything, *he* is everything.

"We need to go right now," Tiger Lily says behind me.

"Please, Wen," he whispers, lifting the hand that's not putting pressure on his wound and trailing his fingertips over the wet streaks on my cheek. "Go with Tiger Lily, make sure Tink gets home. Do it for me."

I sniff hard and wipe my nose with the back of my arm. "I'll come tomorrow night, okay?" He nods and gives me a weak crooked grin. I kiss him gently, not caring about our audience, then press my fingers against his lips to seal it in. "I love you, Peter."

His eyes shine in the moonlight, and his grin spreads into a full-blown smile. It's the first time I've ever said those words, but certainly not the first time I've felt them.

"I love you more, Wen."

Tiger Lily pulls me to my feet and looks down at Peter. "You'll always have an ally in me, Peter Pan. If you ever need anything, you know how to find me."

He nods once. "*Go.*"

The three of us race off in the opposite direction from where Croc is advancing. I do my best to ignore the burning in my lungs and the tears drying on my cheeks from the wind, making my skin tight. Eventually, we reach Lily's car, and we ride in silence to my street with the exception of me giving her my address.

Tiger Lily stops the car a block from my house, and I climb out like a zombie, nothing but fear for Peter roiling in my gut.

"Don't worry about him, Wendy," Tiger Lily says from her open window. "He has a strong mind and heart. He'll heal."

I nod numbly, then begin walking toward my house.

"Hey, wait up." I turn around, surprised Tinker Bell is speaking to me directly. She's not even scowling. "What you did…staying behind like that and trying to save her…that was…brave."

The pixie-sized ten-year-old seems to be struggling with paying me a compliment, but I appreciate her trying. Maybe this can be a fresh start for us.

"I'm giving you a favor—just *one*—that can be collected whenever you want," she says. "You stuck your neck out for one of us—not that she's a Lost Boy, but she's one of Croc's puppets just like we are—so that earns you a favor. From me. *One*," she emphasizes with her index finger in my face.

Okay, so we're not going to be besties, after all. But I have earned a bit of her respect. I'll take it. "One," I say. "Got it. Now hurry and get back to school and into bed."

Oh, look, the scowl's back. "You're not my mom," she says and runs back to the car, tinkling all the way.

I sigh, too tired to argue that I didn't mean it that way, and head home—alternately worrying about Peter and wondering what in the world I could ever ask of Tinker Bell that would make us even.

CHAPTER SIXTEEN

PETER

Now...

"Okay, Tink, start her up." Leaning in through the driver's window of the Bel Air, Tink turns the key and brings the engine in front of me to life. "Yeahhhhh, listen to her *purr*. Nice job, sprite."

Tinker Bell cheers with our success before turning it off again and coming to stand by me. "All we need are the final touches, and she's all done."

I frown. "Speaking of which, shouldn't that shipment have come in already? We only have one week left to install everything."

"Don't sweat it, I'm sure it'll be here Monday," she says, grabbing tools from the ground to put them away.

"Shit, I should've placed the order a lot sooner. But I paid for express shipping to make up for it, so we should be fine as long as it doesn't get held up anywhere." Scrubbing a hand down my face, I mentally kick my own ass for not planning this better. "Do me a favor when you go to the house and check the tracking. I want to know where it is and when it's supposed to arrive."

"Sure thing." Turning around, she leans back with her elbows on the tool bench. "You know, if none of those stuffy asshats bid on the car, we could sell her for a mint. Enough to buy another one we can fix up."

Wiping the grease from my hands on a rag, I raise a brow. "You're telling me you think there's a chance no one will bid on this car? Maybe the new paint fumes are going to your head."

She shrugs. "Of course, they *should*. I'm just saying if they're too dumb not to, is all."

"Let's hope that's not the case, or it'll ruin Wendy's fundraiser."

"She's leaving after it's over, right?" Tink's doing her best to sound casual but *hopeful* would be a better word for it.

Lowering myself into a metal folding chair, I brace my arms on my thighs and prepare for an unpleasant conversation. "I don't know yet. We haven't had a chance to talk much about it. But there's a good chance, yeah."

"Oh," she says, sounding a little too chipper. "Well, it was nice to have her here for a visit, but she does have her own life to get back to. Probably has lots of catching up with friends to do, a boyfriend waiting for her, things like that. Guess life in Neverland will be back to normal, then."

"She doesn't have a boyfriend," I say, barely stopping my eye roll, "and whatever happens, things won't be the same in Neverland again."

Tink freezes. "What do you mean? Why not?"

I think about the ring box I unearthed from my tool chest at the shop. I cleaned the dust off it and polished what had been nestled inside, untouched, for an entire decade. I plan on finally giving it to her when I show her the finished car, when I show her that she can depend on me to always come through for her. Because while I might not be the most mature or grown up when it comes to certain things—or even most things—I'll always be what she needs me to be. I will always love, cherish, and take care of her.

Blowing out a long exhale, I bite the bullet and reveal my intentions. "I'm going to ask Wendy to stay. If she says yes, then she'll be a part of our family for good, Tink, and I'll expect you to respect that *and* respect her," I say firmly.

"And if she says no?" she asks slowly.

I pause, unsure if I want to drop this on her now. But there's never going to be a good time for it. Tinker Bell won't like my answer no matter when I tell her or how I do it. I can only hope that she'll come around eventually. "Then I'll go with her."

Her green eyes flare wide. "*What?* You can't leave Neverland! This is your *home*. She's not your family, *we are*. I can't believe you'd fucking abandon me and the boys for *her*."

Shit, this isn't what I want. I hate it when Tink gets pissed or upset with me about serious stuff. I know it'll be an adjustment for her to be without me—I've been her person since she was a baby—but she'll be fine. Maybe it's even better for her if I *do* leave. If Wendy's right about Tink's feelings for me, she'll be able to move on and find someone easier if I'm not around to confuse her.

Pushing to my feet, I hold my hands up. "Calm down, sprite—"

"Don't you dare tell me to calm down, Peter Pan. I have the right to my feelings, and if I want to rant and scream at you then I'll damn well do it."

"You're right, I'm sorry. I don't mean to sound patronizing. I just don't like seeing you upset."

"Really?" she says sarcastically, narrowing her eyes at me. "You have a funny way of showing it."

"Who wants Chinese?"

Tink and I spin to see Wendy standing under the open bay door in a cornflower blue sundress that matches her smiling eyes, holding up white plastic take-out bags like a game show hostess showcasing what we've just won. Sensing the tension in the air, she falters.

"Is this a bad time?"

Making a sound of disgust, Tink brushes by me, but I stop her with a hand on her arm. "Tink, wait. We still need to talk about this later."

"What for? You've already made your decision. And we all know that the great and mighty Peter Pan always does what he wants." She shakes me off and ignores Wendy as she storms off toward the house.

"I'm sorry," Wendy says on a sigh. "That was about me, wasn't it?"

Pulling her into my arms, I kiss her forehead. "No, it was about me. Don't worry about it, I'll talk to her after she cools down. What'd ya bring me?"

I relieve her of one of the bags, and we take them over to the counter. "Chicken Lo Mein, beef and broccoli, wonton soup, fried rice, and Crab Rangoon."

The aromas of sautéed meat and veggies drenched in sauces hit my nostrils and make my mouth water. I didn't realize how famished I was until now. "Nice. So then what are you gonna eat?"

"It's for *both* of us," she says, backhanding me in the stomach. Big mistake because I capture it and yank her in to tickle her sides. "Ahhh, Peter, *stahhhhhp*!"

I can barely understand her through the staccato beats of her laughter as she does her best to squirm out of my grasp. Remembering that she could only deal with tickling for a few seconds at a time, I take out a few containers of food while she catches her breath.

"You're pure evil, you know that?"

I'm about to answer that I'd love to show her just how devilish I can be when my phone rings in my pocket. It's Hook, and I've been waiting to hear back from him. "Hold that thought, baby, I have to take this."

Kissing her on the cheek, I move to where the Bel Air sits in the middle of the bay and swipe my thumb to connect the call. "Hey, man, what've you heard?"

"Nothing."

"Nothing?" I repeat in disbelief. "It's been a whole week, and you're telling me that *none* of your slimy, underbelly associates have heard about anyone messing with Lily?"

"That's what I said. Look, if you don't like my results then I suggest you get your own fucking contacts. I got enough on my plate as it is. I don't need your ungrateful bullshit."

I plow a hand through my hair, no doubt streaking it with traces of grease, and blow out a breath. "Sorry, man, I'm just worried about her. If someone's fucking with her car…"

"I know," he says in a low voice. For all his acting like he doesn't give a shit about anyone, Hook's still protective of his own. It's the rest of the world he truly doesn't give a shit about. "I'll let you know if I hear anything."

"Thanks. Hey, what's going on with Starkey?"

Two arms snake around my waist from behind, and I feel her lips press into the dip of my spine over the thin cotton of my wifebeater. Unable to resist, I guide her in front of me and kiss her neck as I listen to Hook.

"Nothing. They won't release him, won't let me see or talk to him. They've taken away all his rights. And they call *me* the criminal."

Wendy pulls back and whispers, "Is Starkey out?" I shake my head and her brows knit together. "John's LPD. Maybe he can look into it for us."

"No way," Hook snarls into my ear. "No London cop is gonna give two shits about a Pirate, including her kiss-ass brother. Tell her no fucking thanks and to keep her nose—and especially *him*—out of my business."

When the line goes dead, I pocket my phone. "He says thank you, and he really appreciates your help."

Smiling, she says, "Aww, see? He's not such a bad—" She breaks off and narrows her blue eyes at me. "That's not what he said, is it?"

I chuckle and shake my head as I walk her backward. "Not even close."

"Ugh, *men*."

"I only want you thinking of *this* man right now." Her legs hit the front of the Bel Air and suddenly all I can think about is fucking her on top of it. I want to devour her like the rich pricks I'm building it for devour their caviar. To temporarily defile the car as I defile her until she comes so hard, she sees stars and speaks in tongues.

"It's a good thing that giant hood ornament hasn't come in yet or this would've been a lot more uncomfortable for you."

Grabbing her waist, I easily lift her onto the hood and lean in to claim her mouth, but she stops me with a hand on my chest. Twisting around to look at the car, she starts shooting off rapid-fire questions. "Wait, what else needs to be done? Why hasn't the hood ornament come in? Are there other things that haven't come in?" She gasps. "Oh my God, there's no seats! Or a steering wheel!"

Framing her face with my hands, I guide her attention back to me. "Stop worrying, it'll all be done on time. Come by next Thursday night, so I can show you how pretty it is." *And then we can talk about our future together.*

Her eyes are wide, and I can see her mind racing as she runs through all the disastrous scenarios. "Peter, if I don't have a car to auction off next Saturday, I might as well kiss Second Star Events goodbye. My reputation will be ruined, I—"

"You named your company Second Star Events?" I ask huskily. At every turn, this woman undoes me. Ten years apart didn't stop her from keeping so many things about our relationship alive. And I'd chosen to bury it deep in my mind and in the back corner of an unused tool chest drawer. Out of sight, out of mind was the best way I'd found to cope with the aching loss. I could pretend I had everything I wanted in life as long as that ring box wasn't staring at me. I should've gone after her. What a waste of precious time.

She nods and traps that poor lower lip between her teeth. This time I don't use my thumb to rescue it. I kiss it, embracing her lip with mine, sucking on it lightly until it's free. "I won't let you down. You'll have your beautiful Bel Air, finished and ready for bidding. I'll prove it next Thursday."

"Promise?"

"I promise."

Wendy pulls me in by the scruff of my neck, slamming her mouth to mine, and *fuck yes, that's hot*. If she reacts like this every time, I'll make it my life's mission to promise her everything under the sun and stars. Then I'll damn well deliver.

I follow her lead, and I then take it. She instantly submits, eagerly opening to my hungry demands, letting me control the pace, the depth, the intensity. I bite her lip—the one she loves to imprison so much—staking my claim on every inch of her body with a single, sharp nip. *This lip is mine, everything is mine.* Her wanton moan slips over my tongue and down my throat. The vibrations set my blood on fucking fire and rushing straight to my cock.

I kiss and bite down the column of her neck as I reach under the skirt of her dress, up her smooth thighs and grab hold of her ass.

"Sweet Christ," I rasp out. "A thong?"

She blushes. "You like?"

"Yeah, I fucking like." But I'll like them even better off. Hooking my fingers in the sides, I pull them all the way down and tuck the tiny scrap of blue lace into my pocket for safekeeping. Sliding my hands up her dress again, I guide her thighs open.

"Hey, you can't keep my—"

Before she finishes her sentence, I use my thumbs to part her folds and massage her clit. Her words melt into nothing more than a moan as her head drops back on her shoulders. "What was that, baby? I can't what?"

"N-nothing," she gasps when I insert a finger into her tight pussy. "Do whatever you want."

My lips twist into a satisfied smirk, and I drop to my knees in front of her. "Plannin' on it."

The scent of her arousal makes my mouth water more than the take-out did, and if I could figure out a way to do it, I'd survive on nothing but Wendy for the rest of my life. With my free hand, I push her skirt against her belly, giving us both an unfettered view of my finger working in and out of her slick channel.

She braces herself with her arms behind her and stares down her body, watching my invasion with lust-bright eyes, her breasts rising and falling with shallow breaths. I add a second finger, then a third.

"Oh God, Peter," she groans.

Pumping and twisting, I pick up my speed and graze her G-spot on every withdrawal. Her juices bathe my hand and drip onto the hood, and it turns me on knowing this car will have my mark on it in more ways than just my craftsmanship.

Unable to deny myself any longer, I lean in and taste her. My tongue swipes over her swollen nub, causing her to cry out and grab onto my head. She holds me in place like she's afraid I'll back away—which I suppose is fair since I enjoy teasing the hell out of her until she doesn't remember her own name or what planet we live on—but she doesn't have to worry this time because I'm not going anywhere.

Using everything in my sexual arsenal, I continue to fuck her with my fingers and tongue. I plunge and lick and suck and bite. Her arousal consumes me. The scent of her in my nose, the feel of her on my skin, and the sound of her keening moans—all of it makes my cock hard and my balls ache with the need to bury myself deep inside her. But not until I've made her come.

"Fuck, Wen, you taste so good," I growl between swipes with my tongue. I need more, and my fingers are in the way, so I pull all the way out and move them down, spreading her juices onto the hyper-sensitive nerves around her puckered hole. She jumps in surprise, but my hand holds her steady. "Easy, angel, I'm only touching." *For now, anyway.* Someday I hope she'll let me inside, but we have plenty of time to work our way up to that. "Take a deep breath and focus on the pleasure."

She nods, her lids at half-mast, her hair a wild mess of waves around her shoulders. I pierce her sweet cunt with my tongue and eat at her like a man starved. Her inner walls get tighter, her legs begin to shake, and she gets a whole lot louder as her climax approaches.

"Yes, right there, oh my God, don't stop, *please don't ever stop.*"

I wouldn't stop now even if the gates of Hell opened and threatened to swallow me whole. Instead, I double my efforts, adding a slight pressure to the strokes over her hole and using my other hand to rub her clit while I devour her with my mouth. The fist in my hair tightens, but the pain in my scalp only turns me on more.

She shouts my name and curls her body forward, flooding my mouth with an ambrosia all her own. I groan as I drink every drop, and still I want more. As the orgasm sweeps through her, causing her to shake with mini-convulsions on the hood of the '55 Bel Air, I don't let up. I keep going and going, pushing her back toward the brink of another climax before the first one even has the chance to die down.

"Oh God, Peter, what are you— No, I can't— It's too

much, I—" She tries pushing my head away, but I block her hands with mine and then link our fingers as I stare up her body, my lips and tongue proving her wrong. She *can* come again.

And she does.

With her mouth in the shape of an O, her brows drawn, and her hands squeezing mine for support, she comes hard. After several seconds, I slow my motions and gentle my pressure, easing her through it until most of her aftershocks are gone.

Standing up, I strip off my shirt and use it to clean my face before tossing it to the side. If I thought making Wendy come twice would zap the energy out of her, I was dead wrong. Grabbing onto my shoulders, she pulls me in for a punishing kiss. When she breaks away, she pulls a condom out of her bra and holds it between us.

I break into a huge smile. "Have you been taking lessons from the Boy Scouts?" Despite her brazenness two seconds ago, my teasing makes her blush, and it drives me crazy.

"Shut up, put it on, and…"

My eyebrows shoot up to my hairline. Hell no, I'm not letting her stop there. I want to hear her say it. I *need* to hear her say it. Snatching the latex ring from her hand, I rip it open and sheathe my cock in record time after opening my fly and shoving my jeans past my hips. Gripping my hard cock, I set the head at her entrance and wait.

"And what, Wen?"

She raises her chin a notch. "You know what."

I shake my head. "I shut up. I put it on. Tell me what you want me to do next."

Just when I think she can't bring herself to say it, a sly grin tilts up one side of her lush mouth. Then she leans in and whispers in my ear, "Fuck me, Peter Pan."

Jesus fucking Christ, I think I may have died and went to Heaven. Those sinful words from my angel's lips send me into overdrive, and before I know what I'm doing, I flip her position and have her bent over the hood with a foot up on the bumper. One hand squeezes my cock and presses the tip against her pussy as my other one fists her hair and pulls back, arching her beautifully for me. She moans and tries to push back on my dick, but I don't let her.

"Say it again," I rasp out against her ear.

Wendy turns her head to lock eyes with me over her shoulder, her words pouring out slow like warm honey. "Fuck me, Peter."

"Hell yes." I drive home in a thrust so powerful it moves her several inches higher onto the hood. She cries out and begs me for more, but it's an unnecessary plea because I'm already pounding into her, over and over—harder, deeper, faster.

I don't think I've ever been so turned on in my life as seeing Wendy Darling bent over the hood of a classic car that I poured my blood and sweat into rebuilding, my large hands gripping her bare ass as I watch my shaft disappear between her swollen pussy lips.

"Gonna come again," she pants.

"That's it," I say, adjusting my hold on her, so I can pull her hips back as I thrust forward. "Do it, baby. I wanna feel you coming on my cock."

She screams, and just as I feel her pulse around me, fire shoots down my spine. My balls draw up tight a second before they unload, my cum shooting through the tip of my dick so hard I see double for a good thirty seconds.

Completely spent, we collapse onto the hood and laugh as we try to catch our breath.

"Should we be this winded after sex?" she asks.

"Baby, that wasn't *just* sex. That was Olympic-level screwing is what that was."

She giggles. "You can't say the F-word to me now that we're done, can you?"

Somehow, I find the strength to push myself up. "Look who's talking," I say, smacking her ass for good measure. She squeals and twists her body, dislodging my softening cock, making me hiss through my teeth. "Well, that was abrupt."

"Serves you right for spanking me," she says with a fake pout.

Straightening, she flips the skirt of her dress down, and I instantly regret not taking the whole thing off her, so she wouldn't have as easy of a time redressing. I make quick work of getting rid of the condom and putting myself back together. Then I pull her into my arms and drop my hands to her ass cheeks. "You have no idea what a real spanking is, but if you're interested, I'd be happy to put you over my knee and turn these babies bright pink."

Her blue eyes spark, and she bites her lip for a split second before she schools her expression. I start to get hard again just thinking about it, but Wendy changes the subject on me. "Are you going to return my panties?"

"Hell no, these are mine now." I smile down at her. "I'm thinking I might start a collection."

"Then *I'm* thinking I'll switch to cotton granny-panties."

I frown. "That's not funny, Wen."

"Neither is stealing a lady's panties, Peter." She arches a challenging brow and holds out her hand.

Laughing, I fish them out of my pocket. But instead of handing them to her, I crouch down and help her back into them. Once they're firmly in place—*Christ, those look so fucking hot on her*—I give her a quick kiss on the nose. "There, now that you're all put together, what do you say we eat our cold Chinese food?"

"Oh, I'm not actually hungry. I ate before I came over."

Okay, now I'm confused. "You said you brought lunch for the two of us."

"I lied, silly man. I was in the mood for something much more decadent than Chinese, hence the condom in my bra.

It's so cute you thought sex was your idea, though." Rising up on her on tip-toes, she kisses my cheek, then gives me a brilliant smile. "I have to go, but enjoy the food. I'll call you later."

And with that, she saunters her fine, thong-clad ass out of my garage bay and into the midday sun, leaving me utterly speechless except for the laughter that doesn't stop until I stuff my face with lo mein noodles.

Sex on the hood of a car in the afternoon with the woman of my dreams, followed by take-out she brought over as an excuse to have said sex? Life doesn't get any better than this.

CHAPTER SEVENTEEN

WENDY

The sound of my heels clicking on the floor as I walk into the Children's Hospital is incongruous with how I'm walking on air. I should hear nothing but the soft swooshing as I bounce from one puffy, white cloud to another. But despite the lightness in my steps, I haven't yet learned to fly, so my feet are tethered to this tile like everyone else.

"Hello, Anne, how are you?" I greet the receptionist.

"I'm great, Wendy, thanks for asking. I don't have to ask how you are, you're positively glowing," she says, beaming at me.

"Well, thank you, I am feeling pretty great today."

She picks out a visitor badge and offers it to me. "You ready for the big meeting?"

Big meeting is right. The meeting where I lay out all the things I have planned for the biggest event of my career that's only two days away. The meeting where I have to pretend I've personally confirmed that the main focus of the entire event—the thing that can potentially raise the most money this fundraiser has ever seen—is completed, instead of telling them I haven't seen it yet, but I will tonight, as per my agreement with Peter.

But I'm not worried. I trust him implicitly, and if he's been a little distant this week, it's probably only because he's busy getting it ready. Plus, I think he might be planning an extra something special. I don't know for sure. It's just a hunch, but one I'm excited about.

"Absolutely," I say with confidence. "Everything is falling into place. I think the board is going to be very happy with the update."

"That's wonderful to hear. Oh, look," she says, pointing behind me, "there's some familiar faces."

I turn to see my brothers walking with a teenage girl between them. Her black hair is in a loose ponytail like it got snagged on something and pulled halfway out. Besides the pair of ripped jeans and faded Eminem concert T-shirt, she's wearing a pissed-at-the-world scowl I've seen regularly on a certain blond fairy.

As soon as my brothers notice me, their faces light up and meet me in the middle of the lobby. John and I haven't seen much of each other since I've been back, so I welcome the big hug he gives me, though it's slightly uncomfortable with all the gear on his duty belt and the Kevlar vest under his shirt.

"This is a nice surprise," he says in his deep voice. "How are ya, little sis?"

Pulling back, I scoff. "I'm two years older than you, in case you've forgotten."

"Yeah, *older*—which isn't something I'd brag about by the way—but you're way smaller than us, which makes you our little sister."

Michael chuckles. "I like that."

"It's not my fault you two shot up like the Jolly Green Giant. Come to think of it, all the boys turned out huge. Maybe there's something in Neverland's water," I mutter.

John tenses next to me. "There's definitely *something* going on in Neverland, and I intend to find out what."

John's ominous tone worries me and reminds me that Starkey is still in jail for unknown reasons. I wonder if there's any way he can help, maybe do some discreet digging.

"Can I go now?"

The three of us turn our attention to the disgruntled teen who clearly wants to be anywhere other than here.

Michael raises a single eyebrow, secretly communicating something that has her rolling her eyes. She starts to cross her arms in a huff, then yanks her bandaged hand back on a hiss.

"You okay? Let me see it." Michael reaches for her injured hand, but she pulls it away.

"I told you I'm *fine.*"

My youngest brother tries to hide it, but I see the disappointment flash in his eyes. He wants to help this girl, but she's not interested in letting him. I'm assuming she's one of the kids the foundation works with at the Heart House, a local group home for orphans. Shifting my laptop bag higher on my shoulder, I extend my hand and offer her a warm smile. "Hi, I'm Wendy."

"Hi, I'm not interested," she drolls.

"Jade, enough with the attitude already," Michael says. "Apologize for being rude or you lose your art supplies for a week."

The girl's brown eyes flare like he just threatened her with walking the plank into a shark-infested sea. Michael challenges her with a raise of his eyebrows, and she relents with a dramatic sigh. "I'm sorry I was rude. It's very nice to meet you."

"Nice to meet you, too, Jade," I say, playing along like she's not being forced into politeness.

Looking at Michael, she asks, "*Now* can I go?"

"Since I have a meeting with Wendy soon, yes, you can go. Officer John will take you back to the house."

"I'm almost fifteen. I can get there myself."

"So you can vandalize something else on your way? I don't think so."

"It's *art*," she says, narrowing her eyes.

"Yeah, I know, and it's damn good art, too. But when you put it on the side of a public building—regardless if it's abandoned—it becomes *vandalism*. You're lucky my brother was the one who found you this time. So please just do me a favor and go back to the house with Doughnut Boy here, and we'll talk later."

"Hey," John says, crossing his arms over his big chest.

Jade bites the inside of her cheek like she's afraid cracking a smile might be lethal.

"I don't even like doughnuts," he says. "It's been so long since I've had sugar, I'd probably keel over. And if I resembled half the guys on the London force, I wouldn't have caught up with Jade the Jackrabbit when she took off running."

Jade glowers at her bandaged palm. "I would've gotten away if it hadn't been for that stupid fence."

John hooks his thumbs on his belt and puffs his chest out. "Please, I still would've caught you. I'm in peak physical condition."

"Yeah, for an old guy," Jade counters.

John's mouth drops open, and now I'm holding my stomach and laughing. At twenty-six, John is hardly a geezer, but he's super sensitive about his appearance. Last year at Christmas, he found a single gray hair in his goatee and almost had a meltdown.

"Careful, brother," Michael teases with a chuckle. "Your gay is showing."

"If caring about one's health is gay, then I don't want to be straight," John says.

Jade laughs, and I can tell by the soft look on Michael's

face, this is a rare and precious moment. "You don't want to be straight because you're into dudes."

Smiling, John winks at the young girl. "That too. All right, come on trouble maker. Let's get you back to the house, so I can continue chasing bad guys."

We say our goodbyes while Jade gives a reluctant half-hearted wave. As they start to walk away, she asks John, "Am I getting my spray paint cans back?"

"Not a chance, kid."

Michael watches them until they disappear through the front entrance then checks his watch. "We've got about thirty minutes before the meeting. Wanna grab some horrible coffee first?"

"How could I say no to that tempting offer?" I quip, and we head in the direction of the cafeteria. "Jade seems nice."

"If by nice you mean a giant pain in my ass, then yeah, she's super nice," he says wryly.

I see right through my baby brother's act. His heart's as big as North Carolina, and if he thinks someone needs saving, he does everything in his power to be whatever they need. He's a lot like Thomas in that respect. It's what makes Michael so perfect for social work.

Threading my arm through his, I give his bicep a squeeze. "You care about her that much, huh?"

He sighs. "Yeah, I do. She's been in the system from the time she was a toddler, placed in dozens of homes over the years, none of which worked for very long, which is why she's at Heart House now. No one wants a teenager with anger management and authority issues. But now she's causing problems there, too. It's like she wants to push the whole world away."

"What happens if she keeps causing trouble?"

We enter the cafeteria where Michael buys two coffees then ushers me to an empty table. "They'll look to place her in another home and hope for the best. Then when she gets out of control again, she'll get sent back. Rinse and repeat."

"That's awful. There has to be somewhere she can feel at home. She just needs to learn how to let people love her."

"Yeah, I'm working on it."

He scrubs a hand down his face, trying to hide a stifled yawn. That's when I notice the dark circles under his eyes. He's not getting enough sleep, and I wonder if it's from worrying about Jade.

"How are things with you and Peter? Does he still wanna kick my ass for flirting with you?" He grimaces. "Ew, I can't even say that with a straight face."

I laugh. "He forgave you the second I told him it was you. And now that the black dye is washed out and you're back to your natural golden brown, he'll probably have no issue recognizing you, so you don't have to worry about catching his right hook from a spontaneous sighting."

"Good to know. I thought he was intimidating as a scrawny teenager, but the dude looks like he could go five rounds with John and never break a sweat."

I smile behind my cup as I take a small sip of my coffee, then promptly spit it back out. "Wow, that really is horrible," I say.

"Yeah, no shit, I could run my car on this stuff. You never answered my question about you and Peter."

My smile grows so big my cheeks hurt. "We're…great. When I came home, I wasn't sure how he'd react, but he only had his walls up for all of ten minutes. Then like a switch, he decided to reclaim what we once had, and he didn't hold back."

He gestures to my face with his coffee cup. "From the way you're glowing, I'd say it worked."

"Anne said the same thing." Self-consciously I touch my cheeks, expecting to find them hot or beaming with light. "Am I shiny? Maybe I need more powder."

Chuckling, he leans forward and rests his arms on the table. "You look great, sis. Happy. But I know you're planning on going home after the event. What's Peter think about that?"

I chew on my bottom lip while I mull over my answer. We haven't really had time yet, but I'm hoping that once the stress of the event is behind us, we can talk about where we go from here. "I think I'm going to stay."

My baby brother raises his eyebrows. "What about the life you've built in Charlotte?"

I shrug. "It's a good life, I'm not denying that. But how can I live there when my heart is in Neverland?"

Michael nods, rubbing two fingers over his chin. "Yeah, I get that. I'd just hate to see you give up on everything you've worked for over the years. Maybe Peter would move to Charlotte with you."

"And ask him to leave the Lost Boys? I would never do that. I would never *want* him to do that. He belongs with them and vice versa." I grin. "Besides, I don't want to leave them now either. They're all so wonderful in their own way. Even if one of them *does* wish I'd fall off the face of the earth."

His tired eyes spark to life. "How is the feisty pixie these days? I've been trying to get a hold of her, but she's dodging my calls. Think she's playing hard to get?"

I sigh and swirl the liquid tar around in my Styrofoam cup, wishing I'd stopped at a Starbucks on the way in. "Sorry to break it to you, but she's not playing any kind of game. She's in love with Peter—always has been, always will be."

Michael sits back in his chair and folds his arms across his chest, furrowing his brow in thought. "Nope, not buying it." His firm rejection surprises me and drags my gaze up to his as he continues. "I'm not saying she doesn't love the guy, and for good reason. But *in* love? I don't think so. A woman in love doesn't react to another man, and without going into any details that might otherwise make a sibling uncomfortable, that woman *definitely* reacted to me that day at the hospital."

A tiny kernel of hope dares to flare inside of me. Could Michael be right? I honestly don't see how when Tinker Bell was as friendly as a rabid dog around me. She's very territorial about Peter, that much is obvious, but maybe it isn't because she's in love with him like I thought.

Then again, just because a woman finds another man attractive doesn't mean she's not in love. Ultimately, none of it matters because Tink has hated me for the better part of two decades. Whatever her reasons, I doubt that's going to change any time soon.

My phone dings with an incoming text, and the butterflies erupt in my belly thinking it might be Peter. Then I push past the disappointment that it's not. I'll be with him later tonight and then the butterflies can whip themselves into a frenzy.

"Crap. The caterer had something come up and can't finalize things with me this afternoon. She needs to reschedule for tonight."

"That's no big deal, right? Still getting it done today."

"I know, it's just that I had plans with Peter tonight to go over and see the finished car."

"Call him and see if you can go over earlier."

"That's a good idea." I find Peter's name in my favorites on my phone and give him a call, chewing on my lip while I listen to it ring. And ring. And ring. "That's weird. He's never not answered when I call."

"Probably has the music up loud or he could be under the car or covered in grease. I'm sure everything's fine."

"You're right, it's okay. I'll try again after the meeting."

Michael's watch beeps. "Speaking of which, time for us to go," he says, standing and tossing both our coffees in the trash. "Ready to show the board all the amazing things Second Star Events has lined up?"

I push to my feet, shoulder my laptop bag, and place my hand in his with a smile. "Ready."

When we get to the conference room, all five board members are seated and waiting. But there's an extra man I didn't expect to see, making me stop in my tracks. My stomach sours with an ominous feeling as I paste a smile onto my face.

"Dad, what a lovely surprise," I say, trying to sound sincere as I walk over and bend to kiss his cheek. "What are you doing here?"

He smooths a side of his mustache between thumb and forefinger, a habit he has when he's in professional mode. "Since I handle the finances for the Lost Ones of London foundation, I'm here to get an update for our part of the investment of the event."

"Wonderful." As I take my seat, I catch Michael's gaze and arch an accusatory eyebrow. *Thanks for the warning, butthead.* Except the look he tosses back tells me he's just as surprised as I am, so I cancel my plans to throttle him after the meeting.

I set up my laptop and start the presentation. I show them pictures of the venue, as well as a computer-generated rendering of what the space will look like once fully decorated. I go over the schedule for the evening and the menu, complete with pictures and descriptions of all the food and specialty drinks. I hand out lists of the songs I gave the DJ and make adjustments and additions based on their suggestions of what they would and would not like to hear.

Everything is going great, until we get to the discussion about the Bel Air.

I click through pictures I've taken of it in various stages, the last being the one from a week ago—painted a shiny, bright red but missing the doors and everything that belongs on the *inside* of a car. The final picture I show them is one I pulled from Google that's as close as I could get.

"Is that the same car?" one of the men asks.

"No, but that's what it will look like when it's completed."

"It's not finished?"

"I'm sure it is by now," I say, injecting every ounce of confidence into my voice. "Mr. Pan assured me that it would be done by today. I have plans to go there this afternoon to see the car."

My father taps the end of his pen on the notepad in front of him. "So, you haven't seen it in person yet, but you *have* received verbal confirmation that it's done?"

The dubious arch of his brow shoots an arrow of doubt straight into the heart of my confidence. I actually haven't received confirmation. I haven't heard from Peter at all this week. I assumed it was because he was busy, like me, with last minute details. I'm sure that's it. But still, I'd feel better if I could just hear him tell me everything is fine. I planned on trying to call after the meeting to ask if we can switch our plans around. Now I need to call for reassurance.

"Well, no," I admit tightly. "I haven't wanted to bother Mr. Pan as I know he's hard at work on the car. He told me to stop by today, and I have every confidence that I'll see a beautifully rebuilt 1955 Bel Air when I get there."

"That's another thing," my dad starts, "I looked into this LB Automotive place and couldn't find anything about them on the internet. No website or online presence to speak of other than their number and location. When I called to ask them about their rebuild business, I was told they don't do that type of work."

My stomach churns, and my fists clench under the table. The hospital board never questioned who I hired to rebuild the car. They didn't care as long as I produced what I promised. My dad's trying to find a flaw in my plan, a misstep I've made that will prove I've thrown away my future for a silly dream.

"Is there a question in there somewhere, Dad?"

"Why them? Why go with an unknown shop in Neverland with no prior rebuild experience instead of an established London company with a history of doing this sort of thing?"

Michael squeezes my leg in support as I work to keep my composure. My dad doesn't know anything about Peter or the Lost Boys. As unlikely as it sounds, my parents never discovered my six-year-long secret. I had my fair share of close calls, but that part of my life had never been discovered.

In that respect, my father's concerns are valid. On paper, LB Automotive is a horrible choice, and I could kick myself for not being better prepared for this line of questioning. I didn't even know that Peter doesn't have a website. Who doesn't have a website nowadays? Everyone and their brother has a website for things as ridiculous as pranking people or posing their Chihuahua in different costumes. A credible business should *definitely* have one. That's something I'll talk to Peter about later, but it doesn't do me any good now. And as I meet the gazes of the seven people waiting for me to answer, I realize my blind assurance isn't going to do much good either.

Pulling my shoulders back, I fold my hands onto the table in front of me. "It's true that LB Automotive hasn't done rebuilds as part of their business, but that doesn't mean they aren't experienced in doing them. The owner did a complete rebuild of a 1970 Barracuda, which is a very rare American muscle car. It's beautiful and runs perfectly, as it's his personal car for everyday use. I also know the owner on a personal level, and I'm confident in his abilities to provide us with a car that will impress our guests and raise more money for your event than in previous years."

Mr. Fitzgibbons, head of the board and blunt as a baseball bat leans forward in his chair. "I sure hope so, Ms. Darling. Michael assured us you'd be able to handle the job. I'd hate for that to not be the case."

"Michael?" A chill skitters through me, and my throat tightens. I don't dare turn to look at him, but in my periphery, I see him lower his head in his hand.

"Yes. We liked your idea, but we were going to hire a different company that has a history of planning large events. But Michael vouched for your capabilities, so against some of our better judgements, we took a chance on you."

"I see." Michael whispers my name, a plea to understand, but I can't deal with that on top of everything else. My emotions are stretched too far, like a sheet of paper-thin glass. If I think about how he let me believe I earned this, I'll break.

"Gentlemen, I appreciate you taking a chance on me. Believe me when I tell you that I don't take this opportunity lightly," I say, my nerves fraying more with every word, "I also understand your reservations. I'll head over to the shop and take a picture of the finished product, then email it to the group. Now, if there's nothing else, I have a myriad of last-minute details to attend to."

I don't give them a chance to protest. I don't give my brother a chance to speak privately with me. I don't give my father a chance to ask more probing questions. I simply gather my things with a seemingly calm efficiency, bid them all goodbye, and stride out of the room.

As soon as I hit the hall, I head for the main exit while calling Peter. An hour ago, I was on top of the world. Now I feel as though the ground is crumbling beneath my feet. Peter can make me feel better. He can fix all of this for me just by telling me that the car is done, and I have nothing to worry about. That the Bel Air will be the most beautiful thing these socialites have ever seen, and they'll bid ridiculous amounts of money for the chance to own it, and I'll be the hero of this event.

Peter has the power to solidify my world and rebuild my rusting confidence the way he rebuilds rusting cars. All he has to do is pick up the phone.

Except I'm already out of the hospital and on my third call to him, and he's not answering. With trembling hands, I toss my phone into my purse and tell myself not to freak out. I'll just go to his house, and he can tell me in person. *Show me* that I have nothing to worry about. It might ruin whatever he had planned for us later, but it can't be helped. I need him right now, and he said he'd always be here for me. So I'm about to cash in on that promise.

CHAPTER EIGHTEEN

PETER

"**F**uck!" My arm rears back, ready to launch the offensive item when two small hands wrap around my bicep.

"Hey hey hey, that's *my* phone!" Tink wrenches it from my grip and puts it safely away in her pocket. "There's no reason both of our cells need to meet their untimely death."

She's right, and yet, I can't help but feel cheated at not getting to release this burning frustration through the senseless destruction of property. *What would Wendy say if she saw you throwing shit like the Hulk on a temper tantrum?* I don't know the answer, but I doubt she'd like it very much. Physical rage isn't a very grown up way to deal with your problems, I know that. What I *don't* know is what to do about my current one. And it's fucking huge.

Growling, I kick the shattered remnants of my cell phone, which met its demise earlier. The customer service rep for the trucking company kept insisting the records show that my last shipment for the Bel Air parts have been delivered. After the fifth time of reciting the company's anti-fault stance, I lost my cool, along with my ability to use that phone for anything other than plastic confetti.

Plowing my hands into my hair, I fist and pull to prevent myself from busting my knuckles on a steel support beam. "I can't believe this fucking happened."

"It's not your fault. Putting a rush on the shipment should've gotten it here in plenty of time."

Holding my arms out wide, I gesture to the shipment-less garage. "But it *didn't*. Despite what those assholes are saying, it's most definitely *not* here."

"Maybe they dropped it off at another shop or something," she suggests. "I'll go up to the house and make us some lunch while I call around, okay? Maybe J.R. is over at his Toy Shop staring at a huge crate of parts, wondering what the hell they're for. It's possible, right?"

I highly doubt it, but I force myself to nod. "Yeah, okay, thanks. I really appreciate your help."

She places a hand on my shoulder, pinning me with her soulful green gaze. "Whether it's as simple as making phone calls or as complicated as picking up your pieces to put you back together, I'll always be here for you, Peter."

"I know," I rasp out through a dry throat. "You're a great friend, Tink."

She doesn't move for several seconds, then her hand squeezes me slightly, and she gives me a tight smile that falls short of her eyes. "Of course I am. I'll be back."

As soon as she's out of sight, I drop into a chair on a year-long sigh. Unfortunately, expelling the air in my lungs doesn't relieve the tightness in my chest. It presses on my ribs until it feels like the slightest movement will cause them to puncture my organs.

I'm so fucked. Wendy's coming here tonight to see the finished Bel Air. The car that I promised her would be done. The car that is *not*, in fact, done.

Taking the ring box out of my pocket, I brace my elbows on my thighs and open the top to stare at what's inside. She won't want this now. Not after how bad I messed this up for her…

No. I refuse to believe that the second time I try to give her my heart, Wendy will walk away from it. There has to be something I can do. Maybe it won't completely fix it, but I'm not looking for a miracle. I'll settle for a large damn Band-Aid at this point. Maybe if I—

"Peter? Are you in here?"

Snapping the ring box shut, I shove it into my pocket as I jump to my feet and find my dream girl stepping squarely into my nightmare. "Wendy."

Her eyes land on me, and she practically breaks into a run. In the two seconds it takes her to reach me, I notice her brows are pulled together and the corners of her lush mouth are turned down. Something's wrong with my girl, but she doesn't give me time to ask before she throws her arms around my neck and brings me down for a kiss. A kiss I don't deserve but selfishly accept. My hands frame her beautiful face, and I hold her to me, coaxing her soft lips open and tangling my tongue with hers in a dance of desperation she doesn't yet understand.

Or maybe she does because I can feel it pouring off her, too, drowning us both until we finally come up for air.

"Baby, what's wrong? I wasn't expecting you until seven."

"I know, I'm sorry," she says, pressing a delicate hand to her forehead like she's staving off a headache from hell. "It's just the meeting with the hospital board didn't go well, and I needed to talk to you about everything. I tried calling you a bunch of times, but you didn't…" Her voice trails off as she notices my cell phone on the concrete floor. Or what used to be my phone. "…answer."

"Yeah, sorry about that. It's time I upgrade to a new one, anyway."

"Peter," she says carefully, "what's going on? I haven't

heard from you all week. Everything is fine with the car, right?"

I drag my hands down my face, praying for a miracle. Praying that when I turn around, the car will have been magically finished by tiny fairies in the last fifteen minutes. Or that I have my days wrong, and I still have another week— just *one* is all I'd need—to fix this for Wendy.

But when I meet her concerned gaze, I know that none of those things is going to happen. I'm about to let down the woman I love in an epic way. And I can't do anything to stop it.

"Wen, I'm so sorry," I grind out. "The last shipment of parts for the car didn't make it—or it made it somewhere, but not here—and the car won't be done by Saturday."

The expression on her face transforms from concern to disbelief. She shakes her head like if she denies it hard enough, it won't be true. "No," she says, her voice soft. "You promised me it would be done. You promised you wouldn't let me down."

"I know."

"Please tell me this is your idea of a terrible joke. One that will probably take me a good thirty minutes to recover from and then we'll laugh about it. Just tell me it's a joke."

"I wish to God I could." I gesture to where the Bel Air sits in the same spot it's been for over a month. "But it doesn't look any different than it did last weekend."

Her cheeks flush, and her eyes darken to deep pools of navy, signs she's overcome with passion. But this isn't the good kind. This is the pissed-as-hell angel of fury kind. "I can't believe this. I can't auction off a car *without a car*. I just sat in a meeting where I was grilled about your credibility and the status of the Bel Air, and I assured them that everything would be ready according to plan. *How could you do this to me?*"

"Whoa, hold on. I didn't *do* anything. I don't have control over the delivery company. I put a rush order on it, so I would have it in time. *They* lost the shipment."

"Come on, Peter. I get that the delivery company may have screwed up, but this isn't entirely their fault. I told you from the beginning I thought that car was too much work for the time frame we had, but you brushed off my concern. Then add in all the Friday night partying, hanging at the races, and God knows what else when you should've been working on the car, and it's no wonder it isn't finished!"

The blood rushes in my ears and every muscle in my body locks up, bracing for the kind of attack Croc used to give me as he shouted all the things I did wrong. I know Wendy would never lay a hand on me—even if she did, she couldn't inflict much damage—but my brain isn't listening to logic right now. It's reacting, using muscle memory, and sinking into that place where I learned I could do no right, so why even try.

"You claimed to believe in my ability to do this. If that was all a lie and you were so unsure I could hack the job, you should've taken your business elsewhere."

"Are you kidding me?" she shouts. "I didn't doubt your ability to rebuild the car. I questioned your timeline management skills and sense of responsibility. If you were running out of time, you should've been sacrificing your downtime to spend on the project."

"Why, so I could work around the clock and be miserable like you were? There's a reason I make sure Tink and the boys have fun. Life's not worth living if all you do is work yourself to the bone."

Tears well up in her eyes, severing my anger as effectively as a sword slicing through a limb. Sighing, I move to gather her into my arms, but she holds up a hand and takes a halting step backward.

"No," she says, her voice thick with disappointment. "I

thought I could come back for this job, have an adventure, and show myself I could have both. Now it's only going to make everything harder. I never should've come back."

"Wendy," I croak.

"I guess we were right to go our separate ways all those years ago. Everything is great between us, as long as it's all about having fun and seeking the next adventure." She drags in a shaky breath then releases it, raking a hand through her waterfall of maple syrup hair. "But that's not what being a grown up is, Peter. I love living in the moment when I'm with you because, admittedly, sometimes I'm on the other extreme. I focus too much on the serious things and forget to enjoy the small pleasures. The difference is, I won't get fired or evicted or gain a bad reputation from working too hard. So, if I have to choose between fun and responsibility, I'll choose the latter, whereas you'll choose fun. Every single time."

I'm losing her. I can't fucking believe I'm losing her over a goddamn lost shipment. "If the stuff had gotten here like it was supposed to—"

"Right. The shipment, I know." Her words say she understands, but her tone says different. "God forbid you take any responsibility."

"Wen—"

"To you, it's just a shipment, but to me, it's my entire future." She plows a hand through her hair, fisting it briefly before dropping her arm in defeat. "Never mind. I don't have time for this right now. I have to come up with a way to fix this. Plan B, I guess, which I really should've had in the first place. I assume you can still finish the job once you get the rest of what you need?"

"Yeah." All the heat is gone from my voice like a deflated balloon lying limp on the ground. "I'll finish it."

"Great. Please keep me informed of an estimated completion date, so I can make arrangements with the buyer for pick-up." She glances down at her phone, then says, "I have to go. Take care of yourself. Tell the boys I said goodbye."

She turns and starts walking out of the garage, and with every step she takes, she drives a nail through the coffin around my heart. It will never beat for anyone like it beats for Wendy Darling. It barely survived the first time she walked away from me. The only thing that kept it alive was the foolish, miniscule hope that someday she'd return to Neverland.

And she did.

I had the second chance with her I'd always dreamed about, and now it's gone. This time, there won't be enough left of my heart to salvage. Not that it matters, because without Wendy in my life, I don't need that worthless muscle anyway.

"Wendy," I blurt out before my pride can shove it back in.

She stops, and for a few agonizingly long seconds, I think she won't look back...then she does. I fist the ring box in my pocket, the corners digging into my flesh. A physical pain to match my emotional one.

She blinks, and the tears balanced on the edge of her lashes overflow to run down her cheeks. The moisture clings to her skin as though desperate to stay with her for as long as possible. I realize I'm no different as I stand here knowing I won't beg her to stay but terrified to let her leave.

Such is the story of our love. I've always been the peasant boy clinging to the girl who was too good for me. She's like the ocean tide to my moon. She's free to flow where she wants, but I'm tethered to the sky. I use what power I have to pull her into me, but I can only hold on for so long before she inevitably slips away to where she belongs.

There's nothing I can do to stop it. She was meant for greater things, *is* meant for greater things. I need to let her go. Again.

"I love you, Peter," she whispers between the tears.

I swallow thickly and force out the words I will mean until my dying day.

"I love you more, Wen. Always."

The corners of her lips tug up in a trembling, sad smile that shakes me to my core. And then she walks out of my garage and out of my life.

CHAPTER NINETEEN

PETER

Then…
Age 18

As I race through the streets on my motorcycle with Wendy's arms wrapped around my waist, my chest threatens to burst with happiness. I've been waiting for this day for forever. I've planned every detail of what I'm going to say and how I'm going to give her the graduation gift I made her—or us—that's nestled in my pocket. I had to be sneaky about it, but I managed to swipe her acorn nut "kiss" a couple of weeks ago, so I could make some slight modifications to that and my thimble.

Wendy graduates high school next week, and by then, I'll have taken my final tests with Ms. Mills, making me a graduate, too, minus the fancy ceremony and proud parents, but still a graduate. Wen told me she's going to be super busy next weekend with the thing they have at school and the party with her family, so I decided we could have our celebration a week early.

The closer we get to the ocean, the saltier the air gets, and it stirs emotions inside me with just the scent, knowing it's

PAN

my special spot with the girl I love. I think she senses it, too, because her arms squeeze me tighter, and her body melts against the back of mine.

Pulling onto the sand, I head straight for the ocean then cut right to ride through the shallow water lapping against the shore. The spray from the tires makes her squeal and laugh as she hooks her legs around my waist and leans back with her arms thrown wide.

Unable to wait any longer, I slow the bike and come to a stop right in the foam. I plant my feet to keep us steady then help her spin around in my lap, so we're face to face.

"Hi," she says smiling.

I chuckle. "Hi yourself."

Framing her face in my hands, I kiss her lips hungrily, reveling in the traces of salty mist with her vanilla-flavored lip balm. She sinks her nails into my lower back as I sink into her mouth, tangling our tongues and pouring every emotion I've ever had into this all-important moment.

Eventually, I force us to come up for air before I take things too far and end up inside her. Not that that's not the plan—that is *always* the plan however often I can swing it— but I want us to talk first. I want to give her, her gift and see my "kiss" adorning her body as I paint her with real ones under the moonlight on our beach. I've fantasized about it at least a hundred times, and I don't want my rampant libido to ruin things by going out of order.

"Peter, I need to talk to you about something."

Shit. When I ran the night through my mind, I never took into consideration that Wendy might say or do something to alter the course of events. Good thing I'm excellent at improvising.

"What's on your mind?" Her blue eyes bounce between mine, and she traps her lower lip between her teeth. My mouth quirks to one side as I use my thumb to free it, like I always do. "Come on, Wen, tell me."

"I got accepted into Queens University."

My brows draw together. "I thought you were going to East Carolina and living at home."

"That's because I hadn't heard back from Queens. My dad finally called to ask about the status of my application, and they said they'd sent the acceptance letter months ago. It must've gotten lost in the mail or something," she says with a dismissive hand then continues to chatter excitedly. "Anyway, they assumed I'd chosen to go somewhere else when they didn't hear back, but they still have room for me, so I'm in."

"Wow, that's great. Are you still planning on living at home?"

Her smile falters, and her shoulders sag the slightest bit. Enough to tell me I'm not going to like her answer. "No. Queens is in Charlotte, almost five hours away."

"That's…far."

I'm not sure how else to respond to that. There's no way I can drive ten hours round trip to see her at school. My only mode of transportation is this junker bike I fixed up, but it's not good for anything other than local driving. I'd never trust it on a highway or for long periods of time.

"I know," she says, "but it's where everyone in my dad's family has gone to school, so it's a family tradition. And they have a really great finance department; plus, because of my dad's connections, I can get a job interning at one of the local firms, which will give me a leg up on things once I get my degree."

I nod like I agree that everything she's saying is a great thing when, really, I want to scream and tell her none of it is remotely good. She's not supposed to leave me. She's supposed to stay with me in Neverland like we always talked about.

"When does school start?"

"Not until the fall, but my dad got me into an early summer program that starts next week."

Clearing my throat, I do my best to smile for her. "That's great, Wen. I'm really happy for you. I bet you'll have lots of fun."

Worry flashes in her eyes. "Peter, I want you to come with me. Freshmen have to live in the dorms the first year, but after that, I could move into whatever apartment you have. Charlotte's a big city, you could find a job, and after my first year, I'll get a part-time one to help with expenses. We can make this work, you and me, just like we always planned. It'll just be somewhere else."

The ocean breeze picks up, blowing her hair to the west, the caramel strands rippling sideways like her future is already tugging her away from me.

"I can't leave Tink and the boys. I have to keep an eye on them, or there's no telling what Croc will do."

In the past year, I finally started filling out, and now I'm bigger and stronger than that piece of shit. I made sure he knows there's a heavy price to pay if he ever lays a hand on any of them again. If I go, their assurance of not having to put up with his abuse goes with me.

"Oh, right, of course." She glances down at her hands between us, then nods as though reaffirming her words. "No, you're right. You can't leave them."

She sniffles, and I panic, lifting her chin to get a look at her face. The tears are drying in the warm breeze almost as fast as they fall, and I don't know if I prefer the evidence being wiped away or if it's comforting to, at least know, she isn't unaffected.

"Don't cry, Wen. This is going to be such a good thing for you."

"And you? What will you do?"

"Don't worry about me. I already have a mechanic job lined up. It comes with room and board, so it's a pretty sweet deal."

I'm telling the truth, sort of. The job I can have if I want it

177

is working at Croc's other shop while living at the Jolly Roger Clubhouse, which is basically a biker gang on steroids. That's where I found out Hook went after he left the school. From how it sounds, he's thriving over there, collecting a nice group of criminal ruffians he calls the Pirates. But there's no way I'm joining that crew and getting involved in the illegal shit they deal with. Wendy would be so disappointed in me, not to mention, I'm not dragging the other kids into that kind of life. I'll figure something else out. I always do.

"That sounds great," she says, her tone lacking enthusiasm. After a few seconds, she whispers a confession I don't expect from my normally confident girl. "I'm scared, Peter."

My protective streak flares, ready to battle her demons, whatever or whoever they are. "Scared of what?"

"What if I'm no good? The financial planning business is still such a boys club, what if no one takes me seriously?"

I exhale a sigh of relief that she's not in any real danger. "That's ridiculous," I say with a crooked grin. "Everyone knows one girl is more useful than twenty boys."

Another sniffle, but this time, it's shared with a watery smile. "You really believe that?"

"One hundred percent," I say, and I mean it. "You're going to grow up to do amazing things, Wendy Darling. No matter what you choose to do, you'll be making a difference in people's lives. Just like you did with me and the Lost Boys."

I brush her hair behind her ears and hold her face, willing her to see in my eyes every grain of truth in my soul. "Don't ever doubt yourself. Ms. Mills says the moment you doubt you can do something, you cease forever to be able to do it. That sounds like pretty good advice to me."

"I'm going to miss you so much."

Her last word breaks on a sob, and I gather her against my chest and hold her tight as she soaks my T-shirt in enough tears for the both of us. The ring box in my pocket burns my thigh with the unfulfilled promise it represents: us, together, now and always. It might not be true physically anymore, but that doesn't mean I can cut her out of me any easier than I could my own heart. Wendy will always be with me, always be a part of me. Nothing will ever change that.

Resting my cheek on the top of her head, I close my eyes and memorize the feel of her silky hair on my skin. "You know that place between sleep and awake, the place where you can still remember dreaming?" She nods slightly, her wet eyelashes fluttering at the base of my throat. "That's where I'll always love you. That's where I'll be waiting."

She lifts her head to stare up at me, fresh tears swimming in her eyes. "I love you, Peter."

"Love you more, Wen," I rasp.

Then I show her just how much as we lose ourselves in each other one last time. An hour before dawn, we ride in silence, her cheek resting in the hollow of my spine and her arms clutching my waist for the very last time. I contemplate whether to give her my gift, but I'd meant them as a symbol of us being together forever, and that's not happening. At least not now.

Maybe if I hold onto them, she'll come back to me some-day, and I can give them to her then. They'd be a symbol of a new beginning for us, a way to honor our past and represent our future.

When I pull up in front of her house, she gets off the bike and stands next to me. I snake my arm around her waist and keep her close to my side, reluctant to let her go sooner than I have to.

"I hate goodbyes," she says softly.

"Don't say goodbye. Goodbye means going away, and going away means forgetting. Don't ever forget me, okay?"

She reaches up and fingers an errant chunk of hair hanging in my face. "I could never."

Then with one final kiss, I gently push her up onto the

curb, praying she turns around and leaves before the stinging behind my eyes gets any worse. She needs me to be strong for her, happy, and I'll be damned if I ever give her anything other than what she needs.

My prayer goes unanswered as she walks backward, like she's rewinding the thousands of moments we've had together over the last six years. Finally, she turns and climbs up the trellis to her balcony. Once there, she looks down from the bannister and places her hand over her heart.

I love you, Peter.

My fist presses to mine.

Love you more, Wen.

CHAPTER TWENTY

TINK

Now…

W hat a shitty fucking day. I thought today would be one of the highlights of my year, if not of my whole damn life. Peter and Wendy are broken up for good, which means there's no one standing in my way to claim Peter as *mine*, just like he was always meant to be. So why aren't I ecstatic and jumping for joy or reveling in my victory over Wendy the Sickeningly Good Witch?

Probably because the man I love is more miserable than I've ever seen him.

If he was this upset ten years ago, I didn't know it. We didn't see much of him that last week he was at the school. Then we didn't see him for a long time after he moved out. The boys and I knew he was still around because Croc always checked himself every time he went to raise his hand. If Peter had disappeared, there would've been no stopping that barbarian from doing whatever the hell he wanted.

Eventually, Peter started coming back around and making plans with us for when we got out. Years later, he made good on his promise to keep us all together with a house and a business of our very own. I mistakenly thought that as I got older, Peter would notice me as a woman—not the little girl he convinced was a magical fairy who'd lost her wings. I was content just being with him, certain one day he'd look at me with something in his eyes other than friendly affection.

When Wendy showed up, I realized my mistake. I shouldn't have been so complacent. Lily says that if a woman wants something, she needs to go after it, balls-to-the-wall, not sit back and wait for it to come to her. But by then, it was too late. Peter fell right into her trap, just like he did when we were kids.

Peter didn't come into LB today. Hell, I'm not even sure if he got out of bed. After Wendy left yesterday, he pulled down a bottle of whiskey from the bar and sucked on it for hours. His only communication was to growl at people or tell them to go the fuck away. Not even Thomas could get anything out of him.

I'd sat on the stairs for hours, watching him between the slats on the railing. He didn't shed a single tear, but the expression on his face looked like he was being ripped to shreds on the inside, and it killed me. I hated knowing he was so upset, but I told myself it was only temporary. Pretty soon, he'll forget all about Wendy Darling, just like last time, and then I'll tell him how I feel, and he'll realize how blind he's been. That the woman he needs has been right in front of him all along.

The phone rings, so I pick up the reception handset—I volunteered for desk duty since I'm too distracted to work with tools today—only the phone keeps ringing. Realizing it's my cell, I put the other phone down and swipe to connect the call.

"Hey, Lil."

"Don't you hey Lil me, Ms. Bell. When the hell are you getting this gigantic crate of stuff out of my shop? Why is it even here? Don't you need this to finish that car?"

Pinching the bridge of my nose, I set my elbow on the desk and squeeze my eyes shut against the rising headache promising to wage war on my brain. "Not yet, I don't. I'll grab it on Sunday, okay?"

"But the event is tomorrow. What the hell good is Sun— Oh, bitch, tell me you aren't doing what I think you're doing."

"Fine, I'm not doing what—"

"Yes, you are! Tink, are you fucking kidding me? Is this why Tobias and Ty are blowing up my phone about Peter going off the deep end?"

Quick, change the subject. "Why would the twins be blowing up your phone?"

"Nuh-uh, don't even try that shit with me. This is serious. You're going to ruin everything. Not just Peter and Wendy's relationship, but her reputation as a planner, and her company will take a hit. What the hell were you thinking?"

I spin the chair around to face the back wall and hiss into the phone. "I was *thinking* that if I could hide the shipment of parts and prove to Wendy that Peter won't always come through for her, she'd realize she doesn't belong with us *or* with him, and leave us the hell alone once and for all. *That* is what I was thinking."

"Were you now?"

I yelp in surprise at the deep voice behind me, spinning to face the front with my hand pressed against my racing heart. "Oh, shit," I whisper.

"Yeah," Michael says. "Oh shit is right. Hang up the phone, Tinker Bell."

The combination of Michael's husky and commanding voice and his hazel eyes pierce my free will, rendering it too wounded to fight back. Dropping my hand, my thumb hits the red button that disconnects my call with Lily as she shouts at me to tell her what's happening.

Michael Darling doesn't look like he did that day at the

hospital. He looks *better*. His hair is back to its natural shade of golden brown, and instead of a ridiculous Prince Charming costume—okay, somehow, he made it less ridiculous than it should've been—he's wearing black slacks and a slate gray dress shirt with the sleeves rolled up his muscular forearms. I've never gone for the white-collar type, but I'd be lying if I said Michael doesn't fill out his fancy threads rather nicely.

When we were kids, he was clingy and soft, a naive boy from a good home who had no idea what hardship or abuse was like. It made me hate him, just as I hated Wendy and their other brother, John.

But it's hard to compare that boy with the impressive man standing in our front reception area with steel in his eyes and arms crossed over his wide chest. Clearing my throat, I greet him with plenty of my usual 'tude. "What do *you* want?"

"I came here to ask Peter why my sister's been crying for the last twelve hours, but I guess now I know."

"You don't know anything." *Ooh, good comeback, Tink. Doesn't matter that he literally heard you spill your guts all over the linoleum.*

Michael's eyes dart behind me at Peter's office. "Boss man in?"

"Nope," I say, my smile dripping with sarcasm I don't feel. "He's taking a personal day."

"Good."

Before I know what's happening, Michael crosses behind the counter, grabs my upper arm, and drags me into the office before locking the door and dropping the mini-blinds over the shop window.

Breathing fire, I yank my arm out of his grip. "I don't know who the hell you think you are but—"

"I'll tell you exactly who I am," he says, crowding me against the wall. "I am your reckoning. Your moment of wake-the-fuck-up."

Less than a foot separates us, and the heat from his body

teases my exposed skin like warm fingertips trailing from clavicle to navel. His scent is a mix of starched cotton and city sunshine, like he came from a stroll downtown in his dressy duds. I've never been this close to a man who didn't smell of axle grease and motor oil. It's different. Not bad different, just…fresh different.

"What are you talking about?"

"I'm talking about you coming to the realization that you are, in fact, *not* in love with Peter Pan. Not by a long shot."

I'm so taken aback by that absurd claim from left field that I laugh. "And how would you know that? Last I checked, I'm in charge of my own feelings, not you or anyone else."

"That's right, you are. But you're too innocent to understand the difference between loving someone because he's always been there to care and watch out for you—" His gaze rakes over my body. "—and the kind of things a woman feels when she's attracted to a man on a much more visceral level."

Damn. I'm having a hard time breathing, like he's sucked all the air out of the room with his know-it-all attitude, and it's pissing me off. I think. I'm not entirely sure what I am right now. But I'll rip my nose ring out with a pair of pliers before admitting any of that to this prick.

"I suppose you're going to tell me that I have these feelings of attraction for *you*?"

"Absolutely."

I snort. "That's rich."

"Would you like me to prove it to you?"

I shrug, but my shoulders feel weighted down, so I'm not even sure it works. "Whatever sparks your plugs, London."

Not sure where that nickname came from, but it totally works. Reminds me—*and* him—that we come from two very different worlds. He can no sooner understand me than I can him. Michael braces a palm high above my head and leans in, forcing me to meet his gaze. I lift my chin in a direct challenge. *Take your best shot. You don't scare me.*

"Here's a physiology lesson for you on some of the things that happen to your body when turned on. Your breathing becomes shallow, your heart rate and blood pressure both rise. Your nipples harden and become more sensitive. You also blink more often, and your pupils dilate. Irises darken in color, like yours, going from spring green to a deep emerald."

Shit shit shit. I do my best to steady my breathing, hold my eyes open, and will my heart beat to slow down, but it doesn't seem to be working. His voice is rough and sweetly abrasive, like my favorite vanilla sugar scrub, revealing a new layer I didn't know existed.

Swallowing, I gather the few drops I have left in my normally-endless well of sarcasm and hope it's enough to make him go away. "Looks like those college courses paid off, London. Good for you."

"No, what's good for me is that I can see all of these things on you…right now."

He drags his eyes from mine, down to where my pulse is beating against my neck like a tattoo machine at full speed. Then lower, where my nipples are straining into the cotton of my bra, my heaving chest waving them around like twin flags of surrender. Without ever touching me, his gaze leaves tingles in its wake, and my body starts to arch toward him of its own volition.

What the hell is wrong with me? I feel raw and exposed, like a live wire dancing near water. It's dangerous and seductive, knowing I could fall at any moment and get the shock of a lifetime, and it's starting to feel worth the risk, even if it means I short out and die.

La petit morte. The little death. It's what the French call an orgasm. The thing I've refused to give myself, despite my best friend's insistence, because I wanted Peter to give me my first. But now I'm confused because this…this feels…

Michael cups my face and lifts it with his thumb under my chin, then brushes it over my cheek. "I've always had a crush on you, Tink," he says, his voice thick and sugary like molasses. "I thought you were pretty when we were kids. Then I saw you dressed up as Cinderella with your combat boots and colorful tattoos, and thought you were damn gorgeous. But now…" His eyes drift up to my short, platinum hair, then skate over the various piercings and tattoos adorning my body exposed by my crop top and jean cutoffs. "Fuck, you're so goddamn beautiful."

I frown. "No, I'm not. I'm punk. I've been called cute, hot, fuck-hot, and even sexy by a few drunks at the Lagoon. But never beautiful. That's for girls like your sister."

He's shaking his head before I'm even finished. "Bullshit. I'm the one looking at you, and I say you're beautiful. And sexy. And fuck-hot," he says with a smirk that has me biting my cheek to keep from smiling.

"Whatever," I try. "I don't want you like that."

"Really?" He drops his hand from my face and grazes his knuckles in a circle around my belly button. I drag in a sharp inhale, sucking my stomach in, but he merely follows with his hand. "You don't feel that butterfly sensation in here?"

Oh God, I do. *I do, I do, I do.* Hundreds of tiny wings beating inside my belly so hard they might lift me off the ground. My breath shudders through parted lips, but no words follow. I can't think, can't rationalize. I can only feel, want, need—fucking hell, what is this *need*, this black magic he's weaving to make me want to jump his bones like I never thought I would with anyone other than—

His lips cover mine on a growl, full, warm, and *hungry*. I'm helpless to do anything other than open, inviting him inside to plunder and claim. He eats at my mouth, tasting and twining our tongues. I've been kissed by men before—I wanted to make sure I knew how before doing it with the one man who mattered—but I've never experienced anything like this. Those were boring, almost clinical. An experiment in how to move one's lips and tongue while avoiding the teeth and tonsils.

This…is not that. This is fire and ice and the heat of a good battle.

A moan creeps up the back of my throat as I match his intensity, fisting my hands in his hair and arching against the hard length pressing into my belly. He slips a leg between mine and grinds his thigh against me. Electricity zaps through my body, and I jolt in his arms on a gasp that breaks our kiss.

A devilish smirk carves into his too handsome face. "And *that* is what happens when you're so turned on by someone you can't think straight." He chuckles through labored breaths. "Myself included, *damn*."

Small consolation? At least I'm not the only one ready to melt into a puddle of horniness here. Comparing my libido up to this moment is like a lifelong asexual finally discovering a kink that actually does it for them. Apparently, my kink is Michael Darling. Fuckity Fucksticks.

I snap at him, "What's your point, London?" Because that's what animals do when they're cornered, they lash out at the hand reaching for them.

He takes a step back and adjusts himself, wincing like he's dealing with an uncomfortable situation down there. It amuses me to no end, but I keep my expression schooled with uninterest.

"My point is that you're not in love with Peter. If you were, I never would've had a chance with you just now. You would've ripped off my balls and fed them to me for dinner."

I arch my pierced brow at him. I mean, he's not wrong. I've kneed guys in the junk for looking at me the wrong way. But then that means…

Sighing, I rub my temples. "I don't know what to think. I'm confused."

"I know you are, *chère*. And I don't expect you to fully believe what I'm telling you right away. But what you did to

Wendy and Peter was wrong," he says, his tone going soft and gentle—and did he just use a French term of endearment? "Even if you were in love with him, I'm sorry to say that he will never reciprocate that. He loves you like a best friend, like a sister. But he's deeply in love with my sister. Destroying them as a couple doesn't do anything more than destroy them as individuals. It won't get you what you *think* you want."

"What am I supposed to do? Peter will be so angry with me," I say, my voice sounding as small as when I was a dirty little orphan with a bell around my ankle.

"Yes, he will. But he'll forgive you, especially if he has my sister back. What he won't forgive is if this ends up losing him Wendy forever. I promise you that." Leaning in, he places a sweet kiss on my forehead that turns my insides to mush. "Do the right thing, and do it soon. There's not much time to fix this."

In less than ten minutes, Michael has managed to slice through the armor I've built up for over twenty years, and now I stand here flayed open and vulnerable. Clinging to the bits of what I have left, I raise my chin and cross my arms over my chest. "Thanks for stopping by, London."

"It was my pleasure, pixie," he says and crosses to the office door.

"I'm a fairy, not a pixie." *Jesus, anything to be contrary.*

He cocks his head to the side, then shakes it. "Nah. A fairy is what I call my brother when I feel like getting punched in the face. I like pixie better." He opens the door and walks through, but just before he closes it behind him, he adds with a wink, "Oh, and start answering my calls."

Then he's gone, leaving me to reel from his visit and think about the reckoning he promised and delivered with utter absolution. "Shit," I hiss as I call Lily. When she picks up, I shush her incessant questions and ask one of my own. "Can you bring that crate over to the house?"

CHAPTER TWENTY-ONE

PETER

The garage floor is blurry through my bloodshot eyes, but I push the broom across the concrete floor, sweeping up the shattered pieces of my cell phone as best I can. If only it were this easy to clean up a shattered heart, but that fucker is bleeding out inside my chest so hard, not even a shop mop could soak it up.

Since Wendy left yesterday, I've done my best to numb myself with whiskey and more whiskey. It was a shit plan that worked for shit. The only thing it gave me was severe dehydration and a hangover from hell. I finally rolled out of bed around two, stood under the shower until we ran out of hot water, then chugged a couple bottles of Gatorade before coming out here to clean up and to clear my head. So far, I've only managed one of those things.

"Want help with that?"

I don't even bother looking up at Tink as I push the debris into a dustpan. "No, I got it."

"Peter, listen—"

Before she can launch into whatever speech she's got planned—one that no doubt includes how I'm better off without Wendy—I stop her. "I appreciate you wanting to help, but I'm not really fit for company right now, and I'm sure as hell not in the mood to talk."

I shuffle over to the garbage, where she happens to be standing, and dump the remnants of my phone into the large barrel.

"Then let's not talk," she says, a second before she grabs my face and kisses me, full on the mouth.

In some weird *Twilight Zone* shit, I float outside my body and look down at the two of us with our lips locked like this is a strange riddle I'm supposed to solve. *Why is Tinker Bell kissing me? Better yet, why the fuck am I letting her?*

My brain finally fires up and yanks me back into my body. Grabbing Tink by the shoulders, I hold her out at arm's length. "What the hell are you doing?"

She steps back even farther, her hands covering her mouth, and her eyes blown wide like she's just seen a ghost. "Oh shit," she says in a shaky voice. "Shit, Peter, that was *awful*."

My knee-jerk reaction is to take offense until I remember that hell yeah it was. "*Of course,* it was fucking awful, Tink, you're like my *sister*. Why would you do that?"

"Because I had to know if he was right, and *he was*! Shit, shit, *shit*."

Am I still drunk? Is that why I can't follow along with what's happening? Jesus, I'm never drinking whiskey again. "Who was right? About what? Would you please stop pacing and fucking talk to me?"

"I screwed up. I screwed up bad, and you're going to be so angry with me."

"Come on, sprite, why would I—" When she stops wearing a path in the concrete and slides her misty eyes to the Bel Air, my throat seizes up. "No," I manage to grind out. "You didn't."

She drops her head and swipes at her cheeks, but I don't pay attention because what she's implying sinks in more and more. Every passing second is another shovel of coal tossed on the fire burning inside me until it's a raging inferno to rival the ones in hell.

"Tell me you didn't fuck with that shipment." When she doesn't say anything, I snap. "*Tell me!*"

Her head whips up, and somewhere in my brain, there's a tiny space not consumed with rage that sees the tears streaming down her pale cheeks and the look of torment on her face. But my normal concern for her is overshadowed by the sting of betrayal, and I hold my ground.

"I can't!" she finally shouts back. "I can't because that's exactly what I did. I intercepted the shipment and paid the driver to take it away, so you couldn't finish the car."

Her words are like a stick of dynamite being tossed into the middle of my internal fire. All the pain and loss from the last eighteen hours—the pain and loss I'm destined to feel the rest of my life without Wendy—compresses into a cannon ball of volatile emotions that crashes through me. Roaring, I let it explode through my fist and punch the front of my tool chest. My knuckles blow open, but I don't feel any pain. Yet. Adrenaline is a wonderful thing, but the torn skin and blood means I'll be hurting plenty later.

"Why, Tink?" I ask, the words cutting my throat as I force them out. "Why would you do this?"

"Because I thought I was in love with you. I wanted you to be with me, not her, and I knew if you screwed this up that she'd leave for good."

She leans back against a beam to slide to the floor and props her elbows on her knees, dropping her head in her hands. Suddenly, I'm just as drained, following suit as I collapse onto the metal folding chair. It doesn't matter what Tink did. The damage is done, and I'm not completely blameless.

I should've ordered everything five weeks ago, right after we bought the car. I should've worked on it more often. The rest of the crew could've taken care of things at LB while I worked solely on the Bel Air. I chose to slack off and wait until the last minute for everything. This was my responsibility, and I didn't take it seriously enough. I'm just as much at fault for the car not being done, if not more.

"I've never understood why you hated her so much. When we were young, I thought you were afraid she'd take your place in the group, but I always made sure you knew that would never happen. Then maybe I thought it was the mother thing—which I get—so I asked her to stop pretending that with you, and she did. But that didn't make things better either. Can you just explain it to me, please? Because for the life of me, I can't fucking understand it."

"I told you," she says, "I thought I was in love with you. But now I know that I was confusing regular love with romantic love."

"What brought on this revelation after all these years?"

Her eyes dart to the side, and she chews on her lip for a second before answering. "Someone helped me understand the difference. It's not important who."

I almost press her about it, but she's entitled to her privacy. It doesn't matter other than I'd like to thank whoever it is. Again, this is an area I failed a woman I love. I can't blame myself for not knowing it before, but as soon as Wendy said something about Tink's feelings for me, I should've taken her aside and addressed it. She deserved more than me pushing it off and assuming things would work themselves out.

"I'm sorry, sprite. I should've realized something was up and talked to you."

She shrugs. "I should've manned up years ago and told you how I felt—or thought I felt—so we're equally dumb."

If I wasn't so fucked up over all this, I'd laugh at her usual frankness. "So now that you know what's what, are you finally okay with Wendy?"

It might not matter one way or the other. I still can't finish the car, and I still don't deserve her. But I hate the thought of anyone not liking the woman I love, whether it affects her or not.

Tension seeps back into Tink's body, and her hands curl into fists where they hang between her legs. "She's still not one of us, Peter. She's always been an outsider, pretending to fit in."

That gets my hackles up. Pushing to my feet, I cross to stand over her. "Really. Would an outsider have risked herself to save Lily before we even knew her? Would she have snuck food out of her house every week, so when we didn't get supper, we'd at least have *something* to fill the holes in our bellies?"

Tink's gaze drops to the floor, but I'm not done. Not by a long shot.

"Would she have risked punishment and lied about spending the weekend at a friend's house, so she could hide in the school to take care of Curly when he was so sick, he could barely move? I can keep going, you know. Example after example of how she took care of the boys and made them feel loved—something we sorely lacked in every other aspect of our lives. You and Hook were the only ones to never let her in. But that's not on her." I lock eyes with her. "It's on you."

She's quiet and still, but I don't prod her for a response. I give her the time she needs to process. Slowly, her hands unfurl, her shoulders relax, and she expels a heavy breath as she raises her head, her eyes shimmering with unshed tears.

"I'm sorry," she croaks. "You're right. I've always been jealous of her and her brothers. They had everything we didn't, and it never seemed fair that she could have all of that *and* have what we had, too. But I was wrong. Wendy deserves her spot in our family. I'm so sorry."

Sighing, I reach down and pull her up into a fierce hug

and let her cry it out against me. I've been with this girl from the time she was a baby. I've changed her diapers, fed her a bottle, stayed up with her when she cried at night, talked her through her nightmares, and taught her how to walk. Delia did as little as she could get away with when it came to our tiny fairy, and we'd all loved her from the first time we laid eyes on that blond tuft of hair and those beautiful green eyes.

We're all a product of how we've been raised, one way or another. What matters most is how we grow and learn from our mistakes. How we grow up even when the lure of perpetual childhood is a temptation almost too strong to resist.

If this second chance with Wendy has taught me anything, it's that we can't take things for granted. We can't be happy that something's been given to us and not do the work to keep it. If we don't do our part to earn the good things in our life, eventually, we'll lose them.

Misery squeezes my lungs, making it difficult to draw a full breath. Without Wendy, I might never breathe easy again. There's nothing to do now but adjust and work to make things better.

It's time I grow up. It's time I re-prioritize things, starting with the shop, so we can expand, do more rebuilds, and bring in more money. I need to set a better example for the others and show them that hard work and responsibility are more important than fucking off and having fun. With the right schedule, it's possible to do both, so that's what I'm going to figure out.

And most importantly, I'm going to work to make this up to Wendy. I don't know how, and I don't know how long it will take me to prove myself to her, but it doesn't matter. A life working to get into her good graces again is better than a life where I've given up on us.

Pulling back, Tink gives me a self-deprecating smile. "I've been a bad fairy, huh?"

I wipe the tears from her cheeks and muster a half-hearted grin for her sake. "It's okay, sprite, I forgive you. I even understand where you were coming from. And you're not bad, you just misbehaved. *A lot.* Which is why you're going to apologize to Wendy for treating her like you have since you met."

She steps back and nods as she wipes an arm under her nose in a move that makes her look like the scrappy little girl of years ago. "I will. I'll tell her what I did, too."

"Don't do that," I say, scratching at the several days of beard I've neglected. "No reason for her to hate both of us, and you wouldn't have been able to screw things up if I'd been more on top of my game. This is my mess to clean up."

"But—"

"First thing I need to do is finish the car as soon as I can. Since the driver didn't report *where* he dumped the shipment, I'll have to re-order everything." My wheels start spinning, trying to troubleshoot this clusterfuck. Maybe I can call and make arrangements to pick up the things I need and get it faster.

Tink shakes her head. "No, I—"

"Shit, I need a new phone. Let me borrow your—"

"Peter!"

"*What?*" The rumbling exhaust of a diesel dually reaches me just before Lily's Dodge Ram 3500 pulls in front of the garage with her racing trailer in tow. I frown as she hops out of the cab. "Hey, Lil, you dropping off an old stock car for the boys to play with?"

Her brown eyes cut to her friend, brows raised. "You didn't tell him?"

"I've been trying," Tink grumbles.

The girls walk to the back of the trailer, and I follow, curious what the big secret is. Lily drops the ramp to reveal a gigantic crate stamped with the name of the parts company I ordered everything from on the side.

"Is that what I think it is?"

"Yeah," Tink says sheepishly. "I sent it over to Lil's garage and paid the driver not to report where he took it."

The edge of my anger over the whole situation flares back to life, but I tamp it down. It's over and done with, and Tink's trying to make it up to me. And now that I have all the parts I need to finish the Bel Air, I can try to make this up to Wendy. It might not be enough to win her back, but I won't give up until I do.

I'll prove to her over and over that I *am* the man she can count on. A man who takes his responsibilities seriously, who has his priorities in order, and a man who can still take time out to help her live in the moment and appreciate the magic the world has to offer.

"Ladies, let's get to work," I say, hope filling my chest for the first time in a week. "We have a car to finish. Then I need to find my kneepads, because I have a ton of groveling to do."

CHAPTER TWENTY-TWO

WENDY

In my mind, I'm curled up on my couch in an old T-shirt and yoga pants, shoveling ice cream the flavor of Damsel in Despair into my mouth with a serving spoon in a very unattractive manner.

In reality, I'm standing in the back of the ornately decorated ballroom wearing a silver evening gown and holding a clipboard while watching my seedling company get trampled more and more with every pathetic bid on the as-of-yet unfinished 1955 Chevy Bel Air.

The past forty-eight hours have been a blur of tears, anger, and last-minute prep for this evening's annual Love for Littles gala event. Everything worked perfectly according to my plans—food, drinks, music, decorations, and even the weather turned out beautiful. Everything except for the focal point of the entire theme and the basket I put all my eggs in. So stupid.

I would've preferred ripping off my fingernails with pliers rather than inform the board they were right, but it couldn't be helped. It was better to tell them as soon as I'd had an alternate plan in place, so they had time to cool down before tonight. Thankfully, when I offered to meet them in person with another update, they couldn't make it work with their schedules and requested it via email, so at least I didn't have to see their smug "we knew it" faces when I admitted failure.

I also managed to avoid Michael by texting and asking him to give me until after the event to talk, then I stayed at John's house. I knew Michael's brotherly instinct would be to smash through my walls and work it out right away, but the social worker in him would respect my emotional boundaries, and I used that to my advantage.

As for the board members, after voicing their disappointment for how things turned out, most of them didn't make the effort to speak to me today. All except Mr. Fitzgibbons and my father, neither of whom have wives forcing them into conversations over champagne and canapés.

"It's a shame the actual car isn't here," Mr. Fitzgibbons points out for the dozenth time. "Bidding on the *idea* of a classic car is vastly different than seeing one in front of you."

The temptation to let my eyes roll into the back of my head is strong, but I keep them firmly locked in the forward position. My gaze bounces from the auctioneer who's leaned over his raised podium, desperately trying to drum up excitement and drive up the bids, to scanning the show-room-turned-ballroom floor for any paddles flashing in the crowd.

There aren't many.

"Yes, well, despite the missing vehicle, Tom," my father says smoothly, "you know as well as I that everyone in here can afford to drop a mint on nothing more than an idea and still buy a whole warehouse of classic cars if they wanted. They're aware this is for two well-deserving organizations—they should be bidding regardless of what's in front of them. Their reservations to do so have nothing to do with my daughter's planning."

The support from my dad—backhanded though it was—is

enough to tear my attention away from the floundering auction. "Thanks, Dad."

He acknowledges my gratitude with a stiff nod, but keeps his gaze forward, allowing me a nostalgic moment to study his profile. He's handsome in his tux, reminding me of how he looked when I was young, and he and Mom attended regular charity functions. The only differences are the gray hair, distinguished wrinkles, and the absence of my beautiful mother on his arm. God, I wish she was here. Or maybe not, because I feel like I'm letting her down.

At this rate, this will be the least successful year, and since the money has to be split between two causes, it'll be an epic failure. The Children's Hospital won't have enough for the new beds and other equipment they need, and Lost Ones won't have much to help kids like Jade at the Heart House. And all because I put my faith in the wrong man.

Wrong man. That's a lie, I don't really believe that. There's no universe in which Peter Pan is the wrong man for me, not when comparing his heart to mine. Unfortunately, there's more to life than just love. But that doesn't mean I don't wish differently.

I've replayed that scene in Peter's garage a thousand times, and the things I said to him make me cringe. After that meeting, I was a grenade, held in the trembling hands of my waning hope with the pin already pulled. When I heard the car wasn't ready, that tiny thread of hope holding me together disappeared. Three seconds later, I exploded, hurling verbal shrapnel in every direction except mine.

Could Peter have done things differently that would've ensured the car was done on time? Yes. But it's not like I was turning down his invitations for weekly dates. I could've asked him to use the time to work on the car with the incentive that we could hang out once it was complete. I could've insisted he not wait for me to pick out the accessories and other details, which I'm pretty sure was just a ploy to spend extra time with me since he overruled most of my decisions anyway.

The point is, he's not the only to one to blame in this, and I know he never would've let me down on purpose. If that shipment had come in on time, he would've worked his butt off to make sure I had the car. I'm not saying that realizing these things changes my mind about us not working as a couple. Just that I want to apologize before I go back to Charlotte. I don't want bad blood between us. Regardless of everything else, I still love him. I always will.

But despite what Peter told me when we were seventeen, slow dancing on the beach, happy endings aren't written in the stars, and sometimes love itself is not enough.

Choking back a sigh and blinking the sting of tears away, I stare at the huge banner at the front of the room displaying a picture of what the Bel Air will look like in its finished state. I had to pay out the nose for a rush job and the fancy remote-controlled retractable design, but since I didn't have a car, I needed to go as "big" as I could with its proxy. Unfortunately, as Mr. Fitzgibbons has been so kind to remind me repeatedly tonight, it's not doing the trick.

"Thirty-five thousand, thank you, sir," the auctioneer says, pointing at the last person who raised their paddle half-heartedly. "Can I get thirty-eight thousand? Let me see thirty-seven, thirty-seven thousand…"

I tune out as he starts rattling off nonsensical things between shouting out the car's supposed highlights. "I need a drink," I mutter.

But before I can take a single step in the direction of the bar, Michael skids to a stop in front of me. "Not yet, you don't. Stay right there," he says, his cheeks flushed and chest heaving with shallow breaths.

This is the first time I've spoken to him since the other day. I listened to his impassioned speech earlier about the foundation and our mother's mission, and I was so proud of him. Most guys his age were barely out of their frat party stage, if at all, but Michael was hard at work making a difference in the lives of so many kids.

My baby brother is an inspiration and an amazing human. I can't be mad at him for going to bat for me and giving me an opportunity I wouldn't have otherwise had. I just wish he'd been honest with me from the beginning, and I convey that to him with nothing more than a look.

He nods and takes my hand in both of his. "I know, and I'm sorry. Forgive me?"

I give him an affectionate squeeze and smile. "Already forgiven."

"Great. Oh, shit." He ignores our father's chastising glare for cursing in public to answer his vibrating phone. "Yeah, sorry, I'm coming. Hang on a sec. I said I'm coming, *damn*." Hanging up, he again tells me to stay put then rushes off muttering something about a "sassy dixie," whatever the heck that is.

I watch in confusion as Michael whispers something to the auctioneer who hits the remote to lower the gigantic banner. My stomach leaps into my throat. "What's he doing? They're only up to forty-thousand. It could still go higher, why is he stopping—"

Panic turns to shock as the banner lowers enough to reveal what's waiting on the other side of the floor-to-ceiling glass wall. I chose this venue because of that wall. It has two sliding doors that part to allow large things inside. Like a gigantic sculpture or a decorative courtyard fountain.

Or a cherry red 1955 Chevy Bel Air convertible like the one staring back at us as the glass sliders are pulled open. And standing next to it is the most handsome man to ever look uncomfortable in a tuxedo and dark green bowtie.

I'm speechless, but I'm apparently the only one. Excited chatter spreads through the crowd like wildfire as a platinum-haired girl in grunge band attire slowly drives the car into the spot I'd designed for it at the front of the room. Tink revs the engine a couple of times, showing off the power before it settles back into the purr of a luxury car, then turns it off and hops out.

I think Mr. Fitzgibbons is talking to me—asking if I knew this was going to happen, if I planned it, and something about it not being very sporting of me to not let them in on the dramatic reveal. But I'm not paying attention to him or anyone other than Peter, who's ascending the small stage to get behind the podium. He glances over at Michael standing with Tink—oh duh, sassy *pixie*, not dixie—who nods in my direction.

As soon as Peter's gaze meets mine, my heart flips in my chest and the beating wings in my belly are like fairies on speed. A million and one things are racing through my head, and my emotions are a tangled string of poorly packed Christmas lights. But then he speaks into the microphone— his honey-rich voice echoes through the room, vibrating along my skin—and my knees almost give out.

"Ladies and gentlemen, I apologize for the late arrival of your auction piece, but let me take this opportunity to tell you about how special she is."

Electric blue eyes span the distance and fill the fissures of my heart with their warmth and sincerity.

"This model is absolutely timeless," he continues. "Sleek and classy with understated power and confidence. Whether racing on a straightaway or meandering along life's scenic route, she always reaches her destination with style and grace. She looks great locked up tight, but her true beauty shines when you open her up to the heavens and let her fly.

"Ladies and gentlemen," he says again, still holding my gaze, "it's entirely my fault your car wasn't here on time. But I can assure you…she's worth waiting an eternity for."

I don't even realize I'm crying until tears splash onto my skin above the sweetheart neckline of my dress. I'm going to look like a mess, but I don't care if my mascara streaks down my face and my eyes get puffy and swollen. Because the boy I've loved since I was twelve-years-old is standing before me (and a few hundred socialites) as a man professing his love for me in the language he knows best—mechanic lingo.

Peter jumps off the front of the stage and heads straight for me. The room erupts into a flurry of action as people get up from their tables to inspect the Bel Air, and the auctioneer gets back on the microphone to point out all the features, this time *actual* facts about the classic car and not thinly veiled metaphors for the event planner in residence.

A waiter walks by with flutes of champagne. Without thinking, I snag one and tip it back to drain the entire thing.

"Wendy," my dad whispers in his scolding tone.

"Not now, Dad, okay?" I hand him the empty glass and keep my voice low enough, so no one else can hear. "If Mom were here, she'd tell you to lighten up. The world wasn't ending before, and it sure as hell isn't now that the car is here. So please, give me whatever break you can muster, then lecture me on how I've ruined my life later."

Shock flashes in his eyes, but he doesn't get the chance to respond before Peter reaches us with Michael and Tinker Bell in tow, and suddenly, my two worlds collide. I imagined introducing my parents to Peter and the others a thousand times when I was young, but it was never anything as public or complicated as this. How do you stop a potential train wreck when you don't even know if either train has working brakes?

"Mr. Darling, it's a pleasure to finally meet you," Peter says, extending his work-roughened hand. "My name is Peter Pan, owner of LB Automotive."

My dad studies Peter's hand as he would a rusty bear trap, wondering if it's safe to place his hand inside, or if by playing nice it'll somehow expose his vulnerabilities. After what seems like an hour, he grips Peter and shakes his hand. "Pleasure to meet you, Mr. Pan. You did a fine job on the Bel Air. We appreciate your hard work for the hospital and our foundation."

"I'm glad it's going to help both organizations, Mr. Darling, but truth be told, I did it solely for your daughter."

"Oh? How well do you—"

"*Very* well," Peter says, his words heavy with meaning. My cheeks grow warm, but neither man is paying me much attention as Peter seems to have things he needs to get off his chest. "Wendy's told me so much about you over the years, sir, I feel like I already know you. Which is why I know you're having a hard time accepting that your little girl abandoned everything you worked so hard to give her in favor of something completely unrelated, not to mention financially risky."

"Well, I…um…yes, I-I suppose that's true." Michael and I exchange a look of awe. I'm not sure I've ever heard my father stammer. Drawing his shoulders back, my dad clarifies, "I'm simply concerned for her future. I'm her father, after all, and I care about what she does with her life."

Peter nods. "I understand, which is why you can rest easy. Wendy's an amazing event planner—I've seen what she can do, and I think tonight proves she's capable of creating magic out of thin air—and it won't be long before Second Star Events is a top-tier event planning company."

My dad scans the room as though taking in the decorations and attention to details for the first time. In the background, the auctioneer has resumed the bidding and amidst all the unintelligible sounds, I make out numbers in the two-hundred thousands already.

"Yes," he says, toying with a side of his mustache. "I agree, she's quite good."

It's a good thing I've never been the fainting sort of girl. "Quite good" is high praise from George Darling, and I dare to hope he might start supporting my new career instead of trying to convince me to return to the old one. Cutting a glance at Peter, Dad narrows his eyes as though trying to place him. "How did you say you and my daughter met, Mr. Pan?"

"I didn't." Peter's mouth twists into his innocently mischievous smile, the very definition of dichotomy, which my father will never understand because it doesn't fit into his black and white view of how the world and its people work. "It's not our past that matters, Mr. Darling, it's our future. And I'll travel to the ends of the earth to make sure we have a long and happy one."

My dad's brow crinkles, but Michael swoops in to spare us the rest of this conversation and save it for another time. "Come on, Dad, there's a sidecar with your name on it over at the bar. Let's leave these two to talk."

I breathe a sigh of relief as my brother ushers him out of earshot, but it gets stuck in my chest again when Tink steps in front of me. My nerves are shot, and I'm afraid I won't have my usual patience and understanding when she fires off at the mouth about her disdain for my general presence.

"Hi, Tink," I say, doing my best to offer her a genuine smile. "The car looks amazing, and I know it wouldn't be here without your help, so thank you."

"Actually, it would've been here a lot sooner if I hadn't intercepted the shipment with the hope you'd break up with Peter," she says bluntly. "So, you know, sorry about that."

My jaw unhinges and hits the top of my silver glitter heels.

"Tink, that's not what I told you to apologize for," Peter says.

"She should know it wasn't your fault, regardless of whatever blame you want to place on yourself. Whether you dicked around or not, the truth is, you still would've had it done if I didn't do what I did."

I'm floored. I mean, I knew Tink was territorial over

Peter, but I never guessed she would go so far as to intentionally come between us. "Wow…I'm not sure what to say," I admit.

Anger bubbles hot in my veins, and my initial reaction is to lash out and demand to know if she understands that her actions potentially ruined my relationship with Peter as well as my company's reputation. But then I remember how she was raised—without a mom like mine to teach her empathy and kindness. She was exposed to just as much neglect and brutality as I was shown love. And despite the logical part of me arguing Tink should know better as an adult, my heart pleads with me to be understanding of that little girl.

"Thank you for being honest. I wish you'd tell me what I can do to make you not hate me so much."

"Guess this is your lucky day. Turns out, I don't hate you anymore. I'm not explaining why, so don't bother asking." She glances over at Peter who arches a thick, blond brow expectantly. Sighing, she adds, "But I *am* apologizing for treating you like shit over the years. As long as you make Peter happy, I promise not to do that anymore. Unless you royally piss me off for some reason."

Peter rolls his eyes. "That's enough, Tink. Go keep Michael company for a while."

Her cheeks grow pink, and it looks like she's struggling to keep her disinterested expression. "I'd rather pull my eyelashes out one by one. I did what I came here to do. I'm calling Si to come pick me up. Later."

And with that, the only girl of the Lost Boys clan sashays her punk butt through the throng of socialites, not giving a crap that they're all staring after her like she's part of a circus sideshow, and it makes me laugh. "I'm going to enjoy holding her to that not-hating-me thing. What do you think she'll say to a girly sleepover with face masks and rom-coms?"

"I think it's a good way to make her hate you again," he says with a grin.

I wrinkle my nose in delight. "Yeah, I know. But it'd be so much fun to ask just to see the horror on her face."

Peter steps fully in front of me, effectively eclipsing my view of the world around us. Everything fades away when he's this near, and it brings what I've missed the past couple of days into sharp relief.

"Enough about Tink, Wen," he says, his voice low and deep. "It's time to talk about us."

"Oh, I—"

"Going once? Going twice? SOLD! To the gentleman in the back for *four-hundred and fifty thousand* dollars!"

Did I hear that right? The car sold for almost *half a million* dollars? My heart races as I search for the buyer and almost choke when I see Mr. Fitzgibbons accepting hand-shakes of congratulations as he makes his way over to me and Peter.

"Mr. Fitzgibbons, *you* bought the car?" I ask wide-eyed.

"What can I say, Ms. Darling," he says with a satisfied grin, "once I saw it in person, I couldn't resist. Great job on the rebuild, Mr. Pan. I'd like to discuss doing more business with you in the future, if you're interested."

Peter shakes his hand firmly. "Absolutely, sir. Wendy knows how to get a hold of me. Look forward to talking with you."

"And as for you, Ms. Darling…" I hold my breath as he surveys the room. "Excellent job. The board is extremely pleased, and we hope you'll have another exciting idea for us next year."

Relief and happiness bubble to the surface, and I'm help-less to stop the laughter from escaping with my smile. "Yes, sir, I would love that. Thank you very much."

The older man nods his goodbye and heads toward his new car, inviting people along the way to come and be envious. Somewhere in the last few minutes, the staff pulled the tables and chairs out of the center of the room to reveal the wooden dance floor. The band starts playing an instrumental rendition of "If" by Bread, one of my mom's favorite ballads from the 70s about unconditional love that stands the test of time, even after the universe burns out.

"Wendy Moira Angela Darling, will you do me the honor of high-school-slow-dancing with me?"

I hesitate, glancing from my clipboard of checklists to Peter's offered hand and back to my checklists. Biting my lip, I try to predict who might need me for which reasons. "Peter, I don't think—"

"She'd love to dance with you," Michael says, snatching the clipboard away from me. I try to protest, but he shushes me like a child. "Go on now and let baby bro take care of things. I totally got this."

"Thanks, man," Peter says, taking my newly free hand. "I owe you one."

Michael smirks as though he already knows what he's cashing it in on. "I'll remember that."

Once on the dance floor, my sexy mechanic pulls me in close, and it's like we're seventeen all over again. Except there's a mammoth chandelier dripping with crystals instead of a full moon, barefoot casual is replaced with black-tie attire, and he's about a million times more handsome. But even though we're surrounded by a few hundred people, it still feels as though we're the only people in the room.

"For the record," he says gruffly, "I wanted to let you know I was coming with the car, but the girls suggested I shouldn't get your hopes up before I made sure we didn't have any problems. Then we actually *did* have a hard time getting the seats in right, so we were cutting it closer to the wire than I'd have liked. After all that, I figured I might as well make an entrance."

"Mmm, you definitely did that." I wonder if I'd have even

spoken to him if I hadn't had that time to cool off and think things through. Maybe it was for the best it happened how it did. "As great as it would've been to not to be sick with nerves, even I can admit that the dramatic entrance was pretty cool. It probably even helped with the bidding wars."

"Still, I hated knowing you were hurting and worrying— hated even more knowing I caused it and couldn't comfort you because I didn't deserve to do even that. I don't ever want to see that look in your eyes again."

"What look?" I ask as we sway gently from side to side.

"The one where I've failed you."

His voice is thick with emotion, and it kills me to know he was hurting just as much, if not more. "Peter, it wasn't only you. I should've taken responsibility for my own actions, or inactions. Let's forget about it, okay? It's over and done with. Water under the bridge and all that."

"You've always been the best of us, Wen. I don't deserve you, never have." I open my mouth to argue with him, but he stops me with a crooked grin. "Let me finish before you berate me, okay?"

I nod, amused and curious to hear where he's going with this. "Go ahead."

"Like I said, I've never deserved you, but I never cared either. I had you, so why question it? To me, questioning it was nothing more than tempting fate to take you away, and that was the last thing I wanted. So, I embraced the mentality of 'be thankful for what you have.'"

"Ignoring for the moment that I disagree with your assess-ment of never deserving me," I counter, "that seems like a great mentality to have. It's what we always preached to the boys when they were young. It helped them to think posi-tively about what they did have instead of negatively about what they didn't."

"And in those cases, that line of thinking *is* great. But I've realized that it's the wrong attitude to have when it comes to loving someone."

I swallow and force the words past a throat tight with emotion. "What's the right one?"

He reaches up to brush his knuckles across my cheek before anchoring his hand at the back of my neck possessively. "Instead of being thankful that I've somehow landed an incredible woman I don't deserve, I need to do everything I can to become the man she *does* deserve."

"Peter—" It's difficult to get anything more out as the tears begin to fall. "You already are that man."

"No, I'm not. But I swear to you that I will be. We're going to take things slow for a bit. You have things to do and take care of in Charlotte, and I'm going to hire your dad to help me put a plan together for expanding LB with a rebuild business. I'll visit you in Charlotte on the weekends—if you'll have me—and some weekends, I hope you'll come visit me and the gang in Neverland. How's that sound?"

My head is spinning. I can hardly believe the all-fun, all-the-time Peter Pan is suggesting such practical, responsible things. "That sounds…I mean, it's great, but…so this is like a trial run at a long-distance relationship?"

His brows crinkle together. "Hell, no," he grates out. "I have every intention on us being together-together, even if that means I eventually move to Charlotte. I told you before, I'm not letting you get away again. But first, I'm going to prove to you that I'm worth keeping around. Forever."

Smiling through my tears, I say, "I do like the sound of that, very much."

Peter frames my face with his strong hands and kisses me like our future depends on it. It doesn't—I already know that Peter meant everything he said, and I have no doubt he'll follow through on all of it—but who am I to stop a kiss so all-consuming? This is definitely one of those moments where being happy with and enjoying what you get is perfectly acceptable.

I have no idea how much time passes before he forces us to break apart. More than a bit dazed, I glance around and ask, "Whoa, what day is it?"

He chuckles and gathers me closer. "Wendy Moira Angela Darling," he says, "you just nailed the biggest event of your career, secured the Love for Littles account as their permanent planner, and accepted your boyfriend's groveling apology in the most dramatic fashion. Everyone's dying to know, what are you going to do next?"

Chuckling at his impersonation of a specific line of commercials, my answer is easy. "I'm going to Neverland!"

"Hell yeah, you are," he says, lifting me up and spinning me around before setting me back on my heels. "Okay, you ready?"

I laugh. "No, I can't leave until the event is over."

"Worth a shot." Then, giving me his infamous smirk—the one that's all mischief and sans innocence—he leans in and speaks low for only me to hear. "Then let's go find a janitor's closet and you can check inventory while I check how deep I can bury myself in your sweet body from behind."

Sweet baby Jesus in a manger. Suddenly, it's about one thousand degrees in the ballroom and my face flushes to embarrassing proportions. I'm about to tell him to behave himself when he quirks a challenging eyebrow at me, and I make a rash decision I might regret in fifteen minutes. But probably not.

Bracing my hands on his lapels, I lift up on my tiptoes and whisper into his ear. "It won't be easy getting me to fly in a broom closet, Pan. Let's see how well your magic works in small spaces."

"Angel, if I were a fairytale character, I'd be Harry Potter. A broom closet is the perfect place, even better if it's under a set of stairs. Let's go."

Giggling like I'm seventeen all over again, I let Peter lead me through the empty halls. We don't find a janitor's closet, but we do find a secluded alcove under a set of stairs where we're hidden away from view. Then, pressed into the corner and shielded by his body, Peter rucks my dress up around my waist and reminds me how effortless flying is with nothing more than happy thoughts, a little magic, and a searing kiss from the man I love.

EPILOGUE

.

"**N**ever have I ever keyed someone's car for being a total douchebag," Tink says with a smirk on her face.

Lily's jaw drops in shock as she stares across the bonfire at her best friend. "Okay, I see how it is," she says with a laugh. "Wait till it's my turn, bitch." The rest of us either give Lily shit for defiling a man's ride or encourage her heroism as she takes a long drink of her beer.

The mid-October breeze coming off the ocean makes the flames dance and crackle in the center of our circle. It also makes the woman sitting in my lap snuggle into me a bit more. As Carlos takes his turn coming up with a statement for our friendly game of Never Have I Ever, I kiss Wendy's temple. "You cold, baby? I can give you my flannel."

She gazes up at me with a wide smile and shakes her head. "No, I'm fine. Besides, then you'd be cold with just a T-shirt, and I don't look nearly as good in green plaid as you do."

What she doesn't know is that I could jog the fifty feet behind us and grab another shirt from the beach cottage. The quaint, little two-story home I told her is owned by my friend who's letting us have a bonfire on his stretch of sand while he's out of town. A complete and total lie.

"Bullshit, you look good in everything." She does, too. The cooler temps at night have forced her to cover up more, but she's still sexy as hell in her skinny jeans, pink sweater, and knee boots. Then again, she could be wearing hockey gear, and it wouldn't matter because *I* know what's underneath. Lowering my lips to her ear, I drop my voice. "But if you want the absolute truth, I think you look the best in *nothing*."

She bites her lip and gives me a non-verbal *shhh* with a playful shove against my chest. I love that I can still make her blush, and it's taking every ounce of willpower I have not to toss her over my shoulder and carry her off like the selfish fucking caveman I am. But I have a plan, and that's not part of it, not yet at least. I've waited this long, a few more minutes won't kill me.

It's been two months since the Love for Littles event, and I've worked hard to make good on everything I promised Wendy that night. The Bel Air made quite a splash in the London elite community, and I've gotten several classic rebuild jobs because of it. Silas, Tink, and I are heading up those projects, and we've worked out a new schedule where half of our week is spent in the shop on the normal jobs and the other half on the rebuilds. It means the shop is a bit short-handed on those days, but I'm working on fixing that, too. I plan on asking Chief if he wants some part-time work since he's sticking around for a while, and I also placed an ad for a receptionist, which means Thomas and Carlos won't have to take turns covering the front.

I've spent a lot of weekends with Wendy in Charlotte. She had fun showing me around the city and introducing me to a few of her friends, but my favorite times were when we stayed in and played games or watched movies. Don't get me wrong, I wasn't a saint in any stretch of the imagination, but

I've made a conscious effort not to keep her naked and in bed every hour we spend together. There will be plenty of time for that once we're living together, a topic she's tried bringing up multiple times. A topic I've always brushed off as something "we can discuss later," even as I was making plans behind the scenes. Plans that are about to finally pay off.

At least I fucking hope so.

Our whole family is on the beach with us tonight: the Lost Boys, Tink, Tiger Lily, Chief, and Wendy's brothers who've been hanging out with us occasionally, just like when we were all kids. Even Hook showed up, though not without making sure I knew it was out of respect for Wendy and not because he gives two shits about me, which I'm fine with. I can't tell if his surly ass is playing the game or not by the timing of his drinks, but it doesn't matter as long as he's here. Good beer, great company, a full moon, and a blazing fire. All around, it's pretty perfect.

Tiger Lily raises her beer bottle. "My turn! Never have I ever…" The Piccaninny princess stares down the feisty fairy with a smug grin. "…made out with someone younger than me."

The guys and I drink without hesitation, meaning we *have* made out with someone younger. Wendy doesn't raise her beer—I'm older than her by three months—and neither does Lily. But after a few seconds, we realize that Lily and Tink are staring each other down in some kind of mental stand-off. As our heads swivel from one girl to the other, there's one person in the group who's only interested in what Tink's doing: Michael.

Wendy's baby bro is watching Tink with all the intensity of a cop waiting for his suspect to crack under the pressure. Suddenly, I know how Michael convinced Tinker Bell she wasn't really in love with me. And if I remember correctly, he's about two years younger than her. *Clever bastard.*

Chuckling to myself, I take another sip of my beer and wait for the fireworks.

Tink glances at Michael who challenges her with a raised eyebrow. One that says "either admit it by drinking or I'll refresh your memory in front of everyone." Since my sprite's no dummy, she lifts her beer and takes a long pull of her Corona with everyone cheering her on, though I doubt anyone else caught on to who Tink's younger man is, other than Lily who obviously knows.

"Your turn, Pan," Chief says next to me. "And make it a good one, will ya? I'm not nearly drunk enough."

The past few weeks have been about careful planning and hard work. I never second-guessed myself, never worried if I was doing the right thing, but I thought for sure that when the time came, I'd be nervous as hell. What if I misread what she wants her future to look like? What if she's not ready to take this leap with me? What if she needs another few years to even get to the point I am? Those questions and more are what I'd assumed would plague me in the minutes leading up to this moment. But now that it's here, I've never been so confident about anything in my life.

"Never have I ever," I say with all our friends' eyes on us, "gotten down on one knee and proposed."

Wendy laughs. "Peter, that's a terrible one. None of us get to drink to—"

Holding her gaze, I lift my beer and drain what's left. Her brows knit together with confusion, and I realize my mistake. She thinks I'm referring to something in my past, not our present. Needing to fix the hurt flashing across her face, I toss my bottle to the sand and push to my feet, forcing her to get up with me.

But then I sink to one knee and hold her left hand between mine. Wendy gasps and looks around the circle as though checking if she's the only one seeing this. She's met with knowing smiles, thumbs up, and raised beers.

217

Her shock is adorable and a huge relief since I was worried I've been too transparent in my planning. Chuckling, I say, "Baby, eyes down here."

Her gaze swings back to mine, shimmering with unshed tears and the reflection of my unconditional love. I drink it all in, staring up at the girl I want by my side for the rest of my life. She's bathed in moonlight, just like that first night I saw her on the balcony, as pure as I was tarnished. The angel to my devil, my saving grace. My heart's adventure. And it's time she knows exactly how I feel.

"Sixteen years ago, I was in search of an adventure when I heard a woman in a brick house on Barrie Street telling stories unlike anything I'd ever heard. I returned the next night, and the next, as often as I could to bring the stories back to the rest of the Lost Boys. But no matter how great the stories were, they always rang a little hollow to me because they weren't mine."

Silas snorts. "Also because he sucked at telling stories, as evidenced by this proposal speech."

Nick chuckles. "Always the critic, Si. You think you could do better?"

"There's a stupid question," Tobias and Tyler say in stereo.

"Boys," Wendy scolds, her brow arched with enough sass that she doesn't need to say anything else. She's trying to appear stern, but the hint of a smile tugging at her lips gives her away. She adores these boys, ill manners and all.

Grinning sheepishly, they mutter their apologies, and all I can do is shake my head at their antics. I knew when I decided to involve them that the Lost Boys would be the Lost Boys, which means rowdy and unruly at best, drunk and disorderly at worst. I banned them from those last two until after Wendy and I are gone.

"Thanks, Si, now I lost my train my of thought."

Wendy is all too happy to help me out. "The stories rang hollow because they weren't yours."

"Thanks, baby," I say, kissing her hand then continuing my story. "One night I got to the house and looked up to find an angel standing on the balcony. Her voice was like music, and her beauty took my breath away. I was young and ignorant about so many things, and yet, in that moment, I knew. I knew you were meant to be mine. I knew in my heart that *you* were my adventure, and I was right. When I'm with you, I'm a man who has found his rightful place in this world. Without you, I'm still just a lost boy."

"Ooh, good one, boss."

Someone shushes Carlos—probably Thomas—and I make a mental note to slap them all upside the heads later. I pretend like I didn't hear them and keep going.

"You are my everything, Wen, and I want to give you the fairytale you deserve. I might never be a valiant prince or a knight in shining armor, but I promise to be your responsible, career-minded hero with a fun-loving mischievous streak. Also, a rock-hard body to make all your friends jealous," I say with a crooked grin and wink.

Wendy throws her head back and laughs through the tears as all my friends groan and throw in their two-cents. I tried keeping it serious, I swear I did. But it just wouldn't be a genuine Pan speech without a sprinkling of my signature cockiness. Luckily, Wendy thinks it's part of my charm. I really don't deserve this woman. Just another reason I need to lock this down, once and for all.

With a renewed sense of urgency, I finally retrieve the ring box that's been burning a hole in my pocket since I picked it up this afternoon. Not the one I've kept for a decade that holds memories of our past and promises for our future— that's for later when I don't have to share the moment with anyone but Wendy, like I intended ten years ago. This is

219

something new to represent the new promises and our new life from this point on.

I open the box with the anticipation of weeks and months buzzing through me. Her eyes flare wide, and she presses her right hand over her heart with a sharp inhale as she stares at the ring I had designed for her. The star-shaped center stone is a half-karat in a gold setting with five smaller diamonds nestled into the band on either side.

"Oh, Peter," she whispers.

"Eleven diamonds in all," I explain. "One for each of the eleven orphans you loved and cared for when you were still just a kid yourself. We were siblings through circumstance at that school. But you showed up and made us a true family, Wen."

Hook sits up and takes interest for the first time all night. "You put a diamond on her ring for me?"

"Yup, and Starkey and Smee."

"Don't you think you should've asked if I wanted to be a part of this, Pan?"

"Nope, didn't care," I say, shooting him a *go fuck yourself, with love* grin. "Now shut up and let me finish."

Rolling his eyes, he leans back in his chair, cursing me under his breath. John offers him another beer, but Hook pointedly ignores him like he's been doing since the cop sat next to him. I wonder if Hook's issue with John is that he's on the opposite side of the law or if there's something more to it than that.

"Peter, focus and put the damn ring on her finger already, will ya?"

This from Tink, who's been amazingly supportive. She and Wendy have taken baby steps in their new friendship, and the times I've caught them laughing together gave me feelings so soft not even the threat of a firing squad could get me to admit them out loud. I have faith they'll continue to grow closer now that Wendy will be around a lot more. Like, always.

"Sorry, I was distracted by Captain Surly Ass over there."

Clearing my throat, I take the ring out and pocket the box before reclaiming her left hand. As I hold the ring in front of her fourth finger, I'm suddenly overwhelmed with the weight of the moment crashing over me.

"A long time ago, right here on this beach, I told you that our happy ever after was written in the stars, and no matter what happened, that would never change. Now I'm asking for the chance to prove it to you, to show you that our love *is* and will *always* be enough. So, will you, Wendy Moira Angela Darling, do me the honor of making your already ridiculously long name even longer, and marry me?"

"Yes, Peter Pan, *yes yes yes*!"

Pure joy swells in my chest as I slip the ring on her finger then shoot up to swing her around and kiss the living hell out of her to the tune of our family cheering behind us. As usual, they interrupt the moment, and I'm relegated to standing by as everyone takes turns hugging and congratulating my fiancée.

Damn, that sounds good. Wife will sound even better. I wonder how fast I can make that happen. Though, I suppose the chances of an event planner wanting to elope are pretty close to nil.

After Chief puts Wendy down, he claps a hand on each of our shoulders and grins like a loon. "Congratulations, you two. Now go on up and enjoy a night of wild monkey sex in your new house. Oh, one more thing, Wendy. Your boy Pan bought you that beach house as an early wedding gift. Let me know when you need help moving your stuff in."

"Seriously, man? You're just going to cut my legs out from under me like that?" I'm honestly in too much of a good mood to be pissed he ruined the surprise, but I still have to give him shit for it.

"Hell, yeah, I'm doing her a favor. It took God less time to create the universe than it did for you to pop the question. She'd be too old to climb the steps by the time you got around to telling her."

"You're a dick." *Translation: I love you, brother.*

"I know." *Translation: I know.*

Wendy's gaze bounces between the house and me, a mix of shock, excitement, and a hint of doubt on her beautiful face. "You bought that house? For us?"

Stepping closer, I pull her into my arms. "You've been talking about moving back this way, and I didn't want to be like some college guy moving a girlfriend into his frat house. When I found this place for sale on *our beach*, I knew it was meant to be ours."

Unshed tears shimmer in her eyes. "It's perfect," she says, smiling. "All of this. Everything is perfect."

"Not yet it's not."

Scooping her up in my arms, I carry her up to the house. She wriggles as she laughs and protests, claiming she needs to say proper goodbyes. But I no longer give a damn about sticking around. It's not like we won't see them all soon enough, whenever I decide to finally let her out of our new bed to rejoin society. I nix her request for a tour, taking her straight to the master bedroom where I finally set her on the end of the mattress.

I begin undressing her, pulling her sweater up over her head and dropping it to the floor before removing her boots and socks. "The first night we met, you told me a kiss was something you share with someone you care about. And when I asked you for one, you panicked and gave me a thimble."

Her blue eyes soften with a dreamy look, like she's watching that moment between our younger selves. "And you gave me a gold acorn nut in return. I remember."

I undo her jeans, and she lifts her hips to allow me to peel them down her legs, leaving her in nothing but her white lace bra and panties. As always, my mouth waters with the desire to taste every sexy inch of her, and my cock pulses with the painful need to be buried deep between her thighs. She fidgets in place, and as anxious as I am to move things along, there's a method to my madness. So I let my hands roam, distracting her with my touch as I divest her of the last scraps of material.

"Six years later, before you moved away," I continue, reaching under the bed for the other ring box I stashed there earlier, "I stole your kiss and made you this…"

Kneeling between her legs, I open the faded jewelry box and hold it up so she can finally see what I made her forever ago. With a trembling hand, she picks up the delicate 22" gold chain with her acorn nut dangling as a pendant at the bottom. I'd had to get creative with the power tools in the shop when no one was around to get a hole drilled through the crown for the chain to fit through, but I'd pulled it off.

"Peter…" She shakes her head as though unable to get her words out.

"Here, let me. I've waited ten years to see this on you." I set the box aside and lower the necklace over her head as she sweeps her hair out of the way. The acorn nut sits just above her breasts, directly over where her heart beats for me inside her chest, exactly how I wanted it.

"I thought I lost this," she whispers, fingering the pendant.

"I know, and I'm sorry I let you think that. I'd planned on giving it to you that last night on the beach, but when I found out you were leaving, I couldn't do it. I thought maybe if I kept our kisses, they'd bring you back to me someday."

She smiles. "I guess it worked. Where's yours?"

Reaching back, I peel off my flannel and T-shirt, revealing the silver beaded chain that had originally come with a set of novelty dog tags. I'd taken those off and threaded the chain through the hole I'd made in my thimble. Now it sits over my heart, just like hers.

"Wow," she says on a soft chuckle, trailing her fingers around where my "kiss" sits over my heart, just like hers. "I don't think there's another man alive who can make a Monopoly game piece look this sexy."

"Funny, I was thinking the same thing about you and that acorn nut."

Framing my face in her hands, she kisses me, injecting a shot of lust straight to my groin before pulling back. "Thank you, Peter. You've made everything perfect. The kisses, my ring, the proposal, the *house*—oh my God, I still can't believe you bought us a house on our beach—it's all just so perfect. It's like all of my fairytale dreams plus ones I never knew I had come true. I never thought I could be so happy."

"All I've ever wanted is for you to be happy. We're together now, and this time it's forever. Tonight is the first night of the rest of our lives, the beginning of our happily ever after."

"Then what are we waiting for?" she asks as her hand moves down my stomach toward my aching cock. "Let's start things off right."

A groan escapes my chest, and it's all I can do not to flip her over and show her the filthy things that have been running through my mind since last weekend. I'm going to make love to this woman, so she remembers how I worshiped her and showered her with love on our engagement night. *Then* I'll fuck her six ways from Sunday until she can barely walk.

She almost derails my carefully laid plans when she squeezes me over my jeans. Sucking a breath in through clenched teeth, I grab her wrist and pull her hand away before she gets any more bright ideas. "Fucking hell, Wen, you're gonna kill me."

"It's only fair because if you're not naked and inside me in the next few seconds, I'm pretty sure I'll die."

"Can't have that, can we?" I get to my feet and strip, then stand before her. Blue eyes drink me in as my thick cock strains toward her. "Move up onto the bed, angel."

Biting her lip, she holds my gaze and lays in the center of the mattress as I follow her down, settling my weight over her. She wraps herself around me, and I notch myself into the tight opening between her thighs where I belong, still thankful we moved past using condoms weeks ago, so nothing gets in the way of our connection.

"Take me," she whispers. "Claim my body like you've claimed my heart and soul. Please, Peter, I need you."

She arches her hips, enveloping the head of my cock in her slick heat, and I swear I see stars. "You have me, Wen. I'm yours. Always have been, always will be."

And with that, I plunge home, because that's what Wendy is. I may have always lived in Neverland, but Wendy is my home, just as I am hers.

With the moonlight streaming in from the window, I make love to the woman of my dreams. With every thrust, every invasion, I give her a small piece of myself, of my soul. I kiss her, caress her, and hold her like I'll never let her go. And when her tight walls squeeze and flutter around me with the strength of her climax rolling through her, I hold her gaze and whisper how much I love to watch her fly for me.

"I love you more than anything, Peter," she says, her body still quivering with aftershocks and so much emotion in her eyes that it overflows in the form of tears streaming down her temples.

I kiss the salty wetness away and then kiss her pleasure-swollen mouth. "Still love you more, Wen."

And I do. There's nothing in this world that could convince me that anyone loves another as much as I love her. And loving Wendy Darling for the rest of our lives is going to be an awfully big adventure.

EPILOGUE II

HOOK

I watch Pan carry Wendy up to the house from under hooded eyes, careful that my expression doesn't give anything away. Deep down, in the dark place I shove all my emotions, I recognize that I'm happy for them. If Pan doesn't deserve the fairytale, Wendy sure as hell does. I never bonded with her like the other guys because I never bond with anyone, not even my own brother. Getting close to people is a dangerous game in my life, and one I don't care to play, so I make sure everyone stays the fuck away.

Even still, I got a lot of respect for Wendy Darling. I might never admit it, but I hope Pan makes good on all that flowery bullshit he just spewed. Out of everyone on this beach tonight, she deserves it the most. Which is also why I agreed to come in the first place. But now that I've fulfilled my obligation, and Pan is no doubt already balls deep in his new fiancée and won't know the damn difference, I'm out of here.

I don't bother saying anything by way of goodbye. Pan's the only one who insists I'm a part of his Lost Boy clan. The rest don't give a shit if they ever see me again, which is fine by me. I've got my own crew to worry about. The Pirates aren't anything like Pan's boys. They're a bunch of criminals with loose moral codes when it comes to stealing and dealing, but they're as loyal as dogs, and that's all I require.

Zipping up my leather jacket, I walk through the circle past the fire and ignore the invitations to stay longer as I stride up the beach to where I parked my GSXR-1000—the only thing of value I own in this world. I paid cash for her a few years ago, but everyone assumed I stole it. I didn't bother correcting them. What's the point? Perception is stronger than reality, and it's not like I have a reputation as a law-abiding citizen to worry about.

I round the corner of the small building that houses the public bathrooms when I hear a deep voice behind me.

"James."

A chill races down my spine, even as I instantly break into a sweat. It's been a lifetime since I've succumbed to the call of that name, and I'm not about to let that old bastard start up his twisted shit with me again. Spinning on my booted heel, I fist the front of his shirt in one hand and wrap the other around his neck before throwing him up against the brick wall.

"Don't you fucking call me that," I growl, inches from his face.

The man holds his hands up. "Okay, sorry, my bad," he says. "I just wanted to talk to you for a second, that's all."

Talk? Fuck him, he never wanted— The breeze changes directions, and I'm suddenly assaulted by the scents of polyester, bar soap, and gun oil. An altogether not unpleasant combination but not the tobacco, sweat, and engine grease I expected. *Jesus, it's Darling. Get a hold of yourself.*

"What the hell do you want?" I don't dare let go of him. If I do, he'll see the way my hands tremble without something for them to hold on to. The moon is bright enough, and I'm not about to explain my demons to anyone, much less a fucking nosy cop.

"Wendy told me about Starkey," he says. "I want to help."

For a brief second, hope flares inside my chest. Everything I've tried so far to get to Starkey has failed. The entire Neverland PD is in Croc's pocket, and until he's satisfied I've done my job, they're under strict instructions to keep my brother locked up tight.

Yeah, my brother. The one nobody knows I have.

For the millionth time, I wish I would've killed Croc when I was younger. But I didn't have the stomach for murder and foolishly thought that if I could just make it to my eighteenth birthday, I'd be free. But Fred Croc deals in information. It's how he manipulates the people around him. He'll dig and dig until he finds what he needs to hold over your head and attach those strings to make you one of his personal puppets.

In my case, it was telling me that he finally decided to look through our files and was surprised to find out that Starkey was actually my baby brother. No one had known before then. I made sure to keep it a secret, even from the little boy with shock-white hair and a case of hero worship for the one he called Captain.

If I'm capable of feeling anything close to love for another human being, it's that kid. So hearing that someone wants to help me get him out is like taking my first breath of air after being held under water for the past several months.

Until I remember who I'm talking to.

"You can't help me," I grind out. "Go back to the party, Darling."

He narrows his eyes at me. "Don't call me Darling. Unlike you, I don't have an aversion to my first name. John works just fine."

I scoff, letting him know I don't give a shit what he wants to be called, and push off him to walk away. He grabs my arm to stop me, and once again, I react. This time I slam his chest against the wall, pinning one of his arms between us. "The only reason I'm not rearranging that pretty face of yours is out of respect for your sister. But touch me again, and I'll consider it open season on pigs."

He laughs, the sound vibrating through his back and into my chest from the way we're pressed together. It seeps into my muscles and settles in my bones. I have a strange desire to hear it again, but I don't know how to make anyone laugh; in fact, I don't have a clue what he thinks is so funny in the first place.

"In case no one told you, I'm not a comedian, and I don't tell jokes, so I'm not sure what you found so humorous."

He looks over his shoulder at me with eyes the color of warm honey. The shadows from the moonlight make it impossible not to notice his strong features—high cheekbones, a straight nose, and a jawline like a straight-edge—and with his large frame and muscular build, he's a far cry from the scrawny kid who followed me around like a damn puppy.

"It's just that you told me not to touch you," he says, his chest drawing in heavy breaths. "But I think you like it when I do."

John pushes his hips back, silently directing my attention to the elephant in the room. The elephant being my hard dick pressed against his tight ass.

Jumping back like he's holding a welding torch to my balls, I turn him around and jack him up by his throat again. His body is loose, and he gives me a crooked grin framed by his groomed goatee. Why the hell is he letting me throw him around? Three times I've manhandled him. As a cop, it's not like he's not trained in taking guys down. And if I remember right, he was into martial arts and shit, too; yet, he never so much as blocked me from treating him like my own personal rag doll.

And Jesus Christ, why do I find that hot? It's been so long since I was turned on by anything other than porn and my right hand that I'm not sure what does it for me in the real world anymore. Apparently, I have a thing for cops. Off-duty ones. With honey-colored eyes and a deference to my authority. *Fuck me.*

"I don't know what game you're playing at, *Darling*, but you can stop it right the fuck now. You got no idea who you're dealing with, you hear me? Walk away, and stay away."

"I'll walk away," he says. "For now. But you're not getting rid of me that easily. I have sources that tell me your boss is planning something big. I don't know what it is yet, but I'm going to find out, and then I'm going to take him down. I hope you're not around when the chips fall."

"Same can be said to you," I grind out.

He shrugs a broad shoulder. "Be seeing you, Hook." Then he strolls back toward the beach like he doesn't have a care in the world. Like he didn't feel my erection against his ass, and like he didn't notice me noticing the bulge in his jeans when he turned around.

I curse under my breath and stalk over to my bike. Settling onto the seat, I pull my blacked-out helmet on and turn the key. *Stubborn fucking bastard.* He's going to get himself killed if he starts poking his nose into Croc's business. Then Wendy will be upset, and I'll have Pan's boot permanently lodged in my ass. Great, just what I need—a babysitting job on top of everything else.

As I pull out of the beachside lot and onto the highway, I twist my right hand back and take off like a bat out of hell, trying to put as much distance between me and the man who made me feel more in two minutes than I have in the past two decades. With every mile, the tightness in my chest loosens and the coldness of apathy and detachment returns, allowing me to breathe easier.

This is my comfort zone. This is what I know, how I've survived. And this is how I'll remain. No matter what John Darling and his honey-colored eyes say.

There's more of the Neverland crew coming soon...

HOOK, book 2 of the Neverland Novels will release in Spring 2019

Add it to your TBR shelf on Goodreads

Pre-order on Amazon now!
(or regular order if you're reading this after it releases)

GLOSSARY OF NEVERLAND CHARACTERS

Glossary of Neverland Characters
(as they are when the book starts 16 years ago from the
present timeline)

Lost Boys

Peter Pan: Leader of the small group of children at the School for Lost Boys of Neverland.

Slightly (aka Silas/Si): Self-appointed right-hand of Peter since he's the next oldest and a classic one-upper as he believes he's slightly better than everyone else.

Curly (aka Carlos): Sweet and flirtatious with dimples that would get him out of trouble in most cases; yet, he's blamed for things so often that he adopts the habit of accepting blame even when it isn't his to claim.

Nibs (aka Nick): Most reserved of the boys, quiet and loyal; probably Peter's *actual* right-hand.

The Twins (aka Tobias and Tyler/Ty): Identical, fun-loving twins, no one can tell apart, who finish each other's sentences and argue about everything except girls.

Tootles (aka Thomas): Youngest and sweetest of all the boys; very empathetic and helpful.

Tinker Bell (aka sprite/fairy/pixie): Only girl living at the school for boys; sassy and feisty and fiercely loyal to Peter.

Pirates (a sub-group of the Lost Boys)
James "Captain" Hook: Oldest of the boys at the school, inexplicably hates Peter.

Smee: Red-haired and loyal to Hook unless he isn't around, then joins in with the Lost Boys.

Starkey: White-haired and loyal to Hook unless he isn't around, then joins in with the Lost Boys.

Darlings
Wendy Darling: Young girl who lives in neighboring city of London; enjoys telling stories, nursing wounds, and pretending to be a mother.

John Darling: Wendy's brother, two years her junior; smart, cunning, and a martial arts enthusiast.

Michael Darling: Wendy's brother, five years her junior; genius level IQ and hates being the baby of the group.

George Darling: Father to the Darling children and financial planner in London.

Piccaninnies
Tiger Lily (aka Lily/Lil/T.L. Picc): Princess of the Piccaninny

tribe; getaway driver with an affinity for knives and emasculating men.

Gray Wolf (aka Chief): Tiger Lily's older half-brother; outcast, nomad, and mischief-maker.

Crocs

Fred Croc: Guardian of the Lost Boys, small-time criminal, owner of chop shop.

Delia Croc: Wife to Fred and hates kids.

ACKNOWLEDGMENTS

I have so many people to thank for helping me with this book and starting this series. Apologies in advance if my tired, deadline brain forgets anyone. It is definitely not intentional.

As always, thank you to my loving husband and children who show great understanding and patience when I lock myself away for days and weeks at a time to finish a book, which interrupts our normal life more than I'd like.

Thank you to my work wifeys and soul sisters, Cindi Madsen and Rebecca Yarros, for everything and anything: plotting, reading, sprinting, blurb-shaping, whip-cracking, encouraging, supporting, laughing, and a thousand other things I could never list even if I tried. My life is immeasurably better with them in it, and I seriously don't know what I'd do without our daily conversations and weekly video chats. As a tearful Jerry Maguire once said, they complete me. #UnholyTrinity

To Erin McRae who dropped everything to read every single chapter as soon as I hit send, even at 3am when I was expecting her to be asleep, but she never was, and for helping my brain to plot future books over text conversations. I look forward to future text sessions, especially once she finally gets an iPhone again, because let's be honest green text bubbles suck ass. ;)

To Danielle Rairigh (Danielle Leigh Editorial Services/Spellbound Stories) and Rebecca Barney (Fairest of All Book Reviews), two amazing ladies and bloggers in the romance community who, little by little, have restored my faith in the goodness of humanity by going above and beyond to beta read, offer feedback/proofing skills/advice, and repeatedly lifting me up during a time I thought I couldn't trust anyone. This book was largely finished because of their generosity, and I'm so grateful to both of them.

To Jaycee DeLorenzo of Sweet 'N Spicy Designs who created the beautiful covers for Pan, Hook, and Tink, and is literally the easiest, most pleasant, drama-free designer I've ever had the pleasure of working with. If you need design work done, she's the woman to see.

To Brenda Ambrosius, the most kickass attorney I could've ever asked for. She truly has a gift for crafting legal letters with all the professionalism they require plus a healthy dose of ghetto subtext. Without everything she's done for me over the past six weeks, this book wouldn't have gotten out when it did, and my sanity would no longer be intact. Because of everything she's done for me, I'm naming a heroine after her (with a slight variation) in this series. Look for her to be introduced in Tink's book this summer!

To Aimee Pachorek, Amy Ball, Michelle Macrander, and Shelby Burk for reading early versions of these chapters and getting excited about these characters and the world I built for them. Your enthusiasm and encouragement were bright spots in my days, and I appreciate the time you took out of your busy schedules to read when you could.

To my incredible agent, Nicole Resciniti of the Seymour Agency, for her never-ending advice and support, talking me down from proverbial ledges, and working hard to get me awesome opportunities that allow me to share my stories with wider audiences. She's truly the backbone of my career, and without her, I would be lost. I'm incredibly grateful to have her in my life, and someday I hope to return all the good she's done for me, ten-fold.

To everyone in the Maxwell Mob: thank you for sticking with me all these years and getting excited about my new projects in my ever-shifting publishing schedule. Your constant support, enthusiasm, and posts about Jason Momoa are what keep me going. Every. Single. Day.

A very special thank you to all the bloggers who work tirelessly and *for free* to shout out about my books, make graphics, invite me for takeovers, offer advice, take time to read and review my ARCs, and are just in general super amazing women whose passion is to lift up other women. You are the foundation of this book community we all live in, and we couldn't reach nearly as many readers as we do without you. I'm forever grateful for your help and humbled by your generous spirits.

And finally, thank you to everyone who's read this book. I hope you enjoyed my contemporary retelling of *Peter Pan*, and I especially hope you'll stick around for the remaining eight books I have planned in the Neverland Novels. This series is a passion project for me, one I'm incredibly proud of, and I promise to work hard to make it the best I can for you. If you enjoyed it—or even if you didn't—I would super-duper appreciate your honest review on Amazon, Goodreads, or Bookbub. Sharing is caring, and reviews are what makes an author's world go round. :)

If you'd like to keep up with what I'm working on and when my next releases come out, you can sign up for my newsletter. And if you love sneak peeks, sexy men, dirty jokes, and Jason Momoa memes, make sure you join me in my reader group on Facebook, the Maxwell Mob.

ABOUT THE AUTHOR

Gina L. Maxwell is a full-time writer, wife, and mother living in the upper Midwest, despite her scathing hatred of snow and cold weather. An avid romance novel addict, she began writing as an alternate way of enjoying the romance stories she loves to read. Her debut novel, *Seducing Cinderella*, hit both the *USA Today* and *New York Times* bestseller lists in less than four weeks, and she's been living her newfound dream ever since.

When she's not reading or writing steamy romance novels, she spends her time losing at Scrabble (and every other game) to her high school sweetheart, doing her best to hang out with their teenagers before they fly the coop, and dreaming about her move to someplace perpetually warm once they do.

You can find more information about her and all her online homes at www.ginalmaxwell.com.

OTHER BOOKS BY GINA L. MAXWELL

Fighting for Love series: Seducing Cinderella

Rules of Entanglement

Fighting for Irish

Sweet Victory

Playboys in Love series

Shameless

Ruthless

Merciless

Stand-Alones: Hot for the Fireman

Ask Me Again

Tempting her Best Friend

Connect with Gina: www.ginalmaxwell.com

Newsletter Sign-Up: www.ginalmaxwell.com/newsletter

Follow on BookBub: www.bookbub.com/authors/gina-l-maxwell

Reader Group on Facebook:
www.facebook.com/groups/TheMaxwellMob

Want more from Gina L. Maxwell?
Here's an extended sneak peek at SEDUCING
CINDERELLA, book 1 in her Fighting for Love series—
which soared all the way to #9 on the New York Times
bestselling list—about a sexy MMA fighter who gives
seduction lessons to his best friend's little sister, but soon
realizes he's the one being seduced as he falls fast and hard
for the girl who thinks she wants another man…

CHAPTER ONE

Lucie Miller didn't bother looking up when she heard the knock on her office door. Her next physical therapy patient was early, which irked her since she hadn't even completed the paperwork from the previous appointment. She pushed her glasses back in the proper place. He could just cool his heels in the hallway for the next ten minutes while she fini—

The knock came again, a little more insistently this time, and her resolve to not cater to someone else's wishes crumbled, as usual. Dropping her pen to the sheaf of papers in front of her, she called out, "Come in."

A head of perfectly styled dark hair popped around the edge of the door. "Hope I'm not disturbing you."

Before she could order her heart to behave, it skipped a beat at the mellowy-smooth voice of Dr. Stephen Mann, Director of Sports Medicine and major hottie at Northern Nevada Medical Center. At warp speed, her brain performed an unsolicited catalogue of her appearance, spitting out the usual diagnosis of "plain and dishevelled." Holding back a disappointing sigh and the urge to smooth a hand over the strands of hair that escaped her ponytail, she gave him her best smile. "Not at all. I didn't forget another meeting, did I?"

Twin dimples winked at her. "No, not today."

He turned to close the door, and her pulse raced. As an orthopedic surgeon, he'd visited her less-than-impressive office in the Rehab and Sports Med Center plenty of times to discuss mutual patients. But not once had he ever closed the door.

Trying hard not to jump to conclusions, she gestured in front of her. "Please, have a seat."

"Uh…"

Lucie glanced to the single visitor chair piled high with file folders, old newspapers, and research articles. She swore she felt her cheeks actually change color as she bolted around her desk. "Oh my gosh, I'm so sorry. Here, let me just—"

"That's all right, you don't have to—"

"No, I insist." She gathered the haphazard paper mountain in her arms. Not for the first time, or even the hundredth time, she wished she weren't so disorganized. Spinning in a quick circle, she searched for a place to stash the mess. Stacks just like the one she held lined the walls of her office on the floor and over every square inch of desk and file-cabinet space. Finally she gave up and just plopped the pile into her chair before turning her attention to her guest. God, why couldn't she be smooth and put-together like other women? Like the kind Stephen dated. "So, what brings you down into the bowels of the hospital this afternoon?"

He cleared his throat and shifted in his seat. Normally, the gorgeous doctor was the picture of confidence. It was the reason women literally sighed in his wake. Well, that and his easy charm and Ken-doll good looks, complete with killer smile.

"The hospital's annual charity dinner and dance is only two months away, and whereas a guy only has to rent a tux and show up, I'm aware that a woman needs ample time to shop for a dress and schedule all sorts of hair and nail appointments and whatever else it is that you women do to make yourselves beautiful."

Lucie's throat closed, and her fingers flew to fidget with her necklace. This was it. They'd worked together for years, sometimes even staying hours past their shifts to work on mutual cases, ordering bad Chinese when their brains refused to quit but their stomachs could no longer be ignored. They'd always been intellectually compatible, and their mutual obsession to help patients recover quicker and better bonded them as nothing else could. She'd loved him for years, but he'd never asked her out. Never made a move, instead preferring to date classy businesswomen he met during happy hour at the posh Club Caliente down the street.

But now he was here. In her office. Talking about the hospital ball. Dear God, please don't let her faint. Taking a slow, deep breath, Lucie tried for casual. "Are you trying to ask me something, Stephen?" And failed miserably. *Damn.*

A strong hand rubbed at the back of his neck, and he gave her the cutest look of embarrassment. "Ah, yeah. I'm not doing a very good job of it, am I?"

"No, you're doing fine!" *Too much enthusiasm. Double damn!*

"I know I should've brought this up before. And I really did want to ask that night I saw you at Club Caliente last month, but I hesitated and then you left. I was hoping I'd see you there again because it doesn't quite seem appropriate to inquire about a date here at the office, you know?"

Her mind flashed back to the one night she'd ever stepped foot in the overcrowded, overpriced club. Her best friend, Vanessa MacGregor, had just won a really difficult case and wanted to celebrate with a few drinks and some dancing. Instead of going to their usual hangout, Fritz's, Vanessa convinced Lucie to meet her at the much closer meat market of a club. They'd only been there for an hour tops before leaving. The club was like a frat house on steroids with a country-club clientele. The rest of their night had been spent downing tap beer and hustling guys at darts in a proper celebration.

"Oh, don't worry," she assured him. "I mean, not down here. The only person that could possibly hear us right now is Mr. Kramer on the treadmill out there, but the door is shut, and even if it wasn't, I don't think he remembers to turn his hearing aid up very often, so the chances of him hearing us over the noise of the mach—"

"Lucie."

"Sorry." *Oh my God, would you shut up already? You're babbling like an idiot!* "You were saying?"

He took a deep breath and exhaled like he was preparing to BASE jump from the roof of the hospital instead of asking her on a date. "I was trying to get your friend's number."

"My…*what*?"

"The girl you were with that night. Is she seeing anyone?"

"Vanessa?" Lucie's mind scrambled as it tried to follow the sharp turn off the path the conversation had previously been headed. Or where she'd *thought* it had been headed. She was such an idiot. "Um, no, she's not seeing anyone…"

Every muscle in his body visibly relaxed as he stood, his easy smile returning to hit her with both dimples right between the eyes. "That's great! Can I get her number? I don't want to take the chance of waiting till the last minute to ask her. I'd like to take her on a few dates before the big event, too. You know, get to know each other better. Lord knows you can never have a decent conversation at that charity dinner without someone interrupting with shoptalk. Lucie? Are you listening?"

"What? No. I mean, yes, I'm listening. Yes, you're right. It's definitely not conducive to first-date discussions." Lucie dropped her gaze to the organized disaster on her desk. Vanessa would have a panic attack if she saw it. Her friend was hyper-organized, always put together on the inside and out, never a hair out of place or an emotion uncalled for. Add in the perfect Barbie-doll looks and you had the kind of woman Stephen Mann was drawn to. The kind of woman she was most definitely not.

"Soooo... Can I have her number? Or maybe you're playing the role of protective friend and would prefer to grill me about my intentions first," he teased. "Maybe ask me why I think I'm good enough for her, something like that?"

She couldn't help the small lift at the corner of her mouth. "As if you couldn't be good enough for someone. You're charming, smart, handsome, and successful. How could that amount to 'not good enough' by anyone's standards?"

He winked. "I am quite the catch, aren't I? Be sure to tell Vanessa that when she tells you I called her. That is, if you ever give me her number."

"Oh! Right, sorry. Uh..." She looked around for a Post-it note or scratch piece of paper. She knew she had some, and if she could stop and think for a minute, she'd know right where they were, but somewhere in the last five minutes she'd been given a full frontal lobotomy, and now she couldn't function.

Giving up, she grabbed her pen and his hand and scribbled Vanessa's cell number onto his palm. She had to force herself to release him before she did something stupid like add an exclamation mark and "accidentally" use too much force for the dot, puncturing his smooth skin with the tip of her ballpoint. "There you go. All set. Now you'll have to excuse me. I, um, have a new patient who should be here any minute."

"I won't take up any more of your time then. Thanks, Lucie." Using his ink-free hand, he grabbed the knob and opened the door before looking back and adding, "I owe you one."

She pasted what she hoped was at least a facsimile of a

smile on her face as best she could. "I'll keep that in mind, doctor."

As soon as he was gone, she sank into her chair, not even bothering to move the stack of papers before she did so. This wasn't anything new. In fact, being overlooked for someone else was typical. By now, she should be immune to the hurt that came with it. What was that phrase? Old hat. Yes, that was it. By now, this should be old hat, and it wasn't even the first time a guy she liked was interested in her friend. But it still hurt. A lot.

There was no fooling herself any longer. She would never be the object of the doctor's desire. And though the realist in her said it didn't matter—that all she needed was compatibility and companionship with someone else—as her future came into sharp focus, the dreamer in her allowed herself to shed the tears that blurred the world in front of her.

CHAPTER TWO

"Can you point me in the direction of the physical therapy department?" *Where some arrogant ass will give me exercises fit for a toddler, essentially castrating me in the process...*

To say Reid Andrews was in a foul mood was a total understatement, but that didn't mean the hospital receptionist deserved his wrath. He listened as she gave him directions and thanked her as he set off.

The closer he got to his destination, the more his muscles bunched in irritation. He shouldn't be here. He should be back in Vegas, working his injury out with his coach and team doc. Not Sparks, Nevada—which was practically Reno and way too close for comfort to his hometown of Sun Valley to the north. Now he would be working with someone who had no concept of his sport or how important it was for him to get back in the cage as soon as possible to prep for his rematch.

For as long as he could remember, he'd been fighting. Fighting in the sport he loved above all else—Mixed Martial Arts, or MMA—to get to the top, and then fighting his ass off to stay there. Fifteen years later, he was one of the richest light-heavyweight fighters in the UFC, with a record of 34-3 and a fanbase of millions. Of course none of that mattered now because if he couldn't get healthy in time for the rematch, his career was over.

A doctor talking on his cell and checking his pager crowded Reid around a corner and bumped into him. The guy didn't even look back to apologize as he continued to clip down the hallway. Reid clenched his jaw and held his right shoulder as he waited for the pain to subside. Even from an impact so small, it hurt like a bitch.

He had one of the most aggravating injuries a fighter could have: a torn rotator cuff. To literally add insult to injury, it hadn't even happened in a fight. He'd gotten the damn thing while training for his title fight. Thirty-four was almost ancient for a fighter, especially one who'd been at it for as long as he had, and his body was starting to reflect that, injury by godforsaken injury.

Sidestepping an old lady traveling at the speed of a land snail, Reid cursed his trainer, Butch, for sending him here.

Shortly after Reid had had the surgery to repair his right shoulder, the camp's sports medicine doc needed to return home to take care of his ailing father. Scotty wasn't expected to be back for a couple of months, and since Reid was the only injured one in the camp, Butch set him up with a local PT for the interim. But if Reid kept working with that guy, he wouldn't be ready to fight until he was fifty, so he'd taken his therapy into his own hands.

Unfortunately, Butch got hip to what he was doing and bawled him out for not listening to Scotty's replacement and taking it easy. But Reid didn't know the meaning of taking it easy. His mottos were more than just your average motivational fodder. He lived by things like "give more than your everything or you'll amount to nothing" and "if you didn't come to win, you should've stayed the fuck home." Shit like that had been drilled into him since he was old enough to throw a punch at his old man's command.

He refused to accept the possibility of not completely healing in the next two months, thereby losing his shot at ever reclaiming his title. Every year the sport produced younger and better fighters, and it was becoming increasingly difficult for the older fighters to compete. That's why Reid trained as hard as he did. There would always be some guy who wanted his belt and was working his ass off for a chance to take it, so he had to train and prepare that much harder to keep it. He was pissed as hell Butch had given him an ultimatum: leave camp and do PT the right way or he was pulling the fight.

Fuck. That.

Fine, whatever. He'd make his coach happy and go to this lame PT shit. But that didn't mean he wasn't going to treat it any differently than he did his regular training. He didn't have time to dick around. He needed to get back to Vegas a.s.a.p. so he could reclaim what was rightfully his.

Reid pushed open the double doors and walked through a large room resembling the inside of a YMCA. Treadmills, ellipticals, weight sets, and exercise balls. No sparring cage. No floor mats. No punching bags. However there was an old man of about eighty-plus years walking so slow on a tread-mill that he was practically immobile.

"This blows," he mumbled as he approached the small office with his PT's name, Lucinda Miller, on the partially closed door. He raised his hand to give a quick rap before announcing himself, but paused when he heard soft sniffles coming from the bowed head of a brunette sitting behind the desk. At least he assumed it was a desk. It was hard to tell what was under the stacks of files and papers. Instead of knocking, he cleared his throat. "Sorry, this a bad time?"

The woman spun her chair around to face the back wall, hitting her knee on a file cabinet in the process and muttering an expletive he'd bet she didn't use publicly very often.

Though he hadn't seen her face yet, he couldn't help but find her clumsiness sort of cute. When she grabbed a Kleenex from somewhere on her floor and blew her nose, he was reminded that she was in a vulnerable moment. "I can come back."

"No, no." She blew her nose and then gestured behind her without turning around. "If you could just go have a seat in the next room, I'll be right with you."

Sounded good. As much as he hated to see a woman upset, it was bad enough having to console someone he knew, much less a woman he didn't. Finding the room, Reid leaned his hips on the padded table, absentmindedly cracking his knuckles as he waited. It was only another minute before she breezed in, eyes on his file, while making a beeline to the small desk along the wall.

"I'm terribly sorry about that," she said. "Let me just take a brief moment to look this over and we'll get down to business."

"Take your time." Something about her voice poked at his brain. Almost like he'd heard it before.

"Okay, Mr. Johnson, let's take a look at—"

They froze as recognition took hold.

"Luce?"

"Reid?"

It had been several years—shit, six, maybe even seven or more, he couldn't remember—since the last time he'd seen his best friend's little sister. Her face was blotchy with her eyes rimmed in red from crying. so he almost hadn't realized it was her, but the freckle at the outer corner of her left eye vaguely shaped like a heart gave her away. It was just barely visible under the dark-rimmed, rectangular glasses she wore.

"Oh my gosh," she said, giving his waist a hard squeeze. It'd been so long since he'd seen anyone from their home-town, and besides her brother, she'd be the only person he'd care to see. He returned her hug, tucking his head down to hers. Her hair smelled like a mix of flowers and summer, so different from the heavy perfume concoctions he was used to women wearing.

She released him, taking a seat on the swivel stool in front of the desk while tucking loose strands of hair behind her ear. "I can't believe it's you. Wait, why does my chart say Randy Johnson?"

Reid chuckled at the ridiculous name he used for anonymity. "It's an alias." Wanting to erase the pained look from whatever had happened before he arrived, he gave her a wicked smile and added, "And sometimes a state of being."

Her brows gathered together for the few seconds it took to sink in, then her cheeks flushed with color and her eyes grew wide. "Reid!"

He couldn't have stopped his laugh if he wanted to. The shocked look on her face was totally worth it. "Come on, Lu-Lu, you can't still be that innocent after all these years."

"My innocence or lack thereof is none of your business, Andrews. And be forewarned: if anyone hears you call me one of those ridiculous nicknames, I'll stab you in the jugular with my pen."

He held up his hands in mock surrender. "Fair enough, Lubert." She rolled her eyes, but he interrupted her before she could get a good mad on. "Speaking of names, what's up with Lucinda Miller? I don't see a ring. You in the witness protection plan or something?"

She averted her eyes, suddenly finding that her name tag needed repinning. "No. I *was* married briefly in college. Jackson probably didn't tell you about it because we eloped and it didn't last very long." She cleared her throat and smiled at him, but it barely reached her cheeks, much less her eyes. "You know how it is. Capricious youth and all that. I just never bothered to change my name back. But at least I still have the same initials, right?"

Her attempt at disguising her true feelings reminded him

of what he'd walked in on. Something or someone had hurt her, and it instantly called on his protective instincts. After all, Lucie wasn't just any woman. He'd grown up with her trailing after him and her brother, Jackson Maris. And since Jax, also a UFC fighter, was in Hawaii with his training camp and couldn't help make things right for his little sister, Reid would gladly step in.

"Why were you crying, Lu?"

"Oh, that?" She waved a hand dismissively. "Nothing. I have terrible seasonal allergies and sometimes they get so bad I sound like a blubbering, snivelling mess, that's all."

He scoffed. "This is why Jax and I never let you tag along on our more devious 'misadventures.' You're a terrible liar and wouldn't have lasted five seconds under parental interrogation."

She stood, placing her hands on her hips. "Well according to your trainer, you're a terrible patient, so I guess we both have our faults. Now, unless you want to waste your entire session on pointless chatter, I suggest you let me assess your injury."

Reid recognized a brick wall when he ran into one. She wasn't going to talk about it…yet. One way or another he'd get it out of her. "Fine. Assess away, Luey." Reaching between his shoulder blades with his left arm, he pulled his T-shirt off over his head, taking care not to jostle his right arm too much. He tossed the shirt onto the chair in the corner.

"How much PT have you had since the operation?"

"I don't know, the usual amount, I guess. A session a day or so. But it wasn't enough, so I was doing some extra training on the side."

She paused and arched a brow at him. "In other words, you were overdoing it, which is counterproductive to your recovery."

"'Overdoing it' is such a subjective term."

"No, it's not, Reid. Anything more than what your doctor

or therapist instructs is overdoing it. If I'm going to help you, you need to do *exactly* as I say. If you can manage that, I'll have you as good as new in about four months."

"What? Didn't Butch tell you about my rematch in two months? I need to fight on that card, Luce. Diaz has my belt, and I'm taking it back."

Lucie shook her head. "Reid that's insane. Even if I devoted the majority of my time to you, I can't guarantee you'll be ready to fight that soon."

"Bullshit. You have to say that as a professional, but take into account who your patient is. I'm not like the other people you work on. I'm not your Average Joe trying to eventually get back to normal. I'm a highly trained athlete who's had to recover from more injuries in the last fifteen years than a hundred Average Joes put together."

She sighed. "Let's see what we're dealing with here, first, okay, hotshot? Sit."

Reid hopped onto the table and tried not to tense up at the idea of having his arm manipulated. He had a high tolerance for pain, but that didn't mean her exam wouldn't be enough to set his teeth on edge.

"Extend your arm to the side and try to keep it there as I push it down." He lasted only a few seconds before he released the pose with a muttered curse. She pretended not to notice and put him through a couple more strength tests where he managed to keep his swearing rants inside his head. Yay him.

"Okay, last one, Reid. Place your hand in front of your stomach and try to hold it there as I pull it away from your body."

Clenching his jaw and his left fist he tried thinking of something other than the sickening pain shooting from his shoulder. But as bad as the pain was, the fact that he was so weak and couldn't hide it was much worse.

"All right, you can relax now." She made some notes in

his file, then turned back and asked, "On a pain scale of one to ten, with ten being the worst pain you can imagine, how are you feeling at the moment?"

"A four. Maybe even a three."

She arched her brow and crossed her arms over her chest. "Spare me the macho shit, Andrews. I'm not here to challenge your virility. If you want me to do my job, then you have to be one hundred percent honest with me."

He pinned her with a glare that made men twice her size reconsider stepping into the octagon with him. Lucie didn't even flinch. He would've commended her for it had he not been so aggravated with the whole situation. "Fine. A six," he grumbled. "But some days are better than others."

"Don't worry, that's normal. Now lay facedown on the table. I want to do a couple more things."

"You got awfully bossy in your old age, you know that?" He was a tad disappointed she didn't rise to the bait, but offered a sarcastic *Mm-hmm* instead as he arranged his body on the table. With his left arm up to cradle the side of his face, he let his eyes close as she began to work on him.

Her delicate fingertips probed the muscles around his shoulder. He had no idea what she was looking for, but he hoped she searched for a while. Her touch felt so much better than how he was usually handled. Of course Scotty's hands weren't as soft, but it was more than that. It was the technique she used; like he wasn't just a fighter made of hardened muscle that could handle rough, prodding fingers, but rather a man who'd asked for a gentle massage after a long day.

He heard a soft sniffle, and it set his mind to wondering what had upset her so much. Growing up he'd practically been Lucie's second older brother, and it bothered him to know something was wrong.

Whatever it was, she was doing her best to avoid —"Ah, shit!"

"Sorry."

"Yeah, right," he said wryly. "That was probably payback for using your floppy bunny as a lawn-dart target."

He couldn't see her face, but he heard the smile when she spoke. "I forgot all about that. Jackson got grounded for three days, and my mom had to sew all the little holes together. She told me he was a war hero who was going through surgery to get patched up before receiving a medal from the president."

"Your mom was always good for a story. Jax and I counted on her to give us all our background information for our pretend missions as kids."

"Mom was something special all right. I still miss her bedtime stories."

Lucie's parents had died in a car accident the summer after he and Jackson graduated high school and she was just thirteen. Jackson chose to raise Lucie instead of pawning her off on another relative, which is why he wasn't as far in his MMA career as Reid. It was an honorable thing, and it was obvious he'd done a damn fine job, too.

Just then it hit him. "It's a guy, isn't it?"

Her hands stilled for only a moment, but it was long enough to give him the answer he was looking for. "Is it tender when I press here?"

Like bad heartburn, an unfamiliar lividity rose up for the general male population until he could aim it at the one who deserved it. Pushing up with his left arm he swung his body around to face her.

"What are you doing? I'm not done."

"You are until you tell me who he is and what the hell he did," he growled.

"Reid—"

"Quid pro quo, Lu. You tell me who made you cry and why, and I promise to not find out on my own, hunt him down, and kick his teeth down his throat for putting that look on your face."

He almost regretted throwing down the harsh threat when

her face blanched, but if that was the only way he could get her to open up, then so be it. "Here, hop up on the table. We'll switch places," he said as he stood. When she opened her mouth to brook an argument, he narrowed his gaze to show her he wasn't kidding. With a resigned sigh she did as he wanted, albeit not happily.

"There, now you're the patient." Despite the pain it caused in his shoulder, he braced his hands on either side of her hips, preventing an escape should she decide it was the better alternative. "So, Miss Miller," he said looking into her soft gray eyes, "tell me where it hurts."

Visit Gina's website to get more of Reid and Lucie's story!
http://www.ginalmaxwell.com/books/seducing-cinderella

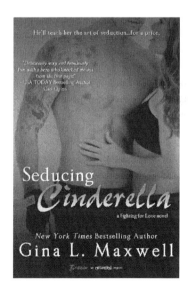